# The Assessment

*Alex Vorn*

**BALBOA.**
PRESS
A DIVISION OF HAY HOUSE

Balboa Press books may be ordered through booksellers or by contacting:

Balboa Press
A Division of Hay House
1663 Liberty Drive
Bloomington, IN 47403
www.balboapress.com.au
1 (877) 407-4847

Print information available on the last page.

ISBN: 978-1-5043-1024-6 (sc)
ISBN: 978-1-5043-1035-2 (e)

Balboa Press rev. date: 10/04/2017

# CONTENTS

*Dedicated to Mary, Jasmine and Haaris, and Feather*

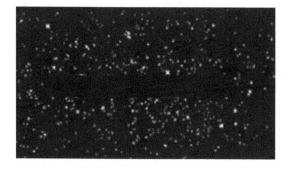

## CHAPTER ONE

# The Visitors

The night sky has always held its secrets.

A good example being the fact that a vast, cloaked ship now resides securely within the confines of the solar system, with one of its several planets currently being assessed. It whirls around with the great scattering of circling planets, unseen. Its inhabitants (the best way to describe them) go about their duties inside this vast, floating metropolis.

In one quadrant of the city a great number of Regional Controllers are briefing their selected Observers. Each Observer has no other purpose than to visit, observe and assess. There would be no further onus placed on it, beyond gathering material sufficient for a report to be prepared. This is managed in a manner beyond any corporal encumbrances.

The method of operation employed by these beings is both prodigious and simple. If it is found that a planet's lifeforms are deemed likely to cause a problem, the visitors clear it of all living organisms and move on.

Hence, the Assessment being undertaken.

A huge army of Observers, all performing much the

same duties, is spread widely across several continents. All categories of human endeavour; education, health, art, science, politics, philosophy and many more are being observed. Visitations are scheduled, so as to place them together, lined up and ready for the Observer to move from one to the next without delay. Each Observer submits its findings to its respective Section Controller for review. All reports are submitted to The Committee for Planetary Development and System Stability, with this committee preparing a final report for the Supreme Council.

This Observer, formally Observer 42817, is newly-appointed and being briefed before embarking on its first mission. The Regional Controller and the Observer have come together.

They are, in fact, two beads of soft, white light hovering in their allotted space.

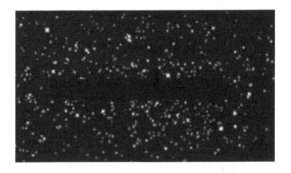

## CHAPTER TWO

# *The Briefing*

The Controller begins. "I see that you have completed your final induction."

"Yes."

"Any problems?"

"No."

"This is your first assignment. Are you familiar with your allotted postings?"

"Yes."

"Are you now proficient with the language?"

"Yes."

"I see you've completed your coordinate transition training."

"Yes."

"Any issues with that?"

"No."

"Any other issues?"

"None."

The Controller continues. "About this planet. There is a primary behavioural drive for survival through reproduction.

Despite this, rapid population growth, together with unprecedented levels of consumption, have brought about massive challenges. There is evidence of a decline in global biodiversity, a depletion of natural resources and a surge of carbon dioxide levels in the planet's atmosphere. With the warming of the planet, the land, plants, animals, oceans, and even the atmosphere, are all under severe threat. Currently, the planet's life-support capabilities are being reduced at an alarming rate due to the ever-increasing impact of human activities.

"However, there are groups on this planet that endeavour to deal with poverty and hunger, access to justice, better management of ecosystems, climate change, water and sanitation, and the consumption of produce.

"You will be witnessing an extremely random selection of human behaviour. Some of the events you witness are designated as strange, while others are commonplace. These happenings are a carefully-chosen mixture of behaviours that lie within your remit.

Go well."

"I go well."

## CHAPTER THREE

# The First Mission

The Observer's mission has begun. It moves silently and unseen through the streets, buildings and homes it has been allocated to enter. It passes through several ceilings, then walls, on to the seventh floor of an apartment building. This was done in only a moment of time. It is at the coordinates provided in order to observe the unfolding event. It is, in itself, a small, dimly lit globe, but now quite unseen.

It floats in a small bedroom, lit only by the glow of distant street lights coming through an uncurtained window. As always, time has been adjusted to enable the observation to begin at the very point of beginning.

It is a boy's bedroom. The television on the corner table is switched off and the boy is in bed. The Observer can hear a low sobbing. In its way it thinks back in time to when the boy was even younger. It delves into the past. It sees what the boy witnessed.

It happened one summer, when the family was staying at a friend's house by the sea. They all went down together from time to time, whenever the Dad could get time away from his business. They were all on the beach when it happened. Something got washed up on the shore and it soon became obvious that it was some kind of animal. It was just a carcass, being rolled over and over as the waves hit it.

They all went to see what it was, but stopped short when it became obvious it wasn't some sea creature, but a dog. It must have been playing in the surf and got caught in a rip. His Mum got very upset because it looked like a well-cared-for pet. Dad sent them back to sit on the towels while he went on to have a closer look.

They just sat there watching while he carried the limp form back onto dryer sand. His Mum thought she had seen a collar but there was nobody in sight either way along the beach. Dad was bending over it for a long time and Mum said he was probably reading its collar.

All of a sudden the dog jumped up, staggered a bit, shook itself dry and raced away up the coastline and disappeared around the point.

The boy's Mum was delighted and clapped and his Dad walked back with a big grin on his face. His Mum told him he was a miracle worker and his Dad just shrugged and said it was nothing really. It was a very happy time there on the beach that day. The incident had a profound effect on the boy.

This night, he had been sitting alone, watching one of those 'Would you believe it?' TV shows, while his Mum and Dad were out. It was running film clips to show how autoresuscitation can occur after resuscitation had been used without success. The presenter said it was called the *Lazarus Syndrome* and it happened in both humans and animals.

He sat quietly for a while, battling the enormous sense

of disappointment that swept over him. His Dad wasn't a miracle worker! Then he left a note for his parents, saying he was very tired and had gone to bed early. Imagination in the young can be very powerful.

Suddenly, the boy turned over and the sniffling stopped. He was now breathing deeply.

The woman turned up just a few minutes early. The Observer can see that she is wanting to impress.

The club was actually closed to customers when she arrived. A large man at the door confirmed who she was and let her in. As they entered the nightclub he pointed across the dimly-lit room to a man sitting at a small table.

"He's waiting," he said and left.

She joined the man at the table, who was now standing. She was not at all sure how this interview would go.

He shook her hand, then waved her into the chair opposite. They both sat. He looked through the paperwork she had submitted.

He looked up and smiled. "Thank you for coming."

She nodded.

"Have you been doing this sort of work for long?" was his first question.

"A few years," she replied.

"I've never heard of you, which is good." He smiled again.

She placed her handbag on the table and said, "I hope I've provided all the information you need."

"Oh! Yes, very thorough. We like to know who we are

taking on, of course. Can never be too careful. No, this looks good."

He sat back and studied her for a few moments.

She was feeling nervous.

He pointed at her bag. "I believe you have something else for me?"

She opened her handbag and produced a small envelope. Sliding it across the table to him she said, "I hope this is what you wanted."

He tore it open and held up a string of pearls. He smiled at her approvingly. "Any problems with the safe?"

"No. Easy job, really."

He shook her hand again and said, "Welcome to the team."

It was now floating above a bench, in a small garage attached to the side of a house. It looked on as a boy stood thinking about past events. He was thinking about how his younger brother had the habit of just sitting there, and how awful it was.

The little brat used to annoy the hell out of him. He would just sit there on the end of the bench looking on, saying "No! No, don't put that there. That won't work." As if the stupid kid would know!

The boy would be under the hood, grease up to his elbows, and his brother would say things like that. In the end he would chuck him out and he'd go running to Mum saying he'd been rotten to him. Then he'd get an earful from her. She would say, "He doesn't mean any harm. He

just wants to help. You should be more patient with him."
Then he would come back in, smirking.

Then came the time when his brother went into hospital.
He had lots of tests done. He was in there for months,
because they couldn't figure out what was wrong with him.
Then he could get on and tinker as much as he liked without
him sitting there being a pain.

He knows he will never forget the shock when his Dad
came out to the garage with the news. He had tears in his
eyes and he looked so old. Mum cried a lot. The funeral
was horrible.

The boy still likes to work on his car occasionally, but
not as often.

His young brother doesn't sit there anymore and he
thinks it's awful!

Nobody could guess why the old lady sat there alone each
night, but the Observer knew. It watched as she closed her eyes.

The seat that she occupied could not be described as
comfortable, being a hard, wooden bench. It was located
across the street from a row of shops. The premises exactly
opposite was a dress shop. It sold ladies' clothes that would
have to be described as 'up market'. It had smartly-dressed
manikins behind a large front window.

Each day, at the end of shopping hours, these
establishments went into a state of semi-darkness, with just
the odd small glow somewhere, serving as a backlight. This,
however, was not the case with the dress shop. Showing that it
was indeed a superior establishment, the large neon sign above

the window that stated its name in fashionable script was left on, lighting the surroundings with its rays of soft green.

It was this elderly lady's habit to arrive at the bench well after dark each evening. She would sit, eyes closed, feeling the light from the shop's bright glow, and she would remember. Her thoughts went back so many years; but the images, the sights and the sounds, became clearer, louder and more real as she bathed in the shop window's glow.

She remembered him. The man that came into and went out of her life. He who had been hers for so short a time. They had made so many plans together. He who was called away to war but didn't come back. She remembered all of this. Especially their dancing. He had talked her into taking dancing lessons. They would go together, although he didn't need them. He was a natural.

Then there were the clubs. The nightclubs where they would dance their way into the night. So many wonderful nights, and their favourite place; The Limelight Club. Such happy times… dancing, talking, and laughing. Intimate moments shared across one of the small tables, bathed in the soft lime glow that coloured everything.

She sits perfectly still, eyes closed, the hint of a smile on her old face, bathing herself in thoughts of days gone by, in so many happy memories… and limelight.

It hovered near the entrance to the Supermarket. It was observing a man looking over the shop's notice board.

He was startled when a voice said, "Anything in particular?"

The man turned. "Pardon?"

"Anything in particular? Are you looking for anything in particular?" She was smiling.

He looked at her. She was quite pretty, and somehow familiar. "Ah, no, not really."

She just stood, smiling at him.

He moved to one side. "Sorry! Did you want to…" he pointed at the board.

"No. That's OK." She was still smiling.

He was beginning to feel awkward. He looked over her shoulder. The shops were very busy, especially the supermarket where his friend had gone in for something. No sign of him yet. He looked back into her grinning face.

"Do we know each other?"

"Aha!" she said. "I was wondering when the penny would drop."

He squirmed a little and said, "We've met, then?"

"You mean you don't remember?"

He frowned in thought for a moment and said, "No. I'm afraid I don't."

She looked surprised. "What, you have no memory of me at all?"

He stared at her for another long moment. She was beaming at him now, and nodding her head up and down in encouragement. There was something vaguely familiar about her but it seemed to be just out of reach.

Finally, he shook his head. "Sorry. Nothing."

Her face fell. "Oh! Really? Well then…" She turned on her heel and joined the crowd spilling out into the street.

The environment that the Observer found itself in was unpleasant. It was looking down at the homeless teenager who was laying, cold and miserable, in the lane.

This was going to be the worst night he'd ever spent sleeping out on the street.

Little did he know just how bad it was going to get. The night was depressingly cold. The wind that blew through the alley brought with it a chill factor that had him continually rubbing his hands together and pushing them up under his dirty pullover to keep them warm. He had searched for some time for any kind of covering. Any old piece of cardboard, or newspapers, or anything would have done; but he could find nothing. Even the skip at the end of the alley was empty save for a small pile of women's magazines. These would have to do if he didn't want to die of hypothermia.

He climbed into the high-walled bin and threw them all out. When he got back out, he gathered them up and returned to the least breezy section of the passageway where he would make his bed.

With his back to the freezing wind he began separating the pages. When this was done, one by one he painstakingly folded and scrunched the edges to produce a thin blanket that he hoped would enable him to survive the night.

As he lay there shivering and continually tucking around and clutching at the crudely made covering, his misery was exponentially heightened by the depressing, yet unavoidable fact that the magazine pages that covered him were crammed full of people a great deal richer than him!

The Observer found them standing in the road peering through a thick blanket of smoke. Orange sparks flew up occasionally, spilling out into swirling patterns on the night's wind, hovering momentarily like tiny Catherine wheels before fading to black.

She waited for it, but it didn't come.

They could just make out the wail of the siren coming through the distant village.

Still she waited.

He let out a great sigh. "If only you hadn't switched the light on."

"Oh! Come on, it was getting dark" she replied. "What was I supposed to do?"

"You were supposed to get someone in, but not him!"

Here it comes, she thought.

"I know he's only an apprentice, but he seemed to know what he was doing."

Even in the dark, she felt him stir with anger. He cleared his throat. Here it comes at last, she thought.

"None of this would have happened if you had hired a licensed electrician like I wanted."

The man's thoughts were being considered by the Observer.

The man sees himself sitting in an old, tattered armchair with the television blaring.

He has the strangest feeling that he's had this same dream before, more than once. It's a case of knowing what comes next. He looks down at two scruffy children, sitting in front of the TV. They alternate between giggling at the TV show and breaking out into sudden boisterous arguments. They continually hit each other, then complain to their mother. She sits in another decrepit armchair, half watching the show and half concentrating on selecting the largest pieces of popcorn from a take-away bag.

He asks for the sound to be turned down but nobody hears him. A mangy-looking dog jumps onto his lap and he knocks it off. There is an acrid smell in the room of burnt fat and steamed vegetables. The children begin yelling even louder and his wife shouts back. He wants to leave the room but can't get up. He feels as if he is grossly overweight and his feet feel swollen.

He looks down to see a beer bottle in his hand. He lifts it to his lips but it's empty. He sees his wife is glaring at him. She seems to be screaming something at him but he can't make out what she's saying. She climbs out of her chair, spilling the bag's contents as she does. She is still bellowing at him as she waves the children out of her way. She treads on the dog's tail and it yelps. She moves the animal to one side roughly with her foot. It growls then slinks away. She now stands in front of him shaking her head. She snatches the bottle out of his hand and cracks it over his head. He wakes with a start… and finds himself sitting in an old, tattered armchair with the television blaring.

It was observing the scruffy old beggar, who was holding out his tin and rattling it.

He is wiry and unshaven, dressed mainly in rags, save

for a bright green beret. The Observer saw the significance of this. The beggar smiles broadly at all his potential customers. He wishes those well who manage to make eye contact. This he does with every city worker that passes by.

Some drop in a coin or two, most avoid him. One of them stops and fishes in his pockets. He is a fresh-faced young man in a cheap suit. He is carrying a case that looks a little battered. It is probably a hand-me-down. Maybe his father's, from times past. He is searching frantically through all his pockets. He is holding up the pedestrians and moves back against a shop window.

The beggar waits patiently. He jiggles his tin from time to time. Eventually, the young man speaks. "I'm very sorry. I thought I had a few coins when I left home. I can't understand it." He looks extremely embarrassed as he searches one last time.

Tipping his tin, the beggar slides a few coins into his palm. He catches the young man's wrist and drops them into his hand.

"Don't you worry about it son. You have a coffee on me. Happy Saint Patrick's Day!

It floated alongside of the man. It knew he was feeling the heat.

The old hobo, stooping under his tatty backpack, approached the edge of town. The day was warm and the flies were bad. A large tree giving good shade, sitting on the edge of a green patch, came into view. Beneath it, a rudimentary bench made up of two brick stacks with a plank laid across them. At one end an even older guy sat smoking a pipe.

He approached and asked "Mind if I sit?"

The old man studied him with cold, grey eyes. "Nah."

"Looks a nice little town. Live here?"

With a nod of his head the other said, "Yep."

The hobo said, "Pub?"

"Yep. Down on the right," came the reply.

"Any work?" asked the hobo.

"Some, not much. Wacha do?"

The other shrugged. "Bit of this…" he paused to spit, "a bit of that."

"Like?"

Scratching his head, the hobo said, "Dunno really. Working in the fields or labouring."

The man took a puff on his pipe and asked, "Looking for work?"

The other grimaced and said, "Nah. Think I'll give it a miss."

The older man nodded.

"Too hot to work," said the hobo.

"Guess so," the older man agreed.

The hobo stood up. "Pub's down on the right, you say?"

The older man looked up with new sparkle in his eyes. "Yep. Not far."

The other said, "Beer nice and cold, is it?"

The man stood up. "Sure is. Wanna go down together?"

The hobo looked surprised and said, "Only if you're buying."

The other looked disappointed and sat down again.

"Think I'll just pass on through," said the hobo, adjusting his straps.

The older man said, "Didn't ask where you came from; or were you were going either."

"Got a policy on that."

"Yeh?"

"Yep. Never like to think that I'm either coming or going anywhere." With that he made off into town.

The man on the seat tapped out and refilled his pipe. He watched the hobo and smiled to himself. Although disappointed about the pub, he reflected on the fact that he hadn't had that much excitement in ages!

It was a noisy, bustling part of the city, despite the late hour. The Observer was aware of the multiplicity of flashing lights and competing music. It concentrated on the girl. She had been making her way to a bus stop and it was only by chance that she saw them.

They came tumbling out of a bar, staggering, laughing, all but falling over. He had his arm tight around the woman's waist while waving for a taxi. He had held her own waist like that. He had often laughed just like that with her in the few weeks they had been together. She saw the car pull up and watched as he made a great gesture of holding the door open for her. She watched the taxi pull away. She couldn't believe how rotten he was. She stood and watched until it was out of sight.

She was crying now. Just uncontrollable sobbing. He had been the one; in so short a time, he had been everything to her. He was her world. She had been so happy, so at ease with him, so sure... She moved to a shadowy doorway and blew her nose. With a mirror and her handkerchief, she tried to fix up smudged lipstick and mascara. She was still shaking as she walked to the corner. She felt weak and unsteady on her feet. The bus stop seemed too far to walk. The whole thing had left her feeling vulnerable. She called for a cab.

She gave the address and settled down in the back still sniffing and trembling. The driver glanced at her from time to time as they made their way out of town. Ten minutes later they pulled up, and after giving her nose another good blow, she fumbled in her purse.

Quite suddenly he turned and said, "If he's done this to you, he's not worth it. Find someone nice, why don't you?" He gave her an enormous grin.

She nodded and almost smiled as she handed over the fare.

He shook his head. "No; on the house. As long as you find someone nice." He smiled again.

She got out and watched the taxi pull away. She couldn't believe how nice he was. She stood and watched until it was out of sight.

It took in the scene. The reoffender was sitting in the prison governor's office, yet again.

The governor shuffled paperwork and sighed. He looked up at the prisoner shaking his head.

He sneered and said, "The way you keep coming back

for more prison time, anybody would think you actually enjoy it in here."

The old lag nodded and replied, "Well, now you come to mention it, I do."

The governor looked at him with an expression of disbelief. "I can't believe that."

"You should. I like it better in here than out there."

"What are you talking about? Why would anybody prefer to spend time in here?"

"Simple," said the man. "Out there I can't afford a car; in here we have a dedicated van service. There's no heating at my place; it's always nice and cosy in here. At home I don't have air-conditioning; it's always kept cool in here. At home there's no indoor toilet; here we have indoor toilets. There's no running water where I live; here there's plenty, cold and hot, always on tap. I can't afford a doctor out there; they provide them in here. I can never afford a dentist when I'm at home; here they are provided free of charge. Out there I'm lucky if I have one square meal a day; in here I get fed three times a day. Out there I have to work; in here I don't."

The governor thought for a bit, then stood up, extended his hand and said, "In that case, enjoy your stay."

The two men faced one another across the fence. The Observer noted a strangeness in the one talking, concerned about recent events. The man was leaning on the fence telling his neighbour about his sister.

"It all started a couple of weeks ago when her pen went missing." He shook his head. "She had been using it moments before… she hadn't even got up from the chair… it was right there on the kitchen table, next to her shopping list… right in front of her! Of course, she went a bit gaga, anybody would. She said she spent nearly an hour, down on her hands and knees, searching all around the kitchen."

The neighbour said, "Wow! Poor girl."

"Yep. Right. As you say, poor girl. But that was only the beginning. When she got home from work the next day, the hat-stand in the hall had gone. I mean, she never really liked it, never hung stuff on it, but her grandfather gave it to her, and you know… anyway, there it was… gone! No sign of a break-in or anything. She called the police. Well, I guess it was the right thing to do. She had the feeling they didn't believe her. Can't blame them for that, I suppose."

The neighbour was becoming a touch agitated, wondering where all this was going.

The other went on. "You know, the strangest part of all this is how it never got into the newspapers. I mean, a story like this… you'd think people would really want to read about it, but no, not a word. Anyway, what happened next was beyond belief."

The neighbour did his best to look interested.

"She drove home from work, parked in the garage and went in to start tea. Five minutes later, no more than five mind you, she found her lipstick wasn't in her bag. So, what does she do? She goes out to see if she had dropped it in the car. You've got it… the car was gone. I mean just gone; without a sound. She would have heard something from the house, but nothing!"

The neighbour looked genuinely surprised for the first time. "Well, that is odd. What did she do?"

The man looked pleased to be getting some sort of reaction. "She reported it of course, but she had the feeling the police considered her to be some sort of looney. But hey! You have to report these things, don't you?"

"Of course," said the neighbour, shaking his head. "That's awful. Was it recovered?"

The other giggled to himself softly. "It wouldn't matter if it was... not now."

"What do you mean?"

"OK. I suppose I should tell you the rest of it?"

"The rest of it? There's more?" asked the neighbour.

"There sure is. Nothing happened for a couple of days. Nothing else went missing I mean. Anyway, she comes home on the bus, later than usual because she was asked to do a bit of last minute overtime. It was dark by then, and when she got to her street she couldn't find the house! She walked up and down the street a couple of times before she realised she had walked past a block of vacant land twice that was exactly where her house was when she left for work in the morning."

The neighbour just stared at the man for a moment, then turned on his heels and headed for his front door.

"There's more! It gets worse; don't you want to know?" the other cried.

"Sorry, must get on," came the reply. The door slammed behind him.

The man was shocked by his neighbour's rudeness. He shook his head and mumbled to himself, "Probably just as well; he wouldn't have believed me anyway. Gee! I'm really going to miss my sister!"

It hovered in the dimly-lit room. It is a quiet house in a quiet street.

The man in the room spent most of the day working in the garden. With his wife away visiting her sister he's been trying to keep himself busy. It's getting dark outside. He lounges, stretched out on the sofa in the front room. The cat's curled up against his leg. He sips his beer. The orange outside light from across the street sends an eerie glow across the net curtains. It's a warm evening and the light flickers as the curtains move with the window slightly open. The effect sends similar patterns onto the ceiling. This was how he remembered envisaging the place the old parish priest would constantly talk about. The place you'd end up in, should you stray from the path. God would know if you swore or if you told a lie or if you stole something. He would know instantly! The old priest was a good man; a servant of God.

He gazed up at the flickering red and orange dancing across the ceiling. This was how he saw purgatory when he was a young man. A place where all was on fire. The vicar had painted such pictures for the young parishioners to think about; such images. It didn't really complicate things that he fell in love with his daughter.

In their late teens it was only natural that they were always conscious of her father's presence; his constant references to how one should live a good life. He reflected on the fact that it had been a good life. One of the best parts of it was the day the priest had married them.

He looked across at the wedding photo, hanging where it had been for so many years. The old man standing on the steps with her on one side and him on the other. He was beaming as though he had just got married himself or had won some major prize or had been selected to represent his country for something or other.

The cat squirmed around making himself more comfortable. He thought for a moment about the old man's funeral; how hard it had rained and how dark the sky was that day; how sad it all was. He stretched and put his empty beer glass down. He'll leave it there and wash it up and tidy around in the morning, before he picks her up from the station. He stood, leaving the animal curled and contented.

He approached the photo. He had always liked looking at it; had always enjoyed the private moments of looking into the old man's face; into his eyes. He was a truly good man.

He crossed to the curtains and pulled them shut.

Purgatory disappeared.

It found itself floating above the passenger seat of the parked car. The man next to it sat quietly, but in very deep thought. It was a rental car and it had been slid off the road and was pulled up on the grass verge. It was a narrow country road with no lights, no white lines, and no traffic. It was pitch black, with only the faint starlight glowing when the driver had switched the lights off. He was now peering up into the emptiness. He felt he didn't need long, just a minute or two. It had happened with some frequency of late. The need to just stop and think for a while.

It seemed so long ago now, when he first met the man. The man he met in his gymnasium, who said he had heard his name at the local gun club. The man who had taken him to a bar for a drink. The man who told him he could offer him a superior lifestyle. Who said he could take him off the sales counter at the local auto parts store. The man who had changed his life.

They had spent more than four hours talking, right up to closing time. When they parted, all he had was a flower shop's business card with a silent number printed in the corner. That had been the first and last time they had ever been face to face. In the whole wide world there was only one man who knew who he was, what he was, what he did.

He had moved away without a word to Jess. He could have had a good life with her. There could have been a house, car, kids, holidays - all the things that went with that… that life style. Not a superior lifestyle, but…

He let down the window, leaned out and stared up at the stars again. He'd been doing a lot of this too. Did he have doubts? Of course he did, every time. These usually evaporated quickly when he thought about his small, but well-appointed city apartments in three countries; his cars, his expensive wardrobe. Were his reservations taking longer to fade?

He opened the envelope and took out the photograph. Not that he needed to, the man's face was indelibly fixed in his memory. Who was this man? He didn't know. He only knew as much about him as he needed to; that's the way it was, every time. He unfolded the sheet that came with it, giving all necessary details: name, address, height, weight, medical conditions, employment, marital status, etc., etc. Every time, it was always the same.

He crouched and unlocked the metal container beneath the dashboard, took out the gun fitted with a silencer, slipped it under his belt and started the engine. He switched on the headlights and slowly moved back onto the road. He moved on with renewed resolve; with a restored and uncompromising determination to maintain his superior lifestyle.

It was aware that the boy who sat at his desk brooding was annoyed that he'd been kept in the dark.

His teacher noted his sullen mood. He was normally such a bright and cheerful pupil; she knew something was wrong.

She stopped her science presentation and looked at him. "Is something wrong?"

He glared at her and answered, "I'll say there is! Why weren't we told about this stuff before?"

"What stuff?"

"Black holes, of course."

She was taken aback. "You weren't told about it before because it wasn't scheduled in the science curriculum until this morning's lesson."

He shrugged. "It just seems to me that we've been kept in the dark about all this."

A girl at the back giggled. He turned to her angrily saying, "That wasn't meant to be a pun."

She giggled some more, and one or two others joined in. He was red in the face now as he turned back to his teacher.

"I mean, this changes everything doesn't it?"

"Changes everything?"

"Yes, of course."

The teacher was frowning now.

He said, "What you said earlier, about antimatter. Why weren't we told about that a lot earlier?"

She wasn't sure how she should answer. "Is it that you don't grasp the principles involved in antimatter?"

He nodded violently. "I'll say it is. I mean, you just said that there's no difference between an antimatter black hole and a regular-matter black hole."

At this point his science teacher was becoming very uncomfortable. "Yes. That's right." She picked up and referred to her course notes. "That is what I said."

"Well, if there is no difference between them, how can they be two different things?"

He looked around the classroom to see if he was getting any support from the others. He wasn't; just a load of glum faces.

He turned back. "OK. You said antimatter has a positive mass, just like regular-matter, and it experiences gravity in the same way…"

She held a hand up to stop him. Knowing full well that she was about to get completely out of her depth she said, "I think it would be best if this discussion was held later. We really should move on with the lesson."

With that, the boy stood gathering his books and made for the door.

Taken aback, the teacher asked, "Where are you going?"

"I've had enough," he said.

"Enough? What do you mean enough?" She picked up two more pages. "There's more to cover in this lessen."

He stood at the door with a look of horror on his face. "There's more?" he shouted. "More?"

He shook his head and slammed the door as he went out.

It looked on as the inventor slowly pushed the door open, saying, "It's all rather Heath Robinson, I'm afraid. I wasn't always able to acquire all of the materials needed."

His friend looked around in amazement. The room, devoid of any furnishings, was literally filled with a great jumble of very strange pieces of apparatus. There were shiny copper pipes and plastic tubes running from one piece of equipment to another. A great assortment of glass containers with coloured liquids, some of which were bubbling. Ropes and pulleys of various sizes, some turning while others were still, and a great many cogs also of various sizes, with only a few of them ticking away and just inside the door, a single lever mounted on a small table.

The friend asked, "Did you say Heath Robinson? Wasn't he some kind of inventor from way back?"

"He was indeed. Born in London in 1872. He created many quite ingenious machines. They were rather complicated and often extremely makeshift." He nodded with a grin. "To be honest, I'm quite a fan really."

The other looked around. "Yes. I can see that."

The inventor said, "Try not to touch anything. I'm still grappling with a bit of slippage."

"Oh! Really? What kind of slippage?"

"Well, put simply, it's the difference between the theoretical and the actual output. When it occurs, it tends to create a backwards jump in time."

The visitor carefully hid a smile. He turned and confronted the other with a straight face and said, "Amazing that we've known each other for so long yet I never realised…"

"No. You have to understand, I couldn't go public with any of this until I had it running perfectly."

The other managed to hold down his amusement. He'd always liked his neighbour and just because he was a little cuckoo he didn't want it to spoil their friendship.

The inventor was saying, "I'm still getting the occasional glitch, otherwise it performs well."

The other felt compelled to ask. "By 'performs', you mean you've used it to travel through time?"

"Oh! Yes. Quite regularly. That is, until the loop slippage I mentioned. I'll have to fix that. It's bad enough that I had an instance of time slippage, albeit for only a few short minutes, but if the things starts to cycle…"

The other said, "Cycle?"

"Yes, that would bring about a looped slippage."

"And a looped slippage means?"

The inventor thought for a moment. "Well, to be honest, I'm not at all sure what would happen. I only know it should be avoided."

The visitor was weaving his way through the great web of pipes and tubes when he saw a label hanging from a copper pipe with the words 'needs work' scribbled on it. "And this?" he asked.

"Yes. That's part of the problem." Looking rather concerned he added "Do be careful in there, won't you."

His friend, understanding the other's anxiety said, "Of course." He started to make his way out. As he did, his elbow jogged something and a plastic tube started to wobble as a stream of red liquid began to travel slowly through it.

"Oh! Dearie me!" exclaimed the inventor. Just as everything went suddenly dark.

The inventor pushed the door open slowly. "It's all rather Heath Robinson I'm afraid…"

The writer sat looking around the room waiting for inspiration. The Observer could tell that he was waiting for a good story.

Nothing was happening. No cracking idea for a tale that would ignite the paper it was printed on. Nothing that would make a reader gasp. He would have to get out. Go among the people. See life as it really is and observe. Watch people in their daily lives. Consider their potential hopes and dreams. Look at what and who they are and draw on what can be inferred, what can be construed, what can be imagined! Yes, it was out there. With a sense of renewed optimism he boiled the kettle, drank another cup of coffee, and then drove into town.

He had hardly parked when he saw an elderly couple arguing as they emerged from a shop. This was it. This was where he would find his story. Out here among the populace. He strode into town. The main street was busy with shoppers. He weaved his way slowly, paying close attention to what he was seeing. A policeman seemed to be giving directions to a tourist. The writer's handy notebook came out as he moved into a doorway. He scribbled a note. Across the street a window cleaner was suspended in a cradle while office workers gawked at him from inside. More scribbling.

At the main cross roads he saw a pigeon swoop low across the windscreen of a waiting car. The driver watched it fly up and away. A car sounded its horn somewhere, but he couldn't see where it came from. He turned into a side mall and looked in shop windows as he went. He could see customers perusing shelves, small children in pushers being negotiated around narrow aisles. Just then, several noisy youngsters came towards him, some with skateboards tucked under their arms, others pushing bikes. He listened to their chatter. He paused to make notes, then headed off to where he could see a café sign.

He entered and took a seat in a cubicle nearest the window - ideal for observing the mainstream of life. As the waitress approached she nearly tripped over the cat that was lounging between the tables. She scowled at it and shooed it away. The cat swore and dived under a chair. The writer ordered a cappuccino and took out his notebook. He was editing his notes when his drink arrived.

Without warning there seemed to be a whisper at his ear. "You're looking for a story? Yes?"

He turned and found the café's cat perched on top of the cubicle's divider. The cat looked around then back again. He was quite certain that the cat raised its paw and rested it gently on his shoulder, saying "At the back of the shop there's an illicit drug lab."

The young girl, a lover of nature and prone to daydreaming, was watched by the Observer as she lay down in the soft grass. She was thinking about her upcoming school assignment (an essay on wildlife) as she drifted off to sleep. In her dream it was a clear, bright morning and the woods were alive with activity. Not always seen, not always visible, but there nevertheless. A multitude of causes and effects, of cycles of activity, of silent and often unnoticed sequences; unobserved, but there all the same.

The summer heat had been slowly building as the hours slipped away, and the smells and sounds of nature grew stronger as the temperature climbed. The scene was green and brown, with only the sparkling, silver-blue water of the lake providing contrast. The grass around the lake was long and thickly-clumped. The blades swayed gently with the soft breeze, dancing rhythmically and in unison with the water's surface. All around the little clearing the trees stood tall and shoulder-to-shoulder, and beyond they seemed to go on forever. On the far side of the lake red and yellow flowers painted the edge, and above it all a clear blue sky canopied nature's picture.

The tranquillity of the scene was suddenly broken by sounds. By running, scampering sounds, made by animals forcing a passage through the long grass.

A dog is chasing a cat. The cat is frantic and wide-eyed; the dog is barking loudly with froth flying from its bared teeth.

A sequence is being played out. A sequence with a noisy and frantic end, but a chain of events with a silent and mostly unseen beginning. It began only a few moments ago with something drifting down through the trees.

A leaf, large, brown and dead, had fallen. With its stem broken, it left its usual place near the top of the tree and swooped without sound to the leafy carpet below. It was silent in flight, but hit the ground with a sharp rustling sound.

A frog was crouched nearby, eyeing insects that swirled around a small plant. Poised to make its move and concentrating on its quarry, the frog was startled by the rustling of the leaf. It jumped. Its own landing was noisier than the leaf that had spoilt its chances of a meal. The second sound echoed through the forest.

A bird, high up in the canopy, heard the thump below and took flight. The branch it had been perched on gave a great whip as the bird launched itself into the safety of the sky. As it went, the leaves danced in unison along the bough.

The frog knew nothing of this.

Among the insects that inhabited the foliage, a fly had been resting on a bright green leaf, bathed in sunlight. The warmth of the upper branches was building, and even this creature would soon be looking for a cooler place to rest. The jangling of the surrounding leaves was a prompt for the fly to move on. It, too, left the tree and came to rest on a leaf beside a lake, suspended above the rippling water - a nicer place to be in the dead heat of summer.

Some instinct had told it that this was where the air was cooler. Instinct also told it that to move further down the weeping leaf would provide refreshment from the cool mist hovering over the water below.

The frog and the bird knew nothing of this.

Dark, beneath the surface of the lake, a fish was swimming in a circular motion, seeking food. As it neared the embankment it made out a dark shape on the green frond above. Knowing this to be suitable prey, but also being aware of the speed with which such insects are able to move, the swimmer remained deep enough to see, but not be seen. It would wait for the fly to move closer.

The frog and the bird and the fly knew nothing of this.

At the edge of the wood, camouflaged by wide, brown trunks, a hungry bear was lurking. The trees that concealed it were close to the water's edge. The animal knew that any fish leaping from the water would be easy prey. It had seen movement for quite some time and was willing to wait until a fish made a play for the insects that lined the water's edge.

The frog and the bird and the fly and the fish knew nothing of this.

Farther around the curve of the lake a man and his dog had come to rest beneath a tree's great leafy spread. The heavy shade provided a well-deserved break as they had been walking for some time through the woods that circled the lake, in search of game. A hunting rifle had been rested against the tree. The dog had fallen asleep. The man had decided to eat. He took something from a bag that had been slung around his shoulder. He had spread the contents out across his outstretched legs. Drinking lukewarm water from a bottle, he eyed the food. A tomato, an apple, a small block of cheese and a large bread roll lay invitingly before him.

As he started to eat the bread and cheese the hunter became aware of movement from along the bank, behind the trees. Without turning his head he had known that a bear was loitering in a clump of trees at the water's edge, probably waiting for fish to surface. With slow, smooth movements he had retrieved his gun and was content to sit silently, waiting for the beast to break its cover.

The frog and the bird and the fly and the fish and the bear knew nothing of this.

In the warm summer air, the cheese had sent an aroma across the surrounding grass. A mouse, deep in the matted surface of the greenery had raised its head to take in the scent. It had watched the man bite off a small piece of cheese and place the remainder on the empty bag that lay beside him. It had seen the movements with the gun, but had been prepared to crouch patiently for the opportunity to race across the short distance and scamper away with a meal.

The frog and the bird and the fly and the fish and the bear and the man and the dog knew nothing of this.

Far back in the heavy undergrowth of the surrounding woods, a cat padded along cautiously, looking for something to eat. As it approached the lake it had climbed silently into a tree. The cat had known that from the branches it could look out over the area. It had also known that small creatures inhabited the banks and were sometimes careless about their movements. The cat, too, had whiffed the cheese, and spied the field mouse squatting nearby. It had deftly moved through the branches until it had come to a spot that would be ideal for springing to the ground between the mouse and the food in one leap. It had settled down to wait.

The frog and the bird and the fly and the fish and the bear and the man and the dog and the mouse knew nothing of this.

Meanwhile, the fly, sitting in the full sun, decided to head down towards the cooling mist of the crystal waters. It edged down a little, and then a little more...

The frog and the bird and the bear and the man and the dog and the mouse and the cat knew nothing of this.

The fish waited until the fly reached a certain spot. Suddenly, with a great beating of its tail, it had risen out of the water and swallowed the fly.

The bear then lurched from behind the tree and with a rapid swoop of the arm had gathered up the fish before it could dive deep enough to avoid its fate.

At this point the hunter had stood bolt upright and levelled his rifle. Before the beast had time to take cover a shot had rung out and the bear had fallen to the ground.

The mouse, startled by the noise, but determined to reap its reward for waiting so patiently, had made a sudden dash.

The cat, not seeing the dog lying motionless in the shade, had taken a mighty leap to the ground between the running mouse and the hunter's food. It was only as it landed that it had seen the dog. The dog had woken and shaken its sleepy head with the sound of its master's gun.

The dog had turned to face the cat. It had barked and made a sudden bound towards the cat.

The cat had squealed and bolted away into the longer grass in an effort to lose his enemy.

The dog, having fully-recovered from his abrupt awakening, is now pounding mercilessly after the cat. The cat is frantic and wide-eyed; the dog is barking loudly with froth flying from its bared teeth...

The girl stirred in her sleep. The sequence was complete. A cyclic pattern of happenings, being played out in rhythmic order, occurring relentlessly in an endless progression of well-ordered events; unobserved, but there for dreamers to see.

It was late evening when it watched the man walk into the living room, holding a piece of paper. His wife was sitting on the couch reading. He walked very slowly to where she sat and stared down at her.

He cleared his throat and said, "I found this in the kitchen a couple of days ago."

She looked up from her magazine. "Oh! Really?"

"Yes. I wanted to ask you about it."

"OK. Ask away," she said very slowly.

"Perhaps I should read it to you."

She put her magazine down and said, "OK."

He unfolded it and read.

"Magazine, hand lotion, cheese straws, see Brad, post letter."

She squirmed slightly. "So?"

"Who's Brad?"

"Pardon?"

"I said, who's Brad?"

"Brad? Don't know." She shook her head. "Must've been a mistake."

"Oh! Come on, what kind of mistake?"

She was blushing now. "I don't know. Maybe it was someone I met."

"What! While you were out shopping you mean?"

"Yes, maybe."

"Give me a break. It wasn't somebody you just happened to meet. It was already on your list."

She shrugged. "Well, like I said. It was probably a mistake."

"A mistake? What kind of mistake? We don't know anyone called Brad. I asked Wendy about it. She doesn't know any Brads either. Then I got to thinking about the day you went out. It was on Saturday. You said you were just popping out for some quick shopping, but you were gone a long time."

She sighed and put her arm out. "Let me see." Her hand shook a little as she took it.

After reading it she said, "I don't know, I must have just had a mad moment or something. Why make such a big thing over it? I must have scribbled it down without thinking, that's all."

He took it back and put it in his pocket. He walked out of the room. Nothing more was said about it before they started to turn in for the night. In fact, very little was said about anything. Finally, they went to bed.

About an hour after turning the light out, he asked, "Who's Brad?"

She sat bolt upright. "OK! I can't take any more of this!"

She jumped out of bed and went to a drawer in the dresser. She came back with a small box, gift wrapped. She handed it to him.

"Brad is the name of the jeweller in the high street. I had him fix your watch because I know how much you miss it. I had planned to give it to you next week on your birthday."

He took it, saying that he'd open it on his birthday. "I'm so sorry!" he said, and they fell asleep, cuddling.

An hour later, without warning, the light came on. He looked up to see her leaning over him.

"Who's Wendy?" she asked.

It could see that the boy was a keen astronomer and had built his own telescope for looking at the night sky.

He imagined it would be wonderful to travel through space and be amidst the stars. Meanwhile, he had saved up for over a year and finally bought the kit he wanted. With just a little help from his father, he had assembled an eight inch Newtonian Reflector telescope. He was lucky to have a large back garden and his parents made sure the lights in the back rooms stayed off while he was out there.

When he set his equipment up near the back fence the immediate environment was as dark as it could be in a residential area. Whenever possible, he would spend an hour or more every evening. Sometimes he would stay out so long his parents would have to call him in. He simply loved gazing up into the blackness, focusing in on tiny points of light. He could name many of the constellations by the patterns they made and he knew where to look for them.

While peering up into the void he knew he was looking at the past. Because the light that he is looking at has taken so long to get to Earth, what he sees, in most cases, is millions of years old. He so often wished he could travel to the stars; to pay a visit to a planet or just be up there looking around at what he was looking at now, but from a different perspective; among it all, surrounded by these shiny gems, so they took on a different pattern from an entirely different point of view. He was sure this would be possible one day, when science had made enough progress to enable such a thing to happen.

Just then, blinking through the eyepiece, he could see something moving. It was probably a fast moving meteor. It was getting larger. He stood back and looked up. Moments later there was a great blinding light that lit up the whole garden. As the light dimmed a great, vibrating saucer came to rest, filling the entire back lawn. The boy stood, petrified, as a hatch opened. A man in a shiny, silver tracksuit climbed out and approached slowly. His face was just a blur at first, then it flickered to something humanoid. He adjusted something on his chest.

"Can you understand me?" he asked.

The trembling boy just managed to say, "Yes."

The man touched the side of his head and announced, "Good. I have been monitoring your thoughts."

The wide-eyed boy just swallowed.

The visitor walked around the telescope. He examined it and the tripod it was mounted on. He looked at the boy.

"You wished that you could travel to the stars; to pay a visit to a planet or just be up there. You wished you could look around the night sky from up there. Is that right?"

The boy found some new courage from somewhere. "Yes, but I don't actually want…"

The visitor said, "I can make this possible for you. I can take you up there. I can let you see what it all looks like, from up there.

The boy shuffled his feet and looked towards the house. Nervously, he said, "I really need to go in. My parents will be worrying about me."

The man from the ship paused for a moment and said, "Are you sure? I can take you wherever you would like to go."

The boy shook his head. "Another time maybe."

The visitor shrugged and turned back to his ship. As the hatch closes he waves to the boy and moments later a great light spreads around the garden again. The saucer rose up with a loud humming.

It was the noise that woke him up, still blinking. Too many late nights can do this…

The student lay bathing in the island sun making the most of the glorious day, while the Observer looked on.

She was on holiday with her parents, content to just stretch out on a beach towel while her mother went in for a swim and her father lounged back at the hotel. This would be their last full day before flying home. The weather on the island was just right and had been that way since they arrived. She was returning to one more round of study before taking up a career. It felt as though she had been studying so hard, and taking in so much, that these few days away from it all had been a great idea.

Her eye was caught by her mother waving from the sea. She sat up and raised an arm in return. This brought her attention to an old beachcomber working his way along the sea's edge, looking for whatever the tide had washed in. He was a small man in shabby shorts and shirt, with brown, weathered skin. He was carrying a small bag that looked almost empty. He was obviously picky about what he collected. She watched him with interest as he came nearer.

All of a sudden he stopped and stooped over. He seemed to be working something out of the sand with his fingertips. He waded a few paces into the shallow and bent down again to wash off his prize. Returning to the beach, he opened his bag and drew out a piece of cloth. He stood drying what seemed to be a pebble. He returned the cloth to his bag, then placed the pebble on the flat of his upturned palm and extended his arm out horizontally. She watched in fascination as the character just stood there for a minute or two, in a pose that suggested that he was offering it to some invisible person.

When his arm dropped he turned and looked directly at the girl. Then, as though recognising her, he gave her a wide grin. She had no idea who he was, but felt compelled to smile back. He walked up the sandy slope to where she had been sun-bathing. He stopped in front of her. "You wonder what I was doing, don't you?" he asked.

She looked up at him while shielding her eyes from the sun with her hand. He looked to be a nice old man with a winning smile and didn't hesitate to say, "I was curious. Yes. What did you find?"

He held up the pebble between his thumb and forefinger. "I was giving thanks for this," he said.

She sat up further and crossed her legs. "May I see it?"

"Of course. After all, it is as much yours as it is mine."

She took it saying, "Oh! Really?"

"Oh! Yes," he said and turned to look out across the waves to the horizon. "Yes." He repeated. He turned back to her and said, "Beautiful, isn't it?"

She turned it over in her hands. As far as she could see, it was just another pebble.

He smiled. "But, don't you see? There is no other pebble like it." He paused to gaze around again and said, "…on this beach, on this island, on this planet or anywhere else in the known universe."

His hands came up in a gesture of prayer. He nodded, and bowing slightly said, "Bless you." With that, he took the pebble back and dropped it into his bag, tightened it with the drawstrings which he looped around his wrist. He then turned and made his way back down the slope to the sea's edge and continued on his way, stopping from time to time to look at something, then moving on.

Her mother was now making her way up the beach.

When she arrived she picked her towel up, shook it free of sand and dried her face. She asked, "Everything OK honey?

Her daughter was deep in thought. She said, "Sure."

"I saw him talking to you. He seemed quite a friendly old thing. No problem then?"

"Oh! No. Not at all."

Her mother pulled a face. "From what I could see he was coming across like he was some sort of loony."

The daughter clasped her hands behind her head and laid back down. She squinted up at her mother and said, "No. On the contrary, I have a sneaky feeling he was one of the wisest people I've ever met!"

It was floating in a small room, listening to the conversation. There was more complaining about having to share the room. It was far too crowded.

Sebastian was a book lover, but was forever having to search for the one he was currently reading. His roommate, Tommy, was always moving his stuff around. Put simply, they were completely different people. Tommy was just naturally messy and Sebastian wasn't. He had been raised in the city above his father's antique business while Tommy had grown up on a farm.

It was quite ironic that these two men should ever end up having to share a room, but they'd been told in no uncertain terms that nothing could be done about it. After all, it wasn't as though it was forever. Neither of them was happy about it. They just had to make the most of it, but it wasn't getting any easier. Arguments were regularly breaking out and this was one of them.

Sebastian: "You've moved my book again."

Tommy: "Which one?"

Sebastian: "The one I was reading."

Tommy: "No. I haven't."

Sebastian: "Yes. It was right here."

Tommy: "You must have moved it."

Sebastian: "Look at this mess. I thought we agreed that you could use that corner, it's bigger than my little space under the window." He looked around, frustrated.

Tommy: "Like I said, you must have moved it."

Sebastian: "I didn't. I know I didn't."

Tommy: "You've got a hell of a lot of books in here. You must expect to mislay one sometimes."

Sebastian: "I didn't mislay it. It was right here."

Tommy: "What was it, anyway?"

Sebastian: "What, the title you mean?"

Tommy: "Of course."

Sebastian: He gave it some thought. "Not sure, now you come to ask."

Tommy: "We should get out more…," he sighed.

He was cut short by a clanging at the door. It opened and the prison psychologist came in with a chair. He seated himself with a clipboard and pen on his lap. He sat looking at the single occupant of the cell.

With an amiable smile he said, "Well now, who would like to talk to me today?"

It knew that the woman wasn't just another itinerant worker, happily picking oranges in Greece. It knew that was only what people saw, on the surface.

It was quite common; people came from all over Europe to work for the farmers, picking fruit. Some were American, but not too many. So nobody found it strange to have a woman with a Yankee accent harvesting alongside them. They may have found it interesting that she didn't return to the States when the season finished.

When others all dispersed back to the countries they came from, she would stay on in cheap digs during the out-of-season months. She would pick up work as a shop assistant or bar work - just about anything really. People were friendly enough and she had been accepted and made to feel welcome by the locals. She was very happy with her life.

Thinking back, it had been so different. A mismatched, childless marriage, with him taking to the bottle. Her life was a misery with no way out. She found herself constantly dreaming up ways of escaping, but he could see this and had made it quite clear that if she ever left him, he would find her.

The only respite she had from her home life were her days in the office. She had been with the same company for several years and had worked herself up into a role that was busy but interesting. She was also lucky enough to have a desk close to a window, and high enough to have a magnificent view out across the city and beyond to the river.

The day that the planes flew found her down at a local store on street level. It wasn't unusual for her to take time out to shop. She heard the first explosion; everybody did. People started running and screaming. When the dust clouds began billowing through the streets she walked, quickly at first, then ran; ran as fast as she could until exhaustion brought her coughing to her knees. She sat on the pavement with her back against a shop front, watching the distant chaos and thinking... a lot of thinking. That's when she saw the way out. That's when she became dead.

Who could imagine that anything good could come out of 9/11?

It floated nearby as the Human Resources Officer met the man at the front desk.

There was nobody on reception when he arrived. The officer came forward and shook the new employee's hand. "Would you like a glass of water or a tea?"

"No, that's fine."

He waved his arm at the elevator. "Follow me then."

In the elevator he said, "You're our new man in accounts, right?"

The other nodded, "That's me."

They stepped out into the corridor. The officer led the way saying, "This is just a brief meet and greet of course, but I think you'll like it here on the thirteenth floor."

They entered a large open-planned office. It was empty

and dark. The new man could just make out several windows with blinds drawn down. The light flickered on and the HR man went to the nearest blind and raised it.

"Magnificent view of the city," he said. "Not that you'll have time to look out of the window." He guffawed.

The new man had reservations creeping in but made an effort to smile.

"Anyway, the truth is the old man…" he coloured and said, "I should say the boss. Truth is he doesn't like the blinds up. Gets a bit worked up about UV rays."

He walked a few paces. "This is your spot. You've got the desk of the guy you're replacing."

Wondering about UV rays, the new man pushed on regardless. "I gather it was an unexpected post vacancy; a sudden need to get a new person in. Some sort of illness, I suppose."

The other dropped his voice unnecessarily. "Just between us, he had a bit of an accident, on one of the outings."

"Oh?"

He sighed. "He was abseiling and he fell… spinal injury is what I heard." He looked uncomfortable and said, "Not too far from the tea machine, eh?"

"Tea?"

"Yes. The boss won't have a coffee machine. Dead against caffeine he is. Says it's addictive and causes cancer and heart disease."

The other stood looking around, thinking about the lack of coffee and natural sunlight.

Finally he said, "Well, I've got to ask, where is everybody?"

"Oh! Goodness. Sorry, I should have said. They're all away at the moment. Boss likes to take everybody on a corporate retreat; a three-day bonding course in the national forest." He seemed to shudder slightly. "He does them every six months. Yes. Saturday, Sunday and Monday; they'll all be back tomorrow."

"How many staff do you have in accounts?" the new man asked.

"Ooh! About a hundred and twenty all up, including the boss and his secretary."

The new man managed to keep down a snigger but it was getting harder. "And he takes them all off for one of these things twice a year?" he asked.

"Oh! Yes. Never misses. He really enjoys it. Gives lots of pep talks. Morale-boosting stuff, you know."

The new man raised his eyebrows. "And you were left behind this time I see; to give me an induction and the grand tour, I suppose."

"Yes."

"So, you missed out this time round?"

The officer looked away and said, "You could say that."

The new man straightened and said, "Well, thank you very much for taking the time today."

On the way down the officer asked, "Any questions?"

"No. You covered it very well I think."

The new man thanked him again in the reception area and left.

The man smiled with satisfaction and relief as he passed through the front entrance, knowing he would not be going back through it. Out on the street he breathed in the air and felt the sunlight wash over him. He went looking for a coffee shop.

He had it sorted in his head. Phone in sick for a couple of weeks, then back to the job ads.

It was alongside the woman who was sitting on the couch. She was sobbing amid the upturned room. She looked up at the man in the suit. "What can I tell you Inspector?"

"Are you able to talk now?"

"Yes. I think so. Sorry, I'll do my best."

"Just take it from the beginning."

"I came back from late night shopping." She stopped and looked at the chaos in the room and the body lying on the floor. She started to cry again.

"You're doing well. Just take your time. When you're ready."

She looked up at him again and nodded. "Yes, of course. You're very kind, and patient. It's the shock of it. Of course, you'd know that in your job." She wiped her eyes.

He nodded.

"I normally catch the bus home from town, but just as I finished shopping I met my neighbour coming out. He was kind enough to give me a lift home. When he dropped me off I saw that the front door was open. I just knew something was wrong. He came in with me."

She sighed and continued. "I'm so glad he did. I don't know how I'd have coped if I'd come in on my own. He was very supportive. He rang the police, then sat me down here with a drink."

"What exactly did you find when you came in?"

"My husband, lying there with blood on the back of his head. My neighbour felt for a pulse. He was... he was dead! I think he must have disturbed a burglar." At this point she burst into tears, burying her face in her hands.

Her neighbour laughed. "That's perfect! If you can keep that up when the police arrive, we'll certainly get away with it. Then, my love, we can be together."

It was observing the man as he disappeared behind the shed. It felt his intense disappointment and a deal of anger. It saw what had gone before with the man looking through the old antique shop's grubby window.

It was the coffee table that caught his eye. He had made a habit of stopping to peer in at the jumble of stuff inside the dingy shop on his daily walk to the station. It was early and he didn't know if it was open. There would be time enough before his train, so he tried the door; a bell clanged over his head. He'd never actually gone in before and just stood gazing around at the wonderful collection that filled the tiny room.

He and his wife had always liked old things, but this table was something really special. He ran his fingers over the intricate pattern of inlayed wooden pieces that covered the rectangular top.

"Can I help?" came a voice from the back, startling him.

He straightened. "Oh! Yes. I was just admiring this table. Queen Anne is it?"

"Yes indeed," came the reply. "It's rare that I get anything close to this quality. It's only been in here a couple of days."

He came up and ran his finger down one of the legs. "These are magnificent, aren't they? As I say, I only just got it in, but I've had enquiries already. It won't be here long, I can assure you."

That was how it started… an offer was made and accepted.

The shopkeeper noted the address it was to be delivered to during the same afternoon. The house had a porch and it could be tucked in there out of sight.

He smiled warmly at his customer. "It will be ready waiting for you when you come home from work."

He caught his train and sat in a happy state of mind for the entire journey, imagining the various places it could go in the house to best show it off. He could hardly wait to give the good news to his wife. During the day he tried to contact her. She was probably at one of her catch-ups.

He arrived home in a state of excitement but found the porch empty. His wife said there had been no deliveries. Naturally, he was very annoyed, but knew the shop would be closed. He would go back in the morning and sort it out.

The next day found the shopkeeper most apologetic. He had written down the wrong street name - Compton instead of Crompton. This was on the delivery note he gave to the driver. All was not lost. The table would be picked up and taken to the correct address as soon as possible. He would call to confirm this had been done; hopefully before noon.

No call had come in until mid-afternoon; when he was asked to call in at the shop on his way home. The shop would remain open until he arrived. This didn't sound good, and it wasn't. The shop owner explained. The driver, discovering that the house had no porch, had dropped it on the front verge the previous day but it had gone when he went back for it. The house owner thought it was strange and figured it was put out for bulk refuse collection, but didn't know why they should choose to put it in front of his house. Refuse pick up wasn't due for several weeks.

However, there was some good news. The lady at the wrong address was pleased to see that it was picked up and taken away from their house, not by the official collectors, but by a local plumber who, thinking the table was up for grabs, had loaded it into the back of his utility vehicle. The shop owner said that he had been in touch with the man, explained the whole situation, and finally had his agreement to allow the driver to call by tomorrow, collect the table and leave it in the porch, as originally arranged.

The following day when he got home, the man was both relieved and delighted to find the coffee table in his porch. His wife wasn't aware that it had been delivered and was shocked as her husband carried it in through the front door.

She didn't like it; not at all, especially the legs! It wouldn't suit their home one little bit. She was quite adamant that she didn't even like the thing coming into the house.

She said, "Put it behind the shed, it can go out with the next bulk refuse collection!

She stands before the mirror carefully checking that she's ready for the morning parade, while the Observer looks on.

Great care has been taken with her hair. The dress is new and sure to turn a few heads. The shoes are very expensive. She always spends big on shoes. Yes, she is ready for her morning parade. A last flick of her hair and she makes for the door.

A few minutes later she arrives at the station. Excitement builds as she approaches the main entrance. Only three minutes before the train. Planned that way to ensure that a full crowd of admirers will be on the platform to watch her enter and walk the walk.

Predictably, heads turn as she strolls gracefully along the front of the platform. She glides the entire length of it to take up her position, then stands poised and graceful. She stands beneath the spotlight where she stands every morning, aware of her audience looking on. She feels good; she revels in the admiring glances. She's a movie star, a celebrity, and a model, all wrapped up in one. With so much attention, she decides to give them all a second show.

Midway back she feels something at her foot as her stiletto heel comes apart, turning her ankle. She falls backwards onto the tracks. There is stunned silence from the commuters, followed by screams. One man starts to climb down but changes his mind when he looks along the track. She cannot see the oncoming train. She cannot move. The rail digs heavily into the middle of her back. She feels the vibration coming through.

Her own scream wakes her.

She is shaking violently. She rolls to one side and with trembling fingers finds the torch. The one she keeps under her pillow. She pulls it out from under her back and drops it to the floor. She lays perfectly still for a very long time, sweating, aching, and feeling nauseous. This was only a nightmare, of course, but she thinks about her morning routine.

With great effort she climbs out of bed and staggers to the bathroom. There she holds onto the sides of the washbasin. Eventually she runs the water and with cupped hands splashes her face. She reaches for a towel. She straightens, and dries her face. She stares at what she sees there. A pale and haggard visage with no makeup, only a few smudged remains from the day before. Hair messy and tangled and bloodshot eyes.

Still trembling, she takes several deep breaths with eyes closed. Another look at her reflection and she knows with absolute certainty that she really isn't a movie star, or a celebrity, or a model, all wrapped up in one.

She may not be any of these things but she is smart enough to know that she really must reappraise how much importance she places on self-image!

The man was strolling slowly, while the Observer floated alongside. He hated waiting for buses. They never seemed to show up when they're supposed to, and his next bus out of town wasn't for half an hour, or more if it was late. That was another thing; they were always running late! He had just fancied a day off from working in the service station at the edge of town. He had phoned in sick. They wouldn't miss him for one day.

He ambled along, looking in shop windows that were of no real interest to him. With so much time to kill he decided to stroll into a narrow lane that he had often seen, but had never had a chance to visit. It wasn't very appealing; the path was dirty and strewn with bits of paper and discarded take-away coffee cups, blown in off the main shopping parade. He was about to turn around when he saw a small, dusty window with a display of curious items. There was no name above the doorway, but it seemed to be some sort of second-hand curio shop.

He stared in at the display as best he could. Some of the strangely laid-out objects seemed to be magic tricks of some sort; playing cards fanned out, large metal hoops, the type that mystically join up somehow, and several top hats with an assortment of wands. He looked at his watch and went in.

A bell clanged somewhere, although he couldn't see it, and a little old man came forward and smiled.

"Anything in particular?" he asked looking around at the jumble of oddments that surrounded them.

He smiled and said, "Just looking."

The old man went back behind the counter and said, "Take your time." He perched himself on a high stool and went back to reading from a very large, ancient looking book bound with leather.

The man took his time, doing a circuit of the shop looking at the strange array of objects, finally ending up back at the front, peering into the front window display from behind. Movement outside made him look up through the murky glass. He got a shock when he saw one of his workmates looking at the objects laid out. He ducked back before he was seen. A sense of panic gripped him and he found a large, comfy armchair with its back to the window. He sank into it and made himself small. He looked at his watch. It must be his workmate's lunch time!

The phone went and the old man turned away and picked it up. The man saw this as his opportunity to find a way of slipping out through the back, just in case the other man came into the shop. He crept silently to the rear of the shop and pulled a heavy curtain to one side. There was a hallway and a door at the end. He move quickly and he was outside, standing in yet another alleyway.

There was a feeling of dampness in the air that took him by surprise, and he could hear water running. He took off down the lane that quickly became some sort of tunnel running beneath buildings, and within a minute found himself staring down into a narrow canal with water flowing gently towards a tiny bridge with flowers running along its rails. In something of a stupor he walked along the side path and crossed the bridge. He entered another laneway; this one became wider and had shops and cafes on either side.

Eventually, he walked out into a great open space. There were a few people around, but they didn't seem to take any notice of him; just another tourist. It had beautiful, old, and very ornate buildings on all sides. He strolled around in a daze looking at the names on cafes. He picked up a menu from one of the tables.

He was in a piazza; he was actually in Venice!

Whichever way he tried to make any sense of it, he was in Venice. He had never been there before but it was totally recognisable from the many magazines and TV shows he had seen about the city. He had no doubt that this would be a wonderful place to visit, but not in the present circumstances.

He stood for several minutes, trying to figure out what he should do. He had never been so frightened. None of this made any sense and he wanted it to end. He wanted to get back to where he was. He wanted to be back to town, waiting for a bus.

He thought very carefully about the route he had taken to get where he was; where he had walked, where he had come from. He had to pull himself together and retrace his steps exactly. This shouldn't be too hard; he had only come a short distance. But this was Venice, notorious for tourists getting lost; very often quite deliberately, as this was part of the place's attraction.

But he wasn't a tourist and none of what was happening to him would ever leave him with fond memories. Fear welled up in him again as he looked back and convinced himself that he knew exactly where he had entered the square. With painful slowness and concentration he made his way back to the rear entrance of the old shop.

As he entered, the shop owner greeted him in the hallway with a smile.

"I'm glad you found your way back alright, come and sit down. You've had quite an experience haven't you?"

He led the way into a tiny parlour off the hall.

"Sit yourself down and I'll put the kettle on. Tea or coffee?"

He was still slowly coming out of the trance in which the whole experience had engulfed him.

"Eh? Oh! Coffee would be good." He rubbed his face. "Thank you," he added, and stared around the room, trying to pull himself back into some kind of normality.

"You must have questions. I'll sit with you and explain."

He brought two mugs to the table and sat down. His eyes were twinkling as he stared at his customer.

"It's a portal," said the old man. "It was set up for me by a great magician and a very good friend. I did him a service once and the portal was, well, it was a reward, if you like.

It allows me to visit my old home without the expense of airfares". He grinned.

"It's… it's wonderful!" The man blurted out. "I mean, you could make an absolute fortune with it. You could…"

The old man held up his hand. "It *is* wonderful, as you say. It is wonderful to be able to tell anybody about it."

He reflected for a moment. "Not a thing that I would normally do you understand."

He got up and went to a cupboard, took out a small object and returned to the table. He held something clasped in his hand and went on. "This was also given to me by that same magician. I would like to show it to you. Again, not something I would usually do, but today you have become a very special customer."

He raised his hand and let a crystal drop; it hung on a fine, almost invisible thread.

"This too is magic. There are beautiful colours hidden inside. Can you see them? You have to look very carefully and concentrate."

The crystal began to swing slowly, and its slight rotation showed small glints of colour.

"Yes! I can see them. Lots of colours… they… they…" His eyelids flickered a couple of times, and then slowly closed.

He felt something pulling on his shoulder. He was being shaken.

"Young man," the voice was saying. "Young man, you can't sleep here, I'm afraid. Somebody may wish to buy this chair."

"What?" He opened his eyes. "Someone might what?"

"The chair," the old man repeated. "Someone may want to buy it and it wouldn't do if you were fast asleep in it."

"Asleep? I've been asleep?"

"Oh! Yes, and dreaming, I think."

"Dreaming?"

"Yes. You kept mumbling something about a bus you had to catch."

He looked at his watch. "Have I really been here for over an hour?"

"I suppose it's my fault in a way. I didn't notice that you had made yourself so comfortable that you had fallen asleep." He peered up at the ceiling. "The light is very poor in here. Sorry, I just didn't see you."

He looked up and saw the solitary naked light globe. For just a moment he thought he glimpsed some colours sparkle, but no, he blinked and it was gone. He struggled out of the chair and felt unsteady as he straightened.

"I've got to go," he said, staring at the shop owner with an apologetic look. "I have a bus to catch."

"Of course," said the old man. "Are you sure you'll be all right? You must have slept very soundly."

"I'll be fine thanks," the man said over his shoulder, as he stepped back into the lane and made his way back to the bus stop.

No sign of his workmate; that had been a close call. He checked the timetable and looked down at his wrist watch again. He still couldn't believe the time. Had he really fallen asleep in that old chair for so long? And… was that all just a dream?

The next bus was due in four minutes. That wasn't too bad, he supposed. He didn't like the idea, but he was going to stand right there and wait this time. He didn't like waiting for buses. They were always losing time.

The doctor was reading, the patient sat across from him and the Observer watched events unfold. It noted the various people who played a role in what was happening.

Harry Brown sat looking around the surgery while the doctor leafed through his patient's notes. He was very nervous. This was not a thing that Harry would normally be comfortable about admitting to. He was, after all, a hardened criminal. He had done a lot of pretty violent things in his lifetime and within his own circle of associates was much admired for his easy going brutality. People didn't mess with Harry.

Yet here he was, waiting for his fate to be determined by this pompous quack.

Doctor Murphy put down the folder and smiled. "That all seems to be in order. As you know, your release back into society is now only dependent on your not having contracted any nasty diseases during your stay with us."

Harry hated this smug bastard, but what he was saying was right. It was only the result of this blood test that could stop him getting out.

He asked "How long do I have to wait before the results come back?"

"Oh! Don't concern yourself with that. We test it straight away. Two minutes, three at the most."

Harry relaxed visibly and rolled up his sleeve.

The needle was pushed gently into his arm and within

seconds Harry's head slumped forward. He had not noted that the plunger was going the wrong way...

A little later, Murphy sat across the desk from Reginald Hardwick, the Prison Governor, in his well-appointed office, waiting for Clive, the computer geek from down the hall. Both men were looking more than a little pleased with themselves, and were having trouble containing their growing excitement at what was about to take place.

When joined by Clive, these three would form a very special group within the prison. Only they were privy to the operation of the Humanitarian Termination Programme; a programme that had been in place for several years, carrying out death penalties as prescribed by law, but without the anguish and suffering caused by the inmates knowing that these sentences were indeed about to be carried out. Harold Brown had been number ten, and with the full set of records, Hardwick was at last able to take his report to the Ministry for approval.

"He knows about the meeting?" enquired Murphy.

"Yes, he'll be here. You know what he's like."

"I do. He worries me sometimes. He's, well... very quiet. Almost secretive in a way."

Hardwick nodded. "That's been an attribute in a way. I've found that has given me confidence over the years that he can keep his part in what we are doing confidential. He's been most particular about managing the programme's database. No-one else has had access to it. He was very careful about that."

After a gentle knock, Clive entered, looking a little scruffy as usual, and carrying several folders. He sat without speaking, nodding at the others.

"Glad you could join us on this very special occasion, Clive. As you know, today sees the end of our programme, allowing me to submit the results. Results that may very well bring about a revolutionary change in the way justice is delivered for future offenders." He glanced at Murphy. "We would both like to thank you heartily for the part you have played."

Clive nodded.

Hardwick opened his own folder. "Brown was number ten in the programme. Any comments on that one Murphy?"

"No. All went according to plan. Presumably he's been added to your database report, Clive?"

Clive grinned. "Eh, yes, he's in there." He squirmed in his chair, staring down at his pile of folders and mumbled, "Bastard!"

Hardwick gave Murphy a shocked stare, leant forward and said, "Pardon?"

Clive rolled his head on his shoulders and repeated, "Bastard. I said he was a bastard."

Hardwick frowned. "Why would you say that?"

"He was very rude to Cynthia when he went for his flu shot."

"Cynthia?"

Murphy interjected. "Yes, Cynthia. She left rather suddenly a couple of months ago. We had a job finding a replacement for her at such short notice."

Clive took out a handkerchief and blew his nose. "She was really upset. She told me about it in the staff canteen. He had been so vulgar. You just wouldn't believe the filthy things he said to her. She was worried about finding another job. She has a sick son, you know."

Hardwick adjusted his tie nervously. "I didn't know, but…"

"Got his punishment though, didn't he? I mean he got what was coming to him. Even if it meant I had to make adjustments to the database."

The two men looked at each other in horror.

Murphy gathered himself and said, "Adjustments?"

"Yeah, it only took a little tweak to the database."

Murphy asked, "Why would you need to do that? He was going to die anyway."

"Not really," said Clive.

"Not really? What do you mean, not really?"

"Well, not until I made sure he got the punishment he deserved." He opened one of the folders he had placed on the governor's desk. "Brown, Harold – fourteen years for attempted murder."

There was a long pause, then Hardwick started laughing hysterically. "You are joking, of course. You have to be joking." He took out his own handkerchief and dabbed at his eyes while Murphy sat shaking his head.

Murphy said "You're not joking, are you, Clive?"

"No, I'm not. The swine got what he deserved."

"Sweet Jesus!" cried Hardwick. "What have you done? What have you done, you fool? You have ruined all our work, all our efforts, our years of research and careful record keeping. All flushed down the toilet, and all because you felt sorry for bloody Cynthia?"

Clive lifted his chin. "She was nice, Cynthia. She was a really decent sort, if you know what I mean. She was very upset by the whole thing. Almost as upset as Audrey. Audrey cried a lot."

Hardwick had his head in his hands mumbling, "Jesus,

what is he going to tell us now? Murphy, you ask him, I can't take much more of this."

Murphy, emotionally reeling from what was going on, pulled himself together and asked, as calmly as he could, "Who's Audrey?"

"You don't remember her, I suppose. It was a couple of years ago. She was very quiet, fragile you might say; but she was a very hard worker and dedicated to her job. She was very happy working in the clinic until Langford turned up."

"Langford?"

"Robert Langford." He opened another file. "Transferred here in September that year. A very nasty piece of work he was. I found Audrey in the linen room crying her eyes out. She went home sick that day and didn't come back. I got off early and gave her a lift home to save her having to wait for a bus. She was in a terrible state. I was hoping she'd come back, but she didn't."

Murphy looked at his own notes and said, "Number seven," under his breath. He continued, "Langford, I remember him, tell me what was he in for?"

Clive glanced down at the open folder.

"Possession of a firearm with intent to endanger life – he got ten years."

"Ten years," Murphy moaned. He looked at Hardwick, who had settled face-down on his desk, with his fingers clasped over his head.

"Did you hear that?" he asked, stretching across the desk and tapping the governor's arm. Hardwick just gave out a childlike whine.

"So," said the doctor "you are telling us that because you felt sorry for these two women you doctored the data held in the database; a database that only you had direct access to, in order to have two men killed for being rude to them. Is that right?"

"Not completely, no."

"Not completely, you say! Not completely! What the hell do you mean by not completely?"

"Well, I haven't told you about Sally, have I? I mean she was a really, really nice girl. A bit prim you could say. I think she might have been religious, but I never asked. That wouldn't really do would it? To ask about a person's religious beliefs, I mean. That would be an invasion of a person's privacy, wouldn't it? Don't you think?"

"For pity's sake, Clive, just tell us what happened. No... don't tell us what happened. Tell us if there are any more!"

Clive shrugged "No, of course not. I wouldn't hurt anyone who didn't deserve it. I mean, that would be wrong, wouldn't it?"

Murphy shook his head wearily and said "Just tell us."

Clive seemed to drift off.

Murphy shouted now, "Just tell us, will you!"

"OK. Well, she was pestered and persecuted for ages by that low-life, but she didn't say anything. She didn't tell anybody until that morning. She'd just had enough, I guess. She kind of snapped. She picked something up and threw it at him; a coffee mug, I think. I'm sure you know about it. There was a hell of a stink and she got the sack, of course."

"Yes, I remember the case. It was decided that she didn't have the temperament for the work and was dismissed. Nothing was said about her being bothered by anybody. What was his name now? It all happened a long time ago."

"Logan, number two in the programme. Here we are, Samuel Logan – breaking, entering and stealing – seven years."

"Logan, I can't say I remember him offhand…"

Hardwick giggled and said, "Offhand!" then wriggled around to make himself more comfortable. He started sobbing quietly again.

"Why didn't any of this come out at the time?"

"You'd have to know Sally to answer that. As I said, she was very shy. One of the wardens who knew her family said she had been so embarrassed by what Logan had been saying to her that she could never repeat it; not even in a court of law."

At this point Hardwick got up shakily and said "I think I'll go and have a lie down." He staggered across to the door, and as it closed they heard another muffled giggle.

Murphy sat staring at the vacated chair for a couple of minutes. He was thinking about what all this meant; to him, to Hardwick, and yes… even to Clive. He could hardly take in the consequences of what Clive had done, what he had made *them* do."

He jumped up suddenly, tipping his chair over. He stood towering over Clive with a raging anger and hate in his eyes.

"You stupid fool!" he shouted. "You obviously have no idea what you have done. These men, these… three people; what were they guilty of, eh? What were these three people actually guilty of?"

"Harassment" Clive muttered.

"Harassment?"

"Yes, harassment. It's illegal."

"Yes. I know it's illegal, but you can't put three people to death for harassment!"

"Clive smiled shyly and whispered, "I did…"

It was now hovering over a back patio, watching a couple sitting together, quietly sipping their morning coffees.

Quite suddenly the man leant across the table and took his wife's hand and said, "If, right now, you could be anywhere, and I mean absolutely anywhere in the world..." he paused for a moment, then went on, "where would you like to be, right now?"

She was obviously surprised by the question, but gazed out across the back garden as if seeing places, taking in their sights and sounds and smells. She fell pensive for a while. He was giving her time to think.

"Like gazing down into the Trolls Pass in Norway?" she asked.

"Yes, if you like," he replied.

"Or wandering through Sri Lankan tea fields."

"That too."

"Maybe standing on a balcony looking out across the roofs of Salzburg."

"Yes."

"I could say, soaking in a hot spring in Fiji."

"You could."

"Or simply strolling across grassy flats within the walls of Cardiff Castle."

"Well, yes, if you like."

"Or maybe sipping wine in a café in one of Montenegro's medieval towns."

"Lovely."

"Or scuba diving in the Mediterranean along the Maltese archipelago."

"Why not?"

"Or just strolling idly through the Red Fort in India."

"Yes."

"Maybe on a wildlife tour through a Madagascan forest."

"Exhilarating."

"Just wandering through the vanilla plantations of Tahiti."

"Ah! Yes."

"Or losing oneself in an olive grove in Greece."

"Yes."

"Or visiting the caves and rock formations in Cappadocia in Turkey."

"Or that."

"Standing on the Great Wall of China."

"That too."

"Kayaking across Lake Baikal in Russia."

"Nice."

"Or taking the tour through the Neuschwanstein Castle in Germany."

"Interesting."

"Visiting the sea turtle nesting grounds in Vietnam."

"That too."

"Maybe just wandering through a Cambodian temple."

"Ah!"

"Visiting the picturesque sand dunes and clay pans in Namibia."

"Lovely."

"Or walking through avenues of orange trees on the Peloponnese peninsula."

"Yes."

"Or flying over the salt flats of Bolivia."

"Exciting."

"Visiting the scenic terraces in the highlands of Iran."

"Beautiful."

"Maybe taking a hot air balloon ride over Buddhist temples in Burma."

"There's that."

"Trekking through bamboo forests in Japan."

"Adventurous."

"Or visiting the Giant's Causeway in Ireland."

"Stunning."

"Or just sunning oneself on an exclusive beach in the Seychelles."

"Sounds nice."

She stopped. He cocked his head, waiting for an answer.

"But to answer you truthfully…, being right here, in our back garden."

He smiled. "Me too."

It was listening to sounds coming from above. She was moving around. It knew that this woman had woken with a massive headache and a really bad taste in her mouth.

She'd had friends around for drinks the night before and things were in a mess. In the kitchen there were empty bottles in the sink and several dishes with food scraps left lying around. She knew there was a clean-up job in front of her. What she didn't see was the spilled water, slowly running behind the toaster. It crept unseen along the work surface. The toaster's cord was frayed and lay in the path of the little stream. Needless to say, this sort of thing was not likely to be noticed by the woman, considering the way her head was throbbing.

She entered the kitchen and stood, staggering a little. She switched on the toaster and began looking for the bread when she caught sight of a shadow moving across her kitchen. At first she thought it was a figment of her imagination due to her hangover, but staring across the room she could just make out a translucent shape forming. It was just a patch of grey at first, slowly swirling and forming the upper torso of a figure. Thrusting her face forward and blinking wildly she could make out a skeletal face buried in a large hood. With the recognition, she let out a cry.

An eerie voice asked "You can see me?"

She squinted. "Sort of."

It seemed surprise. "You can?"

"Well, half of you anyway."

"I apologise. That's not supposed to happen."

She swayed a bit and asked, "What are you doing here?"

"I'm not here really, if you see what I mean."

She shook her head slowly and said "No. I don't see what you mean, I think you should go before I call the police."

It sighed. "Why would you do that?"

"Why? Because this is a home invasion, that's why."

It looked across at the puddle of water now soaking the cord and smiled. "Oh come on, what harm could I possibly do, if as you say, I'm only half here?"

Her head bobbed and she thought very deeply to come up with an answer. "I don't know, I guess I'm just not much of a risk taker."

With that, and hardly aware that she was doing it, she

leant across the counter and yanked out the toaster plug. As she did, she heard a disappointed whisper. When she turned back the thing was gone.

The Observer saw the girl approach the house, making as little noise as possible. It felt the girl's emotional leap as the front gate squeaked.

The girl was musing on how it was always good to spend time with old Mister Fotheringay.

She crept past the sleeping dog and went into the house through the back door and made her way quietly to her room. She knew she was late. It didn't do any good. Her mother appeared at her door.

"You're late. Did you go round to Fotheringay's house again?"

"Yes. He was teaching me more stuff. You know, about magic."

"Magic, you say." She turned to go, then looked back "Did you see Casper?"

"Yep. By the front gate."

"OK. Tea is nearly ready."

"Mister Fotheringay says that some foods have magical properties and that people have known about them for centuries."

Her mother shook her head. "I'm not sure that getting involved with such stuff at your age is a good idea. He seems a nice old guy, a bit weird, but I'm sure he's harmless enough...

"Oh! He is." She interrupts. "He's very kind and tells me all sorts of interesting stuff."

"Well, I don't know."

"He's from a long line of wizards that goes back hundreds of years."

Her mother smiles. "Is he now?"

"Yes, and he has been teaching me spells. He says I'm a natural."

Her mother holds her cheeks and shakes her head again. "I do worry sometimes."

The girl smiles and says, "Nothing to worry about Mum. Everything's cool."

"Cool eh?" She stares lovingly at her daughter.

"What?"

"I don't know. I sometimes wish your father was still around. Maybe he could talk some sense into you."

"But you were always saying you wished he would drop dead."

"Well, yes, but I didn't mean it, of course."

"You didn't?"

"No, of course not."

"Oh! Anyway, Mister Fotheringay said that cats were better than dogs."

Her mother scowled "Does he? Well, I draw the line there. I think he should mind his own business."

The girl didn't seem to hear the anger in her mother's voice. She went on to say, "If I did get a cat, I'd like to call it Fothers?"

Her mother stood speechless, just flapping her arms.

The girl went on regardless. "He says you can really bond with a cat. He says when a person works with a familiar (that's a cat, of course) they pool their resources and the magic is much stronger."

Her mother was now staring into the room with a frantic look in her eyes.

The girl lifted her hand slowly and seemed to be pointing at the ceiling. At that moment from the front of the house there was a screech of tyres and a yelp.

The girl grinned and asked, "Are Siamese expensive?"

Her mother fainted.

It was watching the man standing across the street from the shop, waiting for it to close.

As the man looked on a bus pulled up, temporarily obliterating his view. When it pulled away a girl stood there looking around as though she was lost. Then she crumpled to the ground, not moving. When he got to her she was breathing and coming around slowly. He helped her to her feet and they began to walk slowly. She didn't seem to respond to anything he said. He knew there was a hospital only a couple of blocks away. They gradually made their way there with his arm around her, supporting her, keeping her upright. When they arrived he sat her in the waiting room, pointed her out to the first nurse he saw… and left.

When she came to, she was on a drip in a curtained cubicle. She had been diagnosed as undernourished. A few hours later, after taking a shower and eating the food that came on a tray, the doctor said she could leave. Her rescuer was nowhere to be seen and nobody could give her any information about him. She hadn't managed to get a good look at him. It was late when she walked back out onto the street. She caught the first bus home.

A few months later he was working in an office in the same town. Needing his suit cleaned and pressed, he made his way to a drycleaners after work. He went in and handed the suit over saying to the girl she had better just make sure he hadn't left anything in the pockets.

The girl had got home safely that night but the ordeal had shaken her up. She thought long and hard about the way her life was going. Within a couple of days she was seriously looking for work, eventually getting work behind a counter. She had started a routine of eating properly and getting regular sleep. Some of the people she had been spending more and more time with slowly slipped away.

He had thought a lot about the events of that night. To have been there and been able to help the girl had a profound effect on him. He finally came to a decision about what he really wanted and contacted an old friend, who now worked for an employment agency. After a few weeks he found office work that was different from what he'd been doing, but surprisingly satisfying.

As suggested by the customer, she checked through the suit pockets after he had gone. She soon found a folded sheet of paper.

When she opened it she read, 'I owe you a great deal. On the night you fainted I was waiting to break in and rob the jewellery store near the bus stop. Helping you that time gave me a fresh view on life and a new look at myself. I came away feeling better than any other time in my life. I won't intrude on your life. With your agreement, this can stay between you and me. I just wanted to thank you.'

The suit was cleaned and pressed and made ready for pick up.

The night she got off the bus and passed out she was about to go to an address she had been given. It was a flat above a shop where she was to meet a man that would give her work. She would be given a job in a night club where she could sell the drugs he provided to any customers that went in there looking to buy them. At that time she was spending what little she had on smoking, which wasn't good for her, instead of decent food. She had been really desperate. The kindness shown by the stranger had made her realise that she was travelling down the wrong road. He had rescued her in more ways than one.

When he called in to collect his suit, nothing more than a private smile passed between them. At home he checked his pocket to make sure she had received his note. He found it had been replaced by another piece of folded paper.

It read, 'Thank you for the note. I would like to thank you very much for looking after me that night. It was through your kindness that I saw a better life for myself. I was about to start a life of crime and you stopped me. Just between you and me. Thank you again.'

Andrew was entering the building with high hopes. The Observer was aware of this. It knew that this applicant was elated when he received a call from the agency. He had answered the advertisement a couple of days before, despite the criteria being very thin.

It read:

*A responsible role within an administration office.*
*Males between 25 and 40.*
*Good health.*
*Immediately available.*

It was not a lot to go on, but times were hard at present.

So, at five to eight the following morning, Andrew was entering the agency's reception area to find several people queuing up to be registered. He wondered how many of these might be going for the same job. His turn came. "Andrew Walker."

The guy taking the names said, "Thank you, Mister Walker. Please go through to the interview room with the others. You'll be given further information in there."

When Andrew entered he found several chairs laid out in front of a desk. A woman sat at the desk, patiently watching people coming in and finding seats. He found a spot near the front and looked around with interest. As he scanned them he became acutely aware that there was a submissive air in the room. He wondered what sort of criteria had been used to select the people who surrounded him.

He counted around fifteen, with a few more coming in. The clock on the wall showed three minutes past.

The guy from reception followed the last one in, saying, "All present Miss Grey."

He handed her the list and left closing the door quietly.

Everybody sat in silence. Andrew supposed they were thinking what he was thinking. What's going to happen next? Were all these guys applying for the one position? The job market had been going downhill for a while now, but to have all these candidates going for the one role was pretty weird to say the least.

The woman finished ticking things off on the list she'd been given and looked up.

"Good morning, gentlemen. My name is Miss Grey and I'll be running today's interview session. You will all have met and been registered by Mr Hamilton in reception."

She studied the list for a moment and said, "For those who arrived in good time, thank you. Now, if the following would kindly stand."

The list was referred to as she spoke. "Mister Johnson, Wood, Roberts and Evens. Thank you. On behalf of the agency I would like to thank you for your time today. Please return to reception to receive your vouchers."

The four men moved slowly towards the door. No-one looked back.

In the meantime Andrew had done a proper count and had come up with twenty.

When the door finally closed she said, "For you who remain, I would explain that for some of you, these vouchers are provided to cover any out-of-pocket expenses incurred."

This was followed by a little squirming and coughing from those left in the room.

"OK. Let's get on shall we?" The room went instantly quiet. "I would like to do a quick roll-call, just to make sure we have complete and proper records."

Andrew ruminated on the phrase 'complete and proper'. The whole thing was getting weirder by the minute.

"Please simply reply 'present', when your name is called... King."

"Present."

"Jones."

"Present."

"Wilson."

"Present."

"Clarke."

"Here."

She paused momentarily, then continued on down the list, receiving one more 'here', and an 'OK' as responses, as she continued to call out names.

She made more notations and said "Would Mister Clarke, Kelly and Wright please stand. Thank you. Please make your way out to reception. Thank you."

Kelly, the 'OK' man, who by the look of him may well have said it deliberately, went to say something but changed his mind. The three left and the door closed. Andrew made it thirteen still in the running.

"Well!" she smiled for the first time, "I see we are shrinking fast. Let's move on, shall we?"

She moved a few papers around and said, "I see we have had a few complaints about the chairs in here. Apparently they are rather hard, so I should ask, does anybody want a cushion?'

Slowly six hands went up.

"Thank you. Would those with their hands up please go through to reception?"

Again, as people moved out there was some obvious hesitation, and to some degree anger and resentment quietly brewing with those being evicted. However, the fact that they were being compensated, together with the knowledge that this was one of the best and most prestigious agencies around… well, it made sense to keep your head down and not make a fuss.

Nine remained.

"OK. It feels a little cold in here. Would anybody like the temperature raised a little?"

There were no responses. She looked a tad disappointed and looked back at her notes, while opening a drawer and bringing out a pot stacked with pens. "Alright. If we are all comfortable, will those of you who have already got a pen, please hold it up."

There was a lot of foraging in pockets resulting in just two hands up, holding pens.

"Thank you. Those not holding pens, please make your way out to reception."

A brave voice asked, "Will a pencil do?"

A few giggles were followed by, "No. Not really."

When the door closed once more the two remaining candidates sat looking at each other across the room.

"Um, let me see, I think it appropriate that we're on first names now. Mister Colin Taylor, perhaps you would move to the front here and join Mister Andrew Walker. Thank you."

Andrew smiled at his competition as he sat down next to him.

"Just a simple question should finish it off gentlemen," she said with an air of finality. "Would you please tell me why you should be considered for this role? Take your time, there is no pressure."

They both sat thinking for a while.

Colin spoke up. "Well, put simply, I'm just looking for work."

"OK. Andrew?"

Andrew sat upright and said, "I'm a male, aged between 25 and 40, in good health and immediately available, looking for a responsible role within an administration office."

Miss Grey gave a broad smile and turned to Colin.

"Thank you, Colin. Please make your way to reception." He shrugged, got up and left the room.

"Well, Andrew, let me congratulate you. I should explain that our client, one of our most important clients, is looking for a staff member who is capable of duplicating instructions without complaint."

He smiled and said, "Thank you. So, I've got the job?"

Miss Grey's eyebrows went up. "No, not really; but you're on the short list."

The man's feelings were known to the Observer.

It had happened when he was in the local supermarket when he met the woman from up the street. He knew the family quite well. He was retired now and living on his own. She was married and had a three-year-old daughter, who was with her. She was a happy child. He had always found her to be precocious, but in a nice way. They were passing through the checkout at the same time.

As they had all come on foot they started to return home together, he and she chatting while the daughter happily watched the surrounding activities as they walked through the extensive park with its several separate playing fields.

The mother said, "She loves the park; keeps talking about coming here to play when she's old enough."

He replied by remarking, "I'm not surprised. I must say I've always seen her as a very bright young lady."

The girl looked up and smiled.

The mother stopped abruptly with her hand cupping her mouth. "Oh! Lord! I forgot the chemist!" She made her way to an empty bench and rummaged through her bag. The man and the girl joined her on the seat while she scrabbled around, checking pieces of paper one at a time.

Finally, she brought out a piece of paper and held it up with a sigh of relief. "At least I remembered to bring the prescription. I really must fill it; it's for my husband."

She looked a little awkward. "Would you mind staying with her for just a few minutes while I do this? She loves watching the kids play. She won't be any trouble."

He shook his head. "Not at all, you go on. We'll be fine."

She looked at her daughter with raised eyebrows. "OK, Honey?"

The girl smiled and said, "That's fine, mummy. I'd like that."

The woman left them staring out at the playing fields in a comfortable silence. Two teams were playing their separate ball games, dressed in brightly-coloured tops. She seemed very content to simply sit and look on, but he felt he should say something while they waited. "Well, there are lots of really bright colours out there."

She nodded.

He asked her, "What's your favourite colour?"

Without a pause, she said, "I like all of them."

He smiled. "OK."

He thought for a moment. "What about games, I bet you have a favourite game?"

She shook her head. "I like all of them."

"OK. What's your favourite food then?"

She shrugged. "I like all of them."

He thought for a minute. "What about songs. What's your favourite song?"

She said, "I like all of them."

"OK. What's your favourite flower?"

She seemed to be looking around, making up her mind. She said, "I like all of them."

"Ah!" He said. "What about teachers? I'm sure you have a favourite. I know you go to a play group."

Again, she gave it some thought. She said, "I like all of them."

He sat back a little. "TV shows?" he asked.

"I like all of them," she said.

"What's your favourite ice cream flavour?" he asked, not expecting anything different.

"I like all of them," she said.

Determinedly, he asked, "So, what about the days of the week, surely you have a favourite among them?"

She looked at him directly with eyes wide. "No," she said, "I like all of them."

At that moment the mother returned. "All done," she said with a satisfied expression. "Thank you so much for sitting with her." She looked at her daughter sliding off the seat. "Was that a nice time sweetie?"

She nodded. "Yes, thank you mummy. It was really nice. I'll be coming here to play when I'm older."

The mother looked at the man with a knowing smile. "Yes. You will my love."

They made their way home. At his house, after the goodbyes and thank yous, they left him to go on. As they moved off, the girl turned with a beaming smile and waved. "Good bye," she shouted.

Inside, he put away his few shopping items and put the kettle on. He really needed a cup of tea.

As he sat waiting he was quite overwhelmed by the misplaced but powerful feeling of envy that swept over him.

Looking back, the man wondered how it had come to this. He would never have believed it of himself. The Observer took in what was unfolding before it. The man was thinking about the win, the accident, the weeks of planning… and now; he was sitting in some sort of tug boat in the middle of nowhere. It all seemed so far beyond reality somehow. So incredibly bloody! But he had come too far; much too far. He would see it through to the end now, and then… just walk away.

He lit another cigarette, aware of how nervous he was. But in nothing like the frantic state of mind the man in the next room would be in, when he eventually regained consciousness; when he realises that he is no longer the aggressor.

It had all started on a Friday evening, returning from town, just like any other end of week journey home. The weather was rotten and he had to peer through great slashes of rain to keep his car within the lines. He had just pulled away from a traffic light when he saw the brilliant glow of brake lights come hurtling towards him. The metallic crunch of the impact was sickening. He had sat frozen for moments, coming to terms with the situation, when his door flew open and the altercation began.

It was the worst thing that had ever happened to him. The irate man shouting obscenities, the pounding rain, the traffic jam with cars honking and drivers yelling at them from half-opened windows. He had been dragged from his car and held, back arched, over the hood of his little car, while the maniac he had run into repeatedly punched him in the stomach and screamed at him with a wild hatred he had never experienced before.

He remembers how he had slid down onto the sodden road when the man finally released his grip and climbed back into his expensive saloon car; not even looking back as he drove away.

On reflection, the whole thing had seemed so disproportionate. He knows he must have passed out at that point because the next memory was of the staff treating him at the hospital. Was there anyone they should call? Not really; he had lived alone in his flat for several years and really didn't have many friends outside of the office, and none of them could be called close.

He spent the night at the hospital and returned home the next day. His car was out of service being fixed for a couple of days the following week, but being laid up in bed, he didn't need it. All in all, he was back into something like normal life within a few days and things were almost back to status quo, but not quite. Not completely.

Although it didn't show, he was mad; as mad as hell!

Within himself, he couldn't suppress it. Not a waking moment passed that he didn't recall the thumping he had taken; the humiliation, the disgrace; the pain! He wanted revenge. Yes, that was true he had realised; he really did want some sort of retribution. Little had he known then that this would be handed to him; on a platter, in three servings.

The first incident occurred just a couple of days after returning to the office. Walking out at lunchtime he spotted it… the car. The very car! Even in the gloom and rain on the night of the accident, he saw the distinctive make and model of his attacker's executive saloon. But now, standing so close to it, these memories were reinforced when he saw that not all of the damage had been repaired. He quickly jotted down the number plate and went on his way.

The second event that was to bring him a little closer to where he was now, on this small craft anchored somewhere off some unknown coast, came in the form of a letter. He was being advised of a substantial win in a lottery system that he had been having the odd flutter on for years. Again, on reflection, it was a sign of just how single-mindedly vengeful he had become that he thought very little about it. He just banked it and promptly forgot all about it. Even then, he knew that the hatred that gnawed away at him was, in fact, taking him over.

More than a month had passed since the cheque had been banked when he bumped into an old school friend in his local library. He had regularly kept up his visits there of his own volition since leaving school, where he had been obliged to study material of someone else's choosing. He was scanning titles when a hand came down on his shoulder. It was Bradley Barker, known at school as BB. This heralded the third part of the circumstances that found him sitting, waiting for one of the crew to tell him that all was ready for him in another part of the boat.

As schoolies they had never been chums, not close; there had always been something not quite right about BB. He had always shown a sort of furtiveness that you couldn't quite put your finger on. Nevertheless, it seemed right then to be the sort of thing that Daniel needed, to bring him out of himself. After settling on his choice of books about growing indoor plants, he went to the main desk and waited while BB collected two volumes on the subject of firearms.

That evening they started at a local café with coffees, then taxied back to BB's very expensive hotel suite for a glass or two, went out again to a night club in a neighbouring town until the early hours, returned to Daniel's car, all by taxi, with the arrangement to meet up the next weekend at a public house of which BB was apparently a part owner. It was Daniel's general impression that BB had done very well for himself, regardless of how he had managed it.

That morning Daniel had driven nervously home and fallen into bed in a drunken stupor. It was only after several hours of shaking off a blinding hangover the next day that he realised just how much of his private life and affairs he had shared with his newly-found drinking partner. It had all come out! The accident, the winnings, the beating, the hate, the thirst for revenge - everything!

They met at the pub, as arranged, and were instantly shown into a private room at the rear of the building. It was quickly established that BB did part own the place, apparently along with a mix of several other businesses. He was, it seemed, a successful businessman with a great many connections; including the underworld. Daniel wasn't too surprised at this and they sat chatting about the true power of the criminal fraternity for well over an hour. Then came the proposal. The direct and explicit offer of the very thing that Daniel had hungered for... revenge.

It hung between them for several minutes. Daniel in deep thought about what was being discussed and BB showing a remarkable sense of patience and understanding.

Finally, Daniel broke the silence with a thousand questions. That Saturday in the back room it was settled. The price, method of payment, the timing of the abduction, the meeting at the marina, the names of the parties involved, and the proviso that the final choice of how the victim would be treated would remain with Daniel; it was all arranged. Daniel made a few notes and it was agreed that they would have no contact with each other for at least twelve months when all business had been concluded.

The man that had beaten Daniel so severely that night was a local businessman; he owned two medium-sized companies in town and served on the local council. He was apparently well-respected, but was known to be unfriendly and domineering at times. He was, after all, an important man. He would be missed; but, as BB had assured him, never found.

All this was learned while sitting in the quiet, little room at the back of BB's pub, and Daniel was left with the question. Did he want to commit what in his eyes would be a justifiable homicide and live with the knowledge for the rest of his life?

He had decided that evening, sitting alone in his small kitchen, that he would leave that issue in the hands of his attacker. He would judge him on how he answered the charge that Daniel would put to him. It wouldn't be Daniel's decision at all!

He had agreed to be blindfolded and ear plugged when the time came for his journey. It had taken several hours of transfers between vehicles and finally the boat. He had felt the vibration of the tug's engines as it set out to sea. Daniel had no idea about which sea it was, or how long it had taken to get there. He was fairly sure, however, that he had slept through at least part of the journey.

The small cabin that he sat in, eating some well-needed food that his new business associates had provided, was the first thing he saw when they stripped away the cloth that had been wound across his face; and the chugging of the engines was deafening when the plugs were pulled from his ears. He had started to estimate how much time had passed since being picked up.

He had agreed to drive to a neighbouring town and park behind a small shopping centre, from where he would be collected. Thinking back, things had gone a little fuzzy during the first leg by car… He jolted back from his calculations as one of the crew jerked the cabin door open with a creak and indicated that all was ready. Daniel rose slowly and followed the man down a narrow passage and was shown into a much larger room.

The room was dimly-lit and had a pungent odour of fish. He could see that a square hatch had been opened in the floor; water could be heard lapping somewhere down below. The man pointed to a figure through the gloom, smiled, shrugged, and left the room, closing the door as he went. Daniel moved forward and saw what he had come for; what he had paid for; what he had brought about.

The businessman was hardly recognisable. He had been stripped and beaten. He sat tethered to an old, kitchen chair; one leg of which had a large, concrete block strapped to it very securely with a heavy rope. He raised a blooded face and saw and recognised Daniel. A wildness came into his eyes and he began to shout. He screamed obscenities at Daniel without taking a breath, telling him what he would do to him; how important he was; how powerful he was; and how he would never get away with what he had done. Daniel shook his head and left the room.

The man who seemed to be the boat-owner stood in the passage waiting for him. He laid a hand on Daniel's shoulder with a gentle assurance that he would never be bothered by the man in the chair ever again. He was led back to his little room, and as the bandage was being wound back on, and just before the earplugs were replaced, the distant but incessant screaming stopped… abruptly.

Coming to, gradually, Daniel now realised that he had been drugged on two occasions. The first time was when he was offered a hot drink from a flask at the beginning of his outward journey, and the second, when he had accepted another as the boat had made its way back to land. As far as he could tell, he was now laying on a mattress in the back of a van. When it stopped at the shopping car park, he was unbound and let out. The vehicle sped away and Daniel located his car. He sat for a while until he felt comfortable about the twenty-minute drive home.

He was just entering the outskirts of his home town when an open-topped sports car came out of a side road and came dangerously close to colliding with Daniel's car. Daniel managed to avoid the crash by braking hard and running off the road onto the grass verge. The young man in the sports model stopped and looked back with a silly grin on his face, shouted some expletive that Daniel couldn't hear, made a rude hand gesture and drove off. The car had a cute and easily-remembered licence plate, and Daniel wrote it down.

When he arrived in his home town, still shaking, he pulled up outside the bank. The ATM unit glowed in the dark. He punched a few buttons and a smile spread across his weary face. He stared at his balance... Yes! He just had enough...

The Observer knew that when the man left school, working in a bomb disposal unit wasn't his first choice.

He had wanted to be a ballet dancer. Anyway, the clock was ticking. He was about to open the lid. No, he had to switch the mic on first. He had to remember his training. Wow! So much training. Now, it's the real thing, the real McCoy. There has to be a first time for everything and this is it. Ballet dancing never sounded so good. No! Settle down! He really did have to concentrate. He switched the mic on.

Him: "Hello. Is that control?"

Control: "Control here."

Him: With a sense of relief. "I'm about to open the lid."

Control: "Before you do, please report your situation."

Him: "OK. Situation... well, it's not good. I'm looking at a large metal trunk with a skull and cross-bones painted on the lid. I suppose someone thought that was funny.

Anyway, the bomber's note was correct. It's located in a cleaner's cupboard, in the men's toilet just inside the library's main entrance."

Control: "OK. You would have time to exit the building if, you know, it was about to go off. That's positive, isn't it?"

Him: "I suppose it is, when you put it like that. Anyway…" He wriggles around for a few moments. "God! It's hot in this suit. Anyway, can I open the lid now?"

Control: "Yes, but wait… wait… yes, we've just had word. Yes, I have some positive news for you. The building's cleared."

Him: "The building's cleared? What does that mean?"

Control: "Well, it means that should it, you know, go off, urm, there's only one person in the building."

Him: "But that's me!"

Control: "Yes, but it's now only a case of urm, its urm… the Americans have got a word for it."

Him: "I think the term you're looking for is *collateral damage*."

Control: "Yes, that's it! Thanks."

Him: "You're welcome." With a degree of anger and frustration he adds, "Now, can I open this lid or not?"

Control: "Yes. Yes of course you can. Sorry, I'm doing my best here."

Him: "OK. That's OK. I'm sure you are. I'm just a bit jumpy, that's all. This is my first time you see?"

Control: "Me too."

Him: Long silence. "You know, something really has to be done about all these cutbacks!" A pause. "No offence."

Control: "None taken."

Him: "OK. Opening up now."

Control: "Right. Take your time. Let me know what we have."

Him: "We?"

Control: "Sorry! You."

Him: He lifts the lid slowly, looking for trip wires. You've just got to love that training. Pity the course had to be cut short. No! No time for thinking about that. Concentrate! No trip wires. He switched on his torch and peered in. "Oh! No!"

Control: "What? What is it?"

Him: "Hang on."

Control: "What?"

Him: "I said… hang on!"

Control: "Oh! Yes. Sorry."

Him: "Rotten torch is flickering. I think the battery's going."

Control: "Can you see the clock?"

Him: "What?"

Control: "You know, a clock or a timer or something. They've all got something like that, surely!"

Him: "Oh! Well, if that's the case. I'm in a library! Hey! There's bound to be a book on that in here somewhere. Hang about and I'll have a look around!" A pause. "No!" He shouted. "Sorry to disappoint you but there's no clock or timer of any kind in here!"

Control: "Oh! OK."

Him: Calmer now. "Yes. Oh! OK. Just give me a moment."

What he was looking at was nothing like the set up on the training course. It certainly wasn't anything like in the movies. A blue and a red. Which one should I cut? No. What he was looking at wasn't anything like that. He was looking at a mishmash of different coloured wires. He had an itch under his nose he could do nothing about. "I've got a bunch of different colours here; six of them."

Control: "Oh! That doesn't sound good, does it? Sorry, that doesn't help. Tell me what you've got."

Him: "OK. What I have is black, pale red, dark orange, greenish turquoise, blueish turquoise and musk."

Control: "Musk? Did you say musk?"

Him: "Jees! I don't know, I'd call it musk. I'm just telling you what I see. It's somewhere between a musk and a blanched almond."

Control: "Blanched almond? Where do you get this stuff?"

Him: "School. Did a colour graphics course when the ballet company turned me down."

Control: "Did you say Ballet Company?"

Him: "Look. Can we move on?"

Control: "Yes. Of course." A pause. "I've got... hang on a minute, I've got something coming through. Yes, they've got him talking."

Him: "They have?"

Control: "They have. They've promised him free Foxtel for his mother-in-law."

Him: "Oh! Goody! What the hell is he saying?"

Control: "Yes. Hang on, I'll have to write it down." Long pause. "OK. He says, whatever you do, don't cut the black one."

Him: "Well, that's a start I suppose. What about the rest of them?"

Control: "OK. He says there are six wires, but you only have to cut three of them. He says this will have to be done in the right order. He says if it isn't the thing will..."

Him: "Yes I know – go off."

Control: "There's more. He says if you get it wrong you'll hear a buzzing noise."

Him: "Oh! That's great!"

Control: "Here we go then. The sequence is orange, followed by apricot, followed by turquoise."

Him: "OK. Let's see. Orange or dark orange, that's good. Apricot, looks more like musk to me but no matter. No, it's the turquoise that's a problem. I have a greenish turquoise and a blueish turquoise. I think you're going to have to find out which one. Can you do that?"

Control: "Sure. Wait there."

Him: He sighs and tries to move around a bit. He mumbles to himself. "Wait there, he says." He feels perspiration running down all over his body. "Wow!" He says to a dead mic. "It's getting very hot in here." The itch under his nose has got a lot worse and he is fantasising about scratching it, when he hears the mic crackle.

Control. "We asked if it's the greenish turquoise wire or the blueish turquoise wire." A long silence followed.

Him: "Well? What did he say?"

Control: "He says he can't remember. He says to take a punt."

Him: He laughed maniacally and at that point his torch went out. He took out his cutters and started snipping away in the dark. On the second snip he heard a gentle buzzing and instantly recalled the procedure for this situation from the course.

He ran like hell!

93

It found itself observing a man who sat quietly reading back what he had typed into his laptop.

The man was almost whispering to himself. "She appeared again; a slender figure, crossing the park: his idol, his goddess. She was a child of nature, with something quite mystical about her. She passed into open sunlight, highlighting long, wispy tresses decorated with feathers and beads.

He was smitten, and he knew it. He drew back into the shadows, out of sight. Content to merely watch from afar as she moved gracefully, looking straight ahead with what he always saw as some kind of noble and majestic purpose.

In his eyes, she could command the attention of kings, have young suitors fall at her feet, be asked to consort with other spirits to sow the clouds and bring rain when it was needed. Could he see a wild and untamed spirit behind the elegance on show? Was it only his fancy that imbued her with unsurpassed purity and kindness? What unknown deities might commune with her? How often do hearts beat faster when others meet her gaze? Was it at all healthy to experience this mind-numbing sense of infatuation whenever he saw her?

In his heart he knew that she may not wish to be compared to a goddess or some divine creature; or any other iconic image that displayed such breath-taking grace and beauty, but… she was an angel!

At this point the writer sat back, gazing blindly into the room, allowing the scene with its fanciful images to play across some unseen screen.

He was jolted back into the real world when the door opened and his friend walked in. "Sorry, I just thought I'd…"

He paused as he took in the expression on the other's face. "Everything all right?"

"Oh! Yes." The writer replied. "Just battling with how I am describing someone."

His friend came in and sat down. He smiled across the desk and said, "D'you want to bounce it off me?"

"Yes! Why not?" came the reply, and he read the lines again, this time aloud.

When he finished reading he looked up to find his friend staring back with watery eyes.

"I'm sorry," said the writer. "Look, it's just a description of a character I've dreamt up. She's not real."

The other replied, "Oh! I don't know. When I was a student, I knew a girl who was just like that!"

She was entering the café as the Observer looked on.

It was a routine she used to enjoy, stopping for a coffee before catching her bus.

It was really convenient; the café was on the way and they brewed a good cup. Over the months she had got to know the names of those working there. She would almost always get a window seat and watch the world go by as she let the caffeine shot wake her up, ready for another day.

She was doing just this when she noticed a curious mark in the corner of the paper serviette tucked between the cup and saucer. She pulled it out and saw it was a tiny asterisk drawn with a green pen. Unfolding it she found five small words, also green, written in neat block capitals right in the middle.

'NICE TO SEE YOU AGAIN.'

She looked around, but nobody seemed to be paying any attention to her. Was it really meant for her? Was it somebody who worked there, or one of their regular customers maybe? It was probably a fluke, meant for someone else, or an old napkin that got accidentally used again. She thought no more about it until the following day.

It happened again. The little star.

This time with a message that read, 'YOU'RE LOOKING NICE TODAY.'

She thought about how this could be a plot from a movie. A romantic movie, where the girl gets these secret notes from an unknown admirer, and of course they go on to meet, fall in love… etcetera.

That night she Googled cafes in the same general area and found three. The one even closer to her stop looked good. She would call in there tomorrow. She thought again about the little green notes and shuddered. It was creepy.

She didn't do creepy.

It was floating above the woman when it happened. She had been cleaning through the house for over an hour.

She had just finished dusting when she caught sight of the framed photograph and picked it up. The boy looked sad. She remembered him that day playing with all the other kids. She clearly recalled the sound of the see-saw breaking, and how angry he was. Nobody was hurt really, but it shook the kids up.

As for him? Well, who knows? What had happened

to him that day? Something did. Something must have, but nobody noticed. He seemed to grow up as an entirely different child. They never found out how the fire started at his school. All this time ago and she still felt quite sure that it was him.

Then came the drugs. From the time he left school he never had a proper job. When he was charged with drug dealing it broke his father's heart.

She wiped the frame with her dusting cloth. Then came the murders, of course. Two teenagers, a boy and a girl, both from his old school. He was questioned but nothing was proved. They say the shame of it killed his father.

She looked back at the girl in the photograph. She was one of them. Here she was, a happy young thing, climbing the ladder to the top of the slide. She sighed. And to end the way it did with him crashing a stolen car and the fire that engulfed it, and him being burnt alive. She shuddered. She heard the front door opening and quickly gathered up her things.

The homeowner walked in. "All done?" she enquired.

"Yes. Just finished."

The woman looked around. "You always do such a nice job. Did you find the money?"

"Yes. Thanks." The cleaner stood for a moment looking into the woman's eyes. Sad eyes. So much like those of the young boy in the photograph.

The woman looked a little uncomfortable. "Same time next week then."

"Yes. Yes, of course." she said as she left, carrying her equipment. She waved back from the front gate before making her way to the next customer.

The Observer watched her go, knowing that its next event would be the mission's last.

It watched the proceedings.

They were burying him today. He wasn't going to be missed. Nobody would show up for the funeral, just a priest who'd be stuck for something to say. He'll probably skip it all together. None of his buddies, so called, would want to show their faces in public. Not one of the gang that he ran with had been there on the night it happened to comfort him in his time of need. No hand was held. No softly-whispered words to ease his pain and his passing. No attempt to revive him. No requests to a merciful God to spare him. No last minute words of kindness. No tears; no regrets. In fact, no one there at all as he lay there dying. No one came back for him.

It was a passing stranger who found him. A stranger who lifted and carried his lifeless body to his car and on to the emergency department, not knowing that he was delivering a corpse.

No one would kneel at his grave later, bringing fresh flowers. He would be quickly forgotten. He had done what they had wanted of him. He could be cast aside now. There would be no grieving.

It wouldn't be hard to sum up the kind of person he was.

Truth is, he just wasn't very nice!

## CHAPTER FOUR

# *The First Return*

The Controller: "All reports are received. They are good. Your training has served you well. Collation has begun. Were there any issues with schedules, coordinates or transitions?"

"No."

"Good. It is confirmed that reproduction of the species is being used to maintain a state of continual existence. However, reporting has shown that both the physical and emotional aspects of this method of survival has many drawbacks."

The Controller continued. "Some observations have demonstrated that there are aspects of human nature that provide a moral structure that in itself governs the way life on the planet is supported. We see that there are those that desire war and those that desire peace. It can be surmised that the lifeforms being observed would require a great deal more knowledge about their own human nature before being able to reform it. There is, of course, the same problem we encounter with any unknown species. In this case, it being that in order to fully understand their human nature, we would need to be human.

"Because of the complexity of these ongoing observations and given the significance of such a wide divergence of cultures that show us the ways humans live, we are finding that we are actually dealing with a multiplicity of behaviours.

"It is becoming evident that even the basic concept of whether this species regards itself as being good or bad has been seriously debated over several of their centuries. Any attempt to make a definite association between basic human nature and any perceived moral values is made difficult by the astounding degree of variation in the moral attitudes that are held.

"You return now… go well."

"I go well."

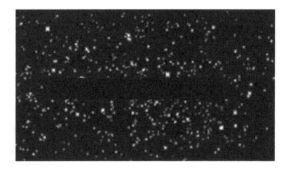

## CHAPTER FIVE

# *The Second Mission*

In an instant, the Observer found itself in a great hall of noise and colour. It saw the frail, elderly lady take a firm grip on the arm.

She likes it here. She has her favourite row. She likes the flashing lights, the colour, the constant background music and the muffled chatter of her fellow gamblers. She likes the people she meets in this giant room. They all have a common purpose.

Her family, her neighbours, her friends, they all know about her weekly trips to this place. Her journey to and from is short and safe. She knows most of the bus drivers. She doesn't drink and she doesn't smoke. She cannot go beyond her allotted outlay.

Last week she heard a jackpot go off. It was in a nearby row, and she closed her eyes and listened to the spewing of coins and the excited conversations that followed. With her eyes closed, she imagined that it was her.

She pulls down really hard on the handle and watches as the tumblers start to spin.

In her mind's eye she can see a row of number sevens come to rest.

Maybe this time…

It was apparent to the Observer that there was simply no way the woman could have predicted the incident.

She had caught up with her boyfriend after work and was on her way home. She was almost there when it happened. One of her neighbour's was holding a garden party and some of it had spilled out onto the front lawn. She slowed her pace and was lost in the music, which was soft and slow. It was almost mesmerising. As she approached she could see a group of young people of around her own age dancing graciously, most of them barefoot, on the grass. She was transported by what she saw. The mood that it generated in her allowed her to see the things in her own life that she felt was most precious.

She thought about her boyfriend.

There was something mystical about their rhythmic agility. They exuded a vibrant sense of vitality. She thought about the insouciance of abandoning all care. She turned her thoughts inward and saw that she longed for, and knew she could attain, the state of tranquillity she was observing. The feeling of wonder and unspoken reverence towards those things in life that are really special.

She thought of him again.

She saw in those brief moments those things that were there for her to grasp. The attainment of harmony, tranquillity and peace of mind. To be able to see through the eyes of a true child of the universe how beautiful nature is. Never to be afraid of allowing the overwhelming experience of pure joy. To constantly settle into a frame of mind that only allows safety and happiness. To fully embrace the art, music and literature that the world has to offer. To actively seek emotionally uplifting experiences.

Her mind turned to him.

She now fully realised that she was innately capable of revelling in moments of stillness and calm. She knew she had the insight to always recognise true goodness and those things that should be admired.

The feeling of complete euphoria was almost overwhelming. The sheer joy of true love and having such positive feelings for, and such a special connection with, another person.

She thought of him again.

And it was in that moment she realised she'd have to get shot of him!

It was floating over the front garden watching the man, who was on his knees weeding the edges along the front path.

His wife, having just reminded him that he hadn't fixed the light in the toilet yet, was turning to go back in, when it happened, when a car suddenly screeched to a halt. A cloud of smoke drifted up behind the back bumper, filling the air with the stench of burnt rubber. Several neighbours, in what was usually a quiet suburban street, stopped whatever they were doing to stand and watch.

He stood up from his gardening and peered at the vehicle, waiting for something to happen. His wife moved forward a couple of paces and stood with her hands on her hips. After a pause, the car door swung open and the driver got out. She was an attractive woman of around thirty, several years younger than the couple she glared at across the roof of her car. She was dabbing her face with a hanky and had obviously been crying.

He was the first to speak. "Can we help you?"

She blew her nose and yelled, "Can you help me, you swine? No, you can't. My life is ruined, thanks to you."

Visibly shaken, he dropped his weeding tool. "I... I'm sorry. I don't understand."

She laughed hysterically and said, "Oh! You don't understand don't you? Well, I did what you wanted, I had the abortion. Are you quite happy now?"

He stood speechless for several moments. He raised his hands and was about to speak when she shouted.

"No! Don't say another word. Not another word! I never want to see or hear from you again!"

With that she climbed back into her car and with gears crashing and finally with wheels squealing again, she took off at great speed.

He turned to his wife who was rushing back into the house. The slamming of the front door was very loud.

Slowing her car to a more respectable pace, the woman giggled maniacally. Creating chaos for complete strangers was her speciality.

The building excitement was evident to the Observer. She had found what she was looking for on the Internet.

It would have been unobtainable if it weren't for the old woman at the travelling fair, who had not only given her the name of the deeply-buried website, but had also sold her the password to open it. She spent time going over the rules to follow, giving special attention to the ingredients that had to be gathered. If all was done correctly, in the right amounts. It could be the very thing she needed to give new meaning to her life.

Day by day, she was getting closer. She was religiously shaking dew drops from the daffodils in the garden into a small tumbler each day, before the sun came up. Into a separate cup she had collected the right amount of moss; and she already had the hairs from a black cat's tail.

She made several trips into a wooded area not far from home to gather some of the things she needed. Wolfsbane and motherwort took a while to find, but in the end she had just about all the ingredients. It was only a matter of collecting the required quantity of daffodil dew before she could blend it all together. This was the final stage. At last, with the precious drops finally captured, she carefully blended everything together into a thick, brown potion.

The instructions required her to fast completely for two days. On the evening of the second, she should take a cold shower then drink the potion before going to bed. It would require only a few short hours for the brew to take effect.

Finally the magic evening came. She had done everything asked of her. It had taken several months to fulfill the requirements as set out on the website. After an uncomfortably cold shower she drank the potion and climbed into bed.

In the morning she woke before the alarm, but was convinced that sufficient time had been allowed for it to work. She jumped out of bed and rushed to the bathroom to see whether she would see the results she had been working towards… and had dreamt of. She stared into the mirror.

No. She still had freckles.

The Observer could see that the boy was deep in thought, thinking about the lady in the blue summer dress and wide-brimmed straw hat, who knew she was playing a dangerous game.

She had done everything she could think of to avoid discovery. She was carrying on as normal as it was possible to be with the war on. Back in the farmhouse the widow had a secret lodger.

As she came out from the Sunday service in the village's church she saw and recognised one of the men that had come to her a week ago. He was leaning on a shovel looking like a grave digger. Nobody would have seen the slightest of nods that passed between them.

She knew what she was taking on when the men brought him. He was upstairs asleep now. He'd been on the run for days. The men told her he was once a teacher with a family, with his wife giving birth to their first born, a child he had never seen. When she had shown a natural tendency to express sadness for his plight, she had been admonished.

"After all," the rebel had said, "this is war and he's a soldier."

She promised to keep him in the attic with the hatch camouflaged until it was safe to move him.

The farm owner and the fugitive had had many conversations during the few days he had been her guest. She knew it wasn't wise to become too emotionally involved. She did feel for him, but more so she found herself festering a growing hatred for the civil war and the ideology that drove it.

There was a sense of panic when the men returned that night to take him away. She would probably never know what would become of him as she handed him a small food parcel, received an unexpected kiss on the cheek, and then stood watching as they took him out into the night.

He thought he had it right now. This was an important school project and he needed to get a good mark for it. The boy went to his room, sat down in front of his laptop and began to type.

'The lady in the blue summer dress and wide-brimmed straw hat knew she was playing a dangerous game.'

It knew that the man sitting at his laptop was deep in thought. It was clear that the writer depended heavily on his muse to provide guidance. Currently this wasn't working out well.

The writer was given a start when she, the muse, suddenly appeared yet again, looking over his shoulder.

She was making tut-tut noises. It had been the same night after night for several days now and he really couldn't put up with it much longer. He had tried so hard to shut her out but she was so persistent. He'd had as much as he could stand and felt it time to have it out with her.

He spun around. "Look. I have to talk to you about appearing as often as you do, far too often."

She went to speak.

"No. Hear me out. I don't like the way you just crash land the way you do, unlike my regular muse. She would just drift in slowly and hover for at least five minutes before offering any kind of guidance. When she did, it was mainly positive, where as you... all I hear is criticism. With your 'No, not like that' and your 'Oh! Dearie me no, that'll never do.' Well, I'm sick of it.!"

She shrugged.

He bristled at her lack of interest. "Where is she anyway, my regular muse?"

She shrugged again. "How would I know, I'm just the stand-in."

"Stand-in," he muttered. "I suppose that explains it. You must have some idea what happened to her. She was lovely; we had a very special rapport going."

She covered a snigger with a cough.

He glared at her. "What were you doing before you became a stand-in?"

"I was in pottery."

"Pottery?"

She looked hurt. "Yes. What's wrong with pottery?"

He softened a bit. "OK. Pottery's fine, but you must have some idea what happened to my regular muse?"

The stand-in flapped her arms. "She went over."

"Went over? What does that mean?"

"She went over... to music."

"Music?"

"Yes. She works with musicians now. Anyway, I don't think I should be telling you any of this."

"Why not?"

"Well, you know, I'm supposed to guide and inspire you, not answer your questions."

He massaged his face and sighed. "Alright, let's move on. I've been working on this piece for ages. Just keep your advice simple, if you can."

He picked up his pen and continued scribbling.

After a few moments he felt a gentle tap on his shoulder.

"What is it?"

"There's no z in miscellaneous."

There had been mounting conflict about where the couple should spend their upcoming holiday; the Observer was aware of this.

The whole thing started as a difference of opinion but over time this had built up into a major disagreement, with both parties continuously squabbling about where they should go. She had always wanted to visit her sister in Canada, while he felt that because of the tidy sum they had saved up, this was the perfect opportunity to do the Mediterranean cruise they had often spoken about. The issue had become so openly hostile between them that their friends and neighbours had all started to wade in with their opinions on the subject. It didn't look as though the matter would end well.

He would visit the gun club more often, gaining some

satisfaction and possibly anger relief from putting holes in a cardboard image. She was spending more time in the crocheting group where holiday plans could be discussed sensibly with people who were willing to listen. It was an indication of the angst in the house that their much-loved Labrador was no longer getting the love and attention it was used to.

With his wife out shopping he decided to spend some quiet time in his little workshop at the end of the garden. There were a couple of fairly important rules that should be kept in mind while cleaning a gun and it was no doubt because of his unhappy state of mind that he ignored both of them. It was a given that you ensure that it is empty before attempting to clean it and it is generally accepted that it is most imprudent to blow into and stare down the barrel while resting a finger on the trigger.

When she returned from the shops there was no sign of him. She eventually ventured out to check the shed. She froze in horror when she discovered him lying on the floor with the gun in his hand and sickened at the sight of the dog licking blood off its master's head. She promptly ran forward and kicked the dog's head away, cracking its skull in the process, before rushing back into the house to phone for an ambulance. At the hospital he was declared dead on arrival.

As time went on there was an inquest where all the previous animosity was aired and a ruling of suicide was made. In the aftermath of the horrible affair most people naturally asked the question, "Why would he feel the need to commit suicide over such a thing?"

The question no one asked was, "Why did he kill the dog?"

It was looking down at the man, feeling the anxiety he was emanating. He had called in at the bar around the corner from his office before catching his train home. He usually caught up with his friend, but he was later than usual. He couldn't help overhearing some of the conversation coming from the table next to him. The two men sitting there were in a huddle. Whatever they were talking about seemed to be pretty serious. Although they were both neatly dressed, he figured that wouldn't necessarily tell you what sort of people they were.

He was pleased when his friend eventually turned up and was quick to tell him that he felt these men were planning something, and from what little he had heard it wasn't very good.

When he'd finished, his friend asked "What? You think they're spies or terrorists or something?"

He said, "Well, not necessarily spies, but I did hear them use the word 'bureau' a couple of times."

The other laughed and shook his head.

The worrier looked hurt. "You may laugh, but something dreadful is about to happen. I'm not kidding."

His friend looked the men over without it seeming too obvious and said, "They just look like a couple of office workers to me."

"Well, that's the point isn't it? Look like everybody else while you're… you know, doing whatever it is you're doing."

His friend leaned forward. "OK. Just what do you think they are doing?"

"I don't know, but whatever it is it's going to happen next week."

"Look, if it'll put your mind at rest I'll ask the barman, he knows just about everybody who comes in here."

"OK, but be discreet."

The other nodded, got up and went to the bar while the jittery man sat and waited nervously.

The man came back grinning and sat down. He said in a soft voice, "If he hadn't had his back to you, you would probably have recognised him. They've been discussing a cyclone warning that's about to come out. He's the TV weather man."

The other sat nodding, taking it in. Then he smiled and apologised saying, "Sorry."

His friend patted him on the arm. "Not a problem," he said, in an understanding tone.

He had always known that the man was the nervous type.

The Observer sensed that it was just lying there waiting.

It wasn't really clear what he was waiting for. Things where changing around him. There were noises that seemed to be coming from outside somewhere. The outside was a mystery to him. He wasn't concerned with the mystery of it, as he was very comfortable where he was. There was a sense of cloistered safety where he was and it felt good. Something told him there was something coming; something imminent. It was just a vague feeling that there was some unknown purpose to his present state and that something was about to change.

Now there were voices. Lots of them. Some quite new. There was a sense of urgency in their tones that he hadn't heard before. He was trying to make sense of the difference he was hearing. It wasn't panic. It wasn't chaos. It was just a strong sense of excitement... out there.

Now, from out there, came this movement. More than that... pressure. A great pressure that was pushing him. He was being moved, maybe to the outside. It wasn't necessarily what he wanted. He had been perfectly comfortable where he was. He had felt warm and safe. But now there was a persistence in the forces that were moving him.

Suddenly, alarmingly, unexpectedly, he was catapulted out into another world. A world of air and light and visions.

A voice, much louder now, said, "It's a boy!"

She dialled absent-mindedly while looking out into the garden. The Observer watched as she saw her husband go into the shed.

She heard a click. "No. Don't say anything. I'm not sure how long I've got." She saw the shed door close. "You're not going to believe this but I saw her. I saw her his morning, bold as you like walking into the butcher's shop in the high street. I mean, how she has the nerve to show her face in public so soon after what happened in the bank is totally beyond me!"

There was silence at the other end.

"Yes. I knew you'd be shocked. That's not all. The woman in the florist shop said she'd been in there asking about lilies. Can you believe that? Anyway, as soon as she had a bunch the shop owner said the woman just stood there quoting *Revelations* at her."

A voice at the other end said, "*Revelations?*"

"Yes." She went on. "I've looked it up. It says 'There will be no more death or mourning or crying or pain, for the old order of things has passed away.' "I mean, how weird is that?"

More silence at the other end.

"The lady from number twelve, who was in there before us, she said it took ages to wash all the blood away, after the forensics people had finished that is. Apparently two women fainted. I didn't even notice that at the time, what with all that commotion going on. One was a customer and the other was one of the tellers. I heard that the pregnant woman who was rushed off to hospital is doing well."

She paused to check the shed.

"I did hear that the chicken was dead before she took it in, and nobody seems to understand what the protest was about anyway. I was naïve enough to ask hubby. How dumb was that? He just said it's all best forgotten. How typical is that? The bank manager was very upset, I think he was crying, because he keeps chickens in his back garden, as pets."

There was a pause. The voice at the other end said, "Really?"

"Oh! Yes, and what's more he never eats them. His wife says when they get old they sell them. He was very upset by the whole affair."

The woman at the other end said, "How do you know all this?"

The caller was shocked. "What do you mean? You were there, and if you hadn't slipped out quietly the way you did the police would have questioned you too."

Another pause.

"Well, just look at the time. I must get on." She looked out of the window. "Oh! He's on his way back in. Sorry, sorry, I know I tend to go on a bit, but I thought you should hear about it. Must go. Talk to you soon, Jackie."

"What was that? What do you mean? No. no, I mean what do you mean you're not Jackie! Oh! Oh! I see. Well, good bye then."

She slammed down the phone... wondering.

The Observer looked on as the man sitting in his tent studied his survey map of the archaeological dig.

His wife entered, she had been digging and only unearthing small items of little interest. She's really keen to make significant finds.

She asked "Anything new?"

He smiled. As leader of the dig, he allocates areas for each member of the team to concentrate on.

"OK." He said, holding up the map. "I know how hard you've been working. They've found some really interesting artefacts deep inside the cave on the north side. They are taking a break at the moment."

"Could I?" she asked, in an excited tone.

He smiled. "All right, but keep it short. The other team will be heading back there in an hour."

She walked over and kissed him on the cheek. "Thanks darling," she said, and hurried out.

Shortly after, his artefact cataloguer entered the tent. She said, "Are you giving her access to the north cave?"

He looked up from his paperwork and said, "Yes, I am."

She responded, "Will she be coming back?"

"Nah! There's a trip wire halfway in; there'll be a cave in."

Her eyes watered up. "Gosh, how I do love you."

He grinned. "Love you too, Poppet."

The Observer looked down at the budding story writer tapping on his keyboard. He sat staring across the dimly-lit room considering the direction his story would take. For him, character development had always been the primary focus of his short story writing. He would agonise for days about this, and lose a number of decent night's sleep at the same time.

Although fairly new to the game of scribbling, the one thing he did know was that making his characters real was very important. After all, the reader (if indeed there should ever be a reader) needed to believe that the players in the story actually exist. This was his biggest challenge and he was prepared to face it; head on!

He had finally got it all together. His main character would be a man of the world; a strong, confident person who knew just what he wanted and didn't shrink from getting it. His name was Bruno. Yes; he had a clear enough idea of the persona and he was at last able to start scribbling.

He reread the few lines he had typed, took a sip from his mug of coffee and looked up at the kitchen clock. The evening was young with nobody expected to call in. He had hours in front of him, sitting alone in his quiet, little flat. He began to write.

*Bruno walked into the estate agent's office. He was enquiring about potential properties for sale in that part of the city. He spoke with an authoritarian tone of voice, giving the impression that he expected prompt service.*

*He introduced himself to the manager as Bruno McBain. He explained that he wanted a large house with good light and extensive grounds, and that money was no object.*

*The manager was visibly excited and showed him a selection of properties, along with photos and house plans. In no time at all, Bruno found what he was looking for, and arrangements were made to meet at the office the following day to inspect the property.*

*On the following morning Bruno was driven across town by the agent.*

*The house was magnificent. It was a beautiful Edwardian style building that overlooked a host of green spaces, with a great spread of lawn at the front and a massive garden behind the house. It was generously proportioned, with an enormous dining room and a light-filled high-ceiling, fitted with the latest digital light system for creating a variety of atmospheric effects. The entire building had designer wall treatment with elegant drapes and lots of luxurious furniture.*

*The main feature was the ballroom; especially the curtains that almost filled the entire wall and its enormous window at one end. The window consisted of a cornice, a valance and two enormous curtains. The supporting curtain pole was extended several inches beyond the window's at the end mouldings to make the expanse of glass appear wider and to admit as much light as possible. The cornice was gilded, and the valance hung below the cornice attached by large, dark wooden rings. The curtains were of a soft damask fabric in aubergine and gold, with...*

There was a sudden knock at the door. He wasn't expecting anybody; not at ten-thirty at night he wasn't. When he opened it he found himself staring at his main character, Bruno. Everything about the man was exactly how he had created him in his head. He just stood gaping.

"Just how long have you been writing?" Bruno asked gruffly, as he pushed past into the flat, and settled into the only armchair. "We have to talk".

Rodney followed him into the small lounge in a stupor and sat nervously on the couch. He was shaking and his head was spinning. His mouth felt so dry, he considered the possibility that he wouldn't be able to talk. He emitted a whimpering groan, cleared his throat and sat staring in disbelief at his main character.

Bruno was getting restless, waiting for the writer to come to his senses. "Are you going to listen to me, or are you completely without any reasonable sense of responsibility?"

The other blinked.

"Well?" Bruno repeated. "How long have you been writing?"

"Not long," he croaked, taking out a handkerchief and dabbing his face.

"Hell! I'm not surprised. What's all this ballroom curtain stuff? For God's sake, I'm a luminary, a big shot, a citizen of the world! Your story is supposed to be about me, not bloody gabardine curtains!"

"Aubergine," he whispered.

"What?"

He straightened a little and repeated, "Aubergine. It's a colour. Gabardine's a coat".

"Are you mocking me?"

"Mocking? No. No I wouldn't do that. I don't know what you are doing here. I don't even know how you can be here. I don't know…"

He fell silent, amazed at his outburst. He was amazed at the whole thing; a thing that couldn't possibly happen. His arm was getting sore from continually pinching himself. He stopped doing it.

"What is it you want? What do you want to talk about?"

Bruno grinned. "That's better. Now we're getting somewhere. You want to know what I want? I want your story to reflect the real me; that's what I want. I'm the central character, remember? OK, so I'm buying a big house. OK. That's good. I like that. It's in keeping with the sort of guy I am. I have plenty of money. Why shouldn't I buy a big house. But, what about women? Eh? Have you thought of that?"

"Women?"

"Well, not necessarily women, but a woman at least. I guy like me would have a woman".

"Well, yes, of course," mumbled the other, not wanting to get on the wrong side of someone who, by all rights, shouldn't even exist!

He was coming to terms with the situation and planned to do whatever it took to get passed what was happening, and return to his silent meditations and character interaction.

That is character interaction on paper! Not this... this nightmare. He tried very hard to smile.

"What sort of woman would you like?"

"Ah! Well now, let's start with a Personal Assistant. That would be in keeping with my status in life. OK. Good. I think we have a better understanding where all this is going now".

He stood up. "Make her a brunette" he said thoughtfully, and then added "Cindy. Cindy would be nice. Can you manage that?"

"Of course... Cindy. I'll fix it as soon as you leave".

With an appreciative nod, Bruno made his way to the front door, gave a cheery wave and disappeared into the night. The writer stood watching the blackness where Bruno had been moments before, wondering if any of what had happened made any sense.

Did it matter? He had been privy to something really special, and as long as he developed the character as agreed, there would be no problem. What a wonderful opportunity it was! To get this close to a character in the interactive process of character development. It was really quite awesome.

He went back to his notes. He read: *the curtains were of a soft damask fabric...* With a few key taps, he obliterated all the house stuff. He was back at the part where he and his Personal Assistant, Cindy of course, arrived at the agent's office to go looking at the chosen property. He wiggled his fingers and began.

*When they arrived at the house Cindy gasped. "Oh! Bruno! It's lovely".*

*Bruno smiled. He had to agree. It was a beautiful*

*Edwardian style building that overlooked an expanse of green lawns, with a spacious garden at the rear. He knew this was right before he entered.*

*Before the morning was out, everything had been signed up and they had moved in. Bruno sat at his large, cherry wood desk in the study, considering who to contact first. He had a number of business deals on the go and it was important that he kept up with them. He picked up the phone and dialled. He was speaking to one of his associates when Cindy stormed into his room with a wild, angry look. Bruno held up a finger, but she ignored it.*

*"You cancelled my lesson. Why?" she blurted. "You know how much my dancing lessons mean to me! You cancelled without telling me. I just heard from the academy; they want to know when I intend to go in to prepare for my next exam". She glared at him. "Why?" she repeated and fell into a chair, sobbing.*

*Bruno was getting more than a little irritated with her obsession of lessons. She was spending too much time with something that could never come to any good. He was sure the woman was kidding herself and wasting time and money; his time and money. He had put his foot down and that was that!*

*After more begging, crying and eventual anger, Cindy ran out of the room threatening something that he couldn't quite hear. He needed to do something about Cindy. She wasn't working out.*

The writer was startled by the noise, although it was only a gentle tapping at the door. He opened it to find a well-dressed brunette holding a tissue to her nose. She slapped his face. If the man had ever harboured doubts about whether these visits were from real people, and not just the result of an overactive imagination, they disappeared as the burning sensation spread across the side of his face.

"So sorry," she said, lowering her head. "I shouldn't have done that". "And this," she looked at him desperately, "the lateness of the hour, I mean. I just had to come and see you".

He looked at his watch; it was almost midnight.

"You must know why I'm here" she said, making no move to enter. "I wanted you to know that you need to make him change his mind you see. You can do it so easily, and he would never know".

She looked back into the gloom of the night, as if she would find someone lurking, a witness to her visit. She lowered her voice. "I can only stay a moment. I don't want to be missed. Could he miss me, even if I am away for just a short time? I don't know how these things work, you see".

She stood, with large watery eyes waiting for an answer.

He felt his heart thumping in his chest, a feeling that overrode the sting on his cheek. He felt for her and what she was going through. No; what he was putting her through!

"I'm sorry too," he said. "We all need our hobbies, our pastimes, and of course our dreams. You go back. I'll fix it. I promise".

Cindy put her hand over her mouth and gave a great sigh of relief. She held it there for a moment, and then blew him a kiss. She turned and hurried off without another word.

Back inside, he stood looking down at his screen. He felt pleased that she had trusted him so completely to put things right, that she had just taken off in full confidence believing he would make it all go away. He would put it right. He would do it now. He began editing and writing again.

*Bruno picked up the phone and dialled the dance academy...*

Roger paused. Should he go back before that? Before the original phone call, he wondered? No; it wasn't necessary. Besides, this way some tension was being injected into the story. He continued.

*Bruno picked up the phone and dialled the dance academy. He established that there was still an evening slot available and rebooked it. However, Bruno felt a question nagging at the back of his mind. He wasn't sure why he had just made that call. In fact, he was so preoccupied with analysing his motives for this that he had forgotten to make another call; to Jeremiah.*

*Jeremiah was a person he only ever called when he wanted somebody roughed up. Because Cindy had dropped hints about disclosing some of his business activities if she didn't get her way, he had decided to have Jeremiah work her over. That was when he was feeling desperate; before making the phone call that had made it all right; or had it? Bruno wasn't sure. There was no need now, because he had rebooked the lesson. Maybe that was why he had made the call.*

*Jeremiah was watching the house when he saw Cindy come out. She made her way to her car unaware of his presence. She was going shopping. As she entered the garage Jeremiah sprang out and struck her over the back of the head with the handle of the axe he carried. She went down like a stone. He looked down at her as he ran his thumb along the length of the blade. He raised the tool high into the air, and then he brought it down, again, and again…*

He stopped writing and sat bolt upright. What was he doing? What had he done? She hadn't deserved this. This ruffian must have gone completely crazy. Bruno wouldn't have wanted this! It was nearly one in the morning and he could feel tiredness beginning to sweep over him; but he had to put it right. He got up and made himself another coffee while he figured out how he could turn it all around.

He had just returned to his laptop when a crash sounded at his front door. Something was pounding on it in a mad fury. Shaking violently, he managed to peer through at the front door, just in time to see the splinters fly in as the blade of the axe broke through.

He woke with a start. His head was resting on his folded arms with the laptop's screen emitting a soft glow. He sat back and read over the few lines he had typed again. He took a sip of coffee. He was having second thoughts about the importance of character development. He sat mulling it over for a while. A thought came to him. Yes! He would write a travelogue.

His older sister was always giving him a hard time. The Observer was aware that it was Chess Night and her brother was getting ready.

Once a week after tea, he would join a group of his peers to play chess. It was held in one of the classrooms and supervised by a teacher. This was the final round and he had a feeling he would win again this year. He was almost ready when he realised it was missing. His lucky coin was missing. He couldn't play without it. In fact, he couldn't do anything without it. His grandfather had given it to him shortly before he died. He'd said it had brought him luck for so many years and he wanted him to have it.

She was talking to her mother when she heard him cry out. She went to his room. "What is it now?"

He stood wide-eyed. "My coin! My lucky coin."

"What about it?"

"It's gone!"

She sighed. "Is that all?"

"What do you mean, is that all? It's my lucky coin, you know that."

She turned to go, saying, "I thought it was something serious."

"It is serious!" he shouted. "It's the final round at the chess group tonight." He started searching again. "I have to have it with me, don't I?"

She turned back. She could see he was really upset. "Where did you see it last?"

"Right there." He pointed to his bedside table. "I always put it there when I get changed. It was right there."

She relented. "OK. I'll help. Although, you don't actually need it, do you? I mean you'll probably win without it."

He said, "How can you say that?"

She shrugged and they spent what little time there was hunting for it. Eventually he had to leave to be there for the first game. He finally left, with a feeling of foreboding about how things would go without his lucky coin.

As it turned out the evening went well, very well. He won the tournament yet again along with the prize that came with the title. At home, he pulled the trophy out of his jacket pocket and held it up with a mighty grin. After congratulations all round he went to the shelf and made room for a third. Later in the evening he stood up saying goodnight and how tired he was.

As he left the room his sister saw a flash of something fall behind him. Unseen, she quickly picked it up and held it in a clenched fist. She sat back down quietly to consider things. On the one hand he was now obviously of the mind that he didn't need his coin to bring him luck, but on the other, the coin had been with him all the time and he had won the contest.

In her bedroom she opened her bedside drawer, took out a small box containing trinkets and dropped it in.

She'd think about it tomorrow.

The Observer saw the nurse making her way through the ward. It watched as she arrived at the new patient's bed and picked up his chart.

"And how are you doing now, pet?"

"Yes. OK Thanks."

The nurse looked nice in her blue and white uniform. She looked back at his chart. She had just come on shift.

"Kidney stone was it?"

"Yes."

She looked around the ward, then back to the patient.

"No visitors, I see".

He looked a little sad. "No. My people... they all have

their own things you see; things they are doing. Important things I'm sure… but no… no visitors tonight".

"Well, perhaps you would like me to ask one of our hospital visitors to pop in for a while?"

He wasn't sure about a stranger standing in for family and friends. He hesitated.

"We have a new m an on duty tonight." She dropped her voice. "I'm told he is a little strange". She looked around again. "Yes, he's there. Shall I ask him to spend a few minutes with you?"

The man in the bed was about to come up with a good reason for not wanting anyone, when the nurse took off in the man's direction.

A few minutes later, a man wearing a shabby grey suit and tousled hair ambled to the foot of the bed. He stood eyeing the patient for a moment, as if checking him out, then pulled up a chair.

The patient smiled and nodded.

The visitor just sat quietly for a few moments, occasionally shifting around making himself comfortable. The patient's mouth was dry and he reached for his glass of water.

Finally, the visitor glared at him and said, "Toothbrushes".

The other paused with his cup at his lips.

"Toothbrushes?" he echoed.

"Yep," the man fanned his fingers, "toothbrushes are indicative of everything that's wrong with the world today."

Although not expecting this topic, it was obviously something that was of great importance to the visitor, and he would have to admit he was more than a little curious about how the other had arrived at this conclusion. "Toothbrushes?" He repeated.

The man settled into his chair a little more, slapped his knees and leaned forward.

"You know, I had to work out of town last week. I was driving along listening to classical music on my car radio." He glared again. "Do you want to know why I was listening to classical music on my radio?"

The other nodded.

"I was listening to classical music because it was the only bloody station I could find playing any music. I had hunted through the stations for ages and all I could find was the news, infantile adverts, and know-it-all disc-jockeys going on and on about what they like and what they think, and gormless-sounding people sitting around discussing bloody TV programs. I mean what's the point in that? If I watched TV I would have already seen the program so why would I want to hear about it again. Even worse, if, like any sane person, I hadn't watched TV because it's so mind-numbingly dull, then why do they suppose I would want to be told about the same rubbish on the radio, when they don't even have the bloody pictures?"

The patient squirmed a little in his bed and was in the process of coming up with a meaningful reply when the man went on.

"It's not just the radio either. Every newspaper is full of what happened on TV the night before, like it's important news or something. Magazines scream about the plot lines of stupid soap operas and treat the actors like they're real people! I just can't understand how we've got to the point where all forms of media have merely become an extension of the most hideous and banal forms of everyday life!"

The man in the bed realised his mouth was hanging open; he quickly took another sip of water.

"Anyway," the other went on, "that's not the reason I was listening to classical music. Not the real reason. The real reason is that it was the only station I could find that had a half decent reception. How is it that we, as a so-called First World country, are unable to broadcast radio signals that remain constant?"

The other raised his eyebrows and shook his head. This seemed to satisfy the visitor.

"Of course, when I did get the radio to play music it bucketed down with rain and I couldn't hear the sodding thing. This was despite the fact that the forecast said fine! Don't these buggers at the Met Office have windows?"

The bedridden man looked longingly at the red emergency button by his bed.

The visitor went on. "Anyway, how can they call it "national radio" when the bloody signal falls out every time you get to the bottom of a hill? One station was actually boasting that they are now live in America; I'd be a bloody sight more impressed if they managed to be live here! Anyway, classical sodding music, that's available everywhere. You could be at the bottom of the deepest mine shaft and you'd still pick up classical bloody music. I mean, surely they've only got a small listening audience, so why is it that they've got a signal capable of reaching the moon? Where's the bloody sense in that?"

The patient squirmed a little and glanced along the ward for the nurse.

"And while we're talking about TV, what's with all these bloody repeats?"

The other wasn't aware that they were talking about TV; he was still trying to work out the connection between classical music and toothbrushes.

"I mean to say," he went on, "I can understand how you might like to see the odd show again, every once in a while, but what makes them think we want to see every show over and over again? I mean, sure, some people might like the chance to see programs again, you know, in case they miss them while they're at work or something. But for God's sake, everybody's got a video recorder haven't they? And it's not just that they repeat the programs, it's the way they repeat them. First, they repeat the whole series in order, then they repeat the whole series again but this time in a random order, then for some strange reason they repeat just series two; twice! Then, in case you still haven't given up on the TV completely, they have a 'special' week, which provides them with the perfect opportunity to play a further random selection of shows in no particular order at all."

Just for a moment the visitor paused to take a breath, but quickly recovered.

"I know there are people that really want to watch it over and over; but they probably have the DVD box-set by now, so why is it still on TV? To my mind there's hardly anything on TV that's worth watching the first time, let alone needing to see it again."

At this point the visitor sat back in his chair and stared, as though waiting for a solution to it all.

The patient just managed to blurt out, "Toothbrushes?"

The man became animated again.

"Ah! The thing is you see, you have to ask yourself, what is a toothbrush? It's a pretty basic item don't you think? It's got no moving parts and, let's face it, it's not like there's a huge variety of mouth shapes out there. So, why is it that there are so many designs of toothbrushes? It's not like we need that many different types, is it? It's just a big con to keep making heaps of money! These clever sods who hire people to design toothbrushes need to convince us that the one we've got now is nowhere near as good as the one that we could have. Jeez! It must be the worst job in the world being an actual toothbrush designer, trying to come up with a new spin on such a basic thing. I mean, once you've made them in umpteen different colours, bent the neck a bit, straightened it out again, bent it back a bit more, changed the size, shape and colour of the bloody bristles - well, what else is there?"

The patient felt for the first time that he was really being asked a question. At this point, and on the general feeling that the conversation was actually coming to a point, he was willing to give it a go.

"Well, I think non-slip handles are a good idea," he said.

His visitor looked aghast, making the sick man feel he hadn't made a positive contribution, and added, "You know, for better grip."

"Oh! For God's sake, how many times have you been brushing your teeth when it slipped from your clasp and clattered to the floor? Have you ever lost control mid-brush and thought to yourself 'Wow! That was a close shave, I do wish someone would make this thing non-slip before I poke my flaming eye out?'"

"Well, no, I can't say it's ever happened to me, the patient replied apologetically.

"Me neither, but someone, somewhere, has invested millions developing non-slip toothbrushes anyway. And that's not even the worst part."

The patient felt that the entire conversation was about to make some kind of sense. He asked, "What's the worst part?"

"The worst part is that there's some poor bugger in a Third World country somewhere slaving away to make me yet another piece of rubbish that I don't want or need. It's no wonder the rest of the world thinks the West is full of rich, decadent slobs when they are scratching a living making that sort of junk."

The man in the bed brightened up. "Oh, I see what you are getting at now. The reason why toothbrushes are what's wrong with the world today…it's Western guilt!"

The visitor slumped. "No, no, of course not! Exploitation of the poor by the rich has always happened and always will. That's perfectly natural. It could even be argued that the need for non-slip toothbrushes provides much-needed employment opportunities for those poor buggers less well off."

He sighed. "No, the reason that toothbrushes are indicative of the world's woes is simple. Of the myriad designs available they all have one thing in common. They all have large, thick handles."

The hospital patient held his breath.

"When I'm staying at a hotel," the other went on, "in the bathroom they provide the usual stuff - plugs that don't fit, glasses wrapped in plastic, soap that doesn't lather and a wall-mounted holder for my toothbrush. The thing is, the handle of my wonderfully-designed toothbrush is always too large to fit into the slot in the holder. Development of toothbrush holders has just not kept up with current toothbrush design. There doesn't appear to be any connection between the creative design side and the practical user aspects; you know, stuff only known to those punters who actually use the bloody things!"

The visitor looked about him as though expecting someone to be eavesdropping.

"So, there you have it! Despite zillions being spent on design and development, together with further exploitation of Third World labour, and the never-ending poxy advertising campaigns that tell me how sodding lucky I am, my toothbrush still has to perch on some grubby windowsill!" He sat back with a contented smirk. "Now then… that's what is wrong with the bloody world today!"

Just then the nurse returned. "Visiting time has been over for several minutes. I'm sure our patient really appreciated your company. Maybe again tomorrow?"

The man in the bed squirmed, "I'm afraid not. I have family coming," he lied.

The visitor looked back. "Ah, OK. Thanks for the chat."

As they walked back down the ward the man in the bed could just catch the visitor asking if he could brush his teeth before he goes. The two stopped for a moment and he could just make out the word 'holder'.

He grinned. After all, he'll let her know what's wrong with the world today.

It was located in a high street, watching a bus approach and learning about the woman that was about to arrive.

She had been on a long journey by train and bus, but a very special one; one of penitence.

The elderly lady got off at the stop on the corner of the high street and stood looking around. It had been so long since she was there that she was getting her bearings. Things had changed. In seventy years, things had changed. In all that time she had never come back; but this was an anniversary she had planned for several years.

There was both sadness and a sense of excitement as she turned the corner and saw the church. It hadn't changed, nor had the graveyard that surrounded it on three sides with its lawns and narrow paths.

It was mid-morning and one or two locals were strolling through, but in the main she had the place to herself. It didn't take long to find it. A tombstone with two decades of weathering, the resting place of the only man she had ever loved.

She had never married; never loved a man the way she had loved him. For such a brief time in her long life, he was everything to her. But it was wrong and they both knew it. He had been married for two years when the madness took them. Her private disgrace had made her forgo a good job in the town and start a new life elsewhere.

As she read the words cut into the stone, thoughts of the times when she could have begun a full life of her own came flooding back, but it had never quite happened. She stood quite still, filled with remorse, for a long time, not noticing that more and more people were using the little footpaths, taking short cuts through the yard; including another elderly woman pulling a shopping trolley on wheels. The elderly shopper had almost made it to the street beyond when she stopped and looked back.

The woman paying homage became aware of this sudden lack of movement and turned. As she did, the woman left the path and pulled her trolley across the grass. Moments later she was standing beside the other, staring at the headstone with tears in her eyes. In the same moment they turned to face each other, and full recognition was there. The woman with the trolley spoke first.

"I knew, you know."

"You did?"

"Yes."

"How long did it last?"

"One night."

"One night?" The other repeated.

"Yes."

As they stood in respectful silence a light drizzle began to fall and so much was washed away as the widow touched the spinster's arm with compassion and said, "I am sorry for our loss. Would you like to come back for a cup of tea?"

The other nodded.

Their hug was the beginning of a new friendship.

The Observer was aware of the fact that Howard Spencer considered that he was surrounded by human leeches.

It all seemed to come to a head the day he exited the railway station, returning from a day in the city. He was making his way out through the main entrance when he was accosted by a young man with his hand out.

He was grinning and saying, "Can you spare any change, mister?"

Howard stopped and carefully looked him up and down. The apparent beggar seemed fairly well-dressed and was showing no signs of being destitute in any way, shape or form.

The silence between them obviously unnerved the young man and he repeated, with less conviction "Do you have any loose change at all?"

Howard, although standing very still with hardly any meaningful expression on his face, was in fact experiencing some kind of epiphany. He held down the anger he felt welling up and said in a firm and uncompromising manner, "I have, yes."

The other asked in an unconvincing mumble, "Can you spare any?"

Howard almost shouted a resounding, "No!" causing the other to turn and make himself scarce further away from the door, plainly shaken up by the incident.

It was generally accepted that Howard was 'something in the city'. This fact, together with the reasonable assumption that he was well off, gave rise to people constantly asking him for favours; everything from investment advice to financial assistance. He was subconsciously aware that he had let this get out of hand over time, with the resulting sense that he was being taken for a ride in such matters.

It was his resentment of this ongoing state of affairs that had brought him to the episode at the station. Something had snapped, and he'd been turning it all over in his mind ever since. The result of all this soul-searching had been to bring about a fierce determination to nip it all in the bud.

Two days later his brother-in-law, Charles, rang. These calls were not uncommon; in fact they had become more frequent of late. Howard was always being asked for advice concerning his brother's investment portfolio. This call was much like so many others.

His brother was saying, "It's all a bit topsy-turvy at the moment. I mean, it's a horrible prognosis for emerging markets. The NASDAQ is down, gold is up a little, but the S&P 500 is down, oil and stocks are heading south and the dollar has slipped again. What do you think I should do? With these latest acquisitions I mean, should I buy or sell?"

Howard drew in a long breath. "What does your stockbroker say?"

Charles said, "Oh! He's useless!"

Howard hung up.

As time passed Howard was pleasantly aware of the fact that he was feeling much better about it all. He had always been too soft. This was going to be a new life for him; a more positive way of not falling prey to leeches. It was with this newfound sense of handling his personal commitments that he received a call from Aunt Jess.

She had to be one of Howard's wealthiest relations, but this was never really evident. She had been set up very nicely when her husband passed away. Her flat was about to be 'spruced up' as she put it, with all rooms receiving a new coat of paint, including the ceilings.

Howard listened patiently as she went on. "It's all going to be such an awful mess when they start next week. I was hoping you could put me up for a week while the workers are in."

He steeled himself and said, "No. Sorry, I can't help you there." There was a long silence on the other end.

Finally she said, "Oh! Really? It would only be for a few days, Howard. I'd be out of your hair before you knew it."

He replied with an easy, casual, but resolute conviction, "Sorry Auntie, but like I said, I'm afraid I can't help you there." The phone went dead. Howard smiled.

One morning, a little later in the week, he was pottering in the garden (a form of relaxation that was getting better by the day, along with his new outlook on life) when his rose pruning was interrupted by an unexpected and definitely unwanted intrusion. It came from across the fence. His neighbour, a man he had never liked, was calling him over.

Howard took his gloves off and wiped his hands as he approached.

"Look, I hope you don't mind my asking, but I have a bit of a problem with my tree." He waved his arm at the large tree taking up most of his back yard. "I've had the tree people in and they say that some of the upper branches need pruning. Because of its age it no longer fully supports them. I'd hate to lose it."

Howard was beginning to wonder what this man wanted. He was thinking that it was ironical that he'd been divesting himself of leeches, and he was sure that this man from right next door to him was about to become yet another one.

He was thinking this when the neighbour's words broke through "…and I just don't have one long enough you see."

Howard blinked, "Sorry. Long enough?"

The man frowned "Yes, long enough... ladder, you see."

"Ah! Ladder. You want to borrow a ladder."

"Well, yes, as I say, I can easily save money by getting up there and doing it myself. Could get the main upper branches off today. These people charge a fortune."

He smiled at Howard with raised eyebrows. "I've seen your ladder; it's a good size. OK if I borrow it? It shouldn't take more than a couple of days all up."

Howard couldn't believe that this sponger was leering at him over the fence, almost demanding that he save himself money with Howard's ladder. How much were ladders, for goodness sake! He certainly wasn't going to let him have it, but he needed time to think.

"Ah! Just a minute," said Howard, holding up a finger. "Let me check."

With this, he turned and made his way down the other side of the house and entered the shed. He stood for a while thinking.

When he returned he said, "Sorry, just as well I checked; I knew there was something. Loose rungs... not safe... shouldn't take the risk."

He turned before the other could say anything, picked up his pruners and went back into the house.

That evening Howard treated himself to an extra-large whiskey before going to bed. He was rewarding himself for maintaining his new technique for eradicating leeches. That night he slept so deeply that he wasn't aware of the storm that raged through the neighbourhood, and was only partly roused by the thundering crash of the tree falling into his garden.

On the following morning Howard was holding an even

larger glass of whiskey than the one the night before; and he was gulping it down for a very different reason.

As he gazed out through his back window, taking in the scene of his flattened rose bushes and flower beds, Howard had another epiphany. Namely; the response provided for any given request should always be weighed carefully against that request's individual merits.

The boy clambered out onto the narrow ledge of the building's twenty-sixth floor as the Observer looked on.

There was a cold wind blowing across the face of the large apartment block, occasionally threatening to scoop him off the piece of narrow concrete that held him. He had been standing, palms flat against the building, for several minutes. He sobbed silently to himself. The drugs had really messed things up.

He turned his head slowly back to the window. Nobody yet. Was he really expecting her? Yes, of course he was. Another minute passed and he heard noises from inside. There, he knew it. He swivelled his head and looked straight into the face of a stranger.

He frowned. "Who the hell are you?"

"Oh! Just a passing stranger, you might say," the man said as he looked down into the yard below.

The teenager stiffened even more and said "What are you talking about - passing stranger?"

The man shook his head. "Not important right now, is it?"

"No?"

"No," he replied. "The important thing right now is whether or not you're going to jump. Wouldn't you say that was more important?"

"Suppose so."

"Only suppose?"

The boy fought back tears and said, "What's it to you, anyway."

"This, right now? Not a lot."

"Come on, you're just trying to use some clever psychology stuff to get me back in."

"No, I'm not."

"Yes, you are. You pretend to be so casual about it all but you're really playing mind games with me."

"No, I'm not."

He shouted, wobbling a little as he did. "Yes you are!" He steadied himself. "Anyway man, my girlfriend will come out of the bathroom any minute, then you'll have some explaining to do."

The man smiled. "I doubt that."

The boy turned his head to look at him. "What do you mean?"

"Oh! Yes. She's in the bathroom, but she's not coming out. Not yet anyway."

"Not coming out?" The boy croaked.

The man now laughed openly. "Nah. She's tied up, gagged and blindfolded, curled up in the bath tub. It's alright, she didn't see me. All she'll have are the bruises you gave her earlier."

The boy looked as hard as he could past the wind whipping across his face and the haze of drugs and alcohol. "I... I... I don't believe you," he said.

"Irrelevant," came the reply.

"I don't get it! What are you playing at, man?"

"Ooh! What am I playing at? That's rich coming from you. You and your girlfriend using your workmate's apartment to get drugged up and spend the weekend whenever he has to go away."

"But, how…"

He carried on. "Now, here you are. Drugged up to the eyeballs, I'd say, and after your blazing row you're waiting for her to come out and talk you in. How dramatic! How romantic!"

"How could you…"

Cut off again, the man went on. "Let's not waste time on how I know all this. As I said, irrelevant. No, what I'd really like to talk about is what happened in the laneway behind my house, last month."

He paused, then went on. "Nothing eh? No memories flooding back? No memories of you running over a cat and tumbling off your motorbike?"

His voice was now taking on an edge. "No recollection of grabbing the animal by the tail and throwing it into the dumpster?"

The boy on the ledge said nothing.

"I will tell you this much. When you lifted your bike upright I got a good look at your number plate; the rest was easy.

"And I'll tell you one last thing. The cat was mine."

He leant out very slowly and gave the boy the gentlest of prods.

The woman's thoughts were made known to the Observer. She was musing on the fact that sometimes it takes lots of ups and downs before things get evened out.

She was thinking about a woman she had heard about recently, who certainly had several rises and falls in her life; good times and bad times. Apparently, it had all started when she met and fell deeply in love with this man. In no time at all they were married.

That was good.

However, he soon turned out to be a no-hoper. He took to drink and became abusive and violent.

That was bad.

It was only a matter of time before the booze got to him and he died of alcoholism.

That was good.

In that short time he managed to run up a lot of debt.

That was bad.

Nevertheless, she had a good job that she really liked and it paid well.

That was good.

Unfortunately, the business went downhill and she was made redundant.

That was bad.

Eventually, she found work again.

That was good.

It was only part time and didn't pay at all well.

That was bad.

Things turned around when she won some money in a competition.

That was good.

On the day she went out to collect her prize, she left the gate open and the dog got out and was hit by a car.

That was bad.

But she had never liked the dog, as it barked a lot.

So, that was good.

As it turned out the extensive surgery was successful and the dog survived.

Ah! That was bad.

Because of the damage to the dog's throat it was no longer able to bark.

That was really good.

She received a huge bill from the vet.

No… that was bad.

Regardless of all the medical treatment, the dog died.

Wow! That was good.

Her sister, thinking she was doing the right thing, gave her another dog.

Oh! No! That was bad.

So, when she went out shopping, she left the gate open…

She had been watching numbers dance across her TV screen. The Observer felt the surge of emotion when she hit the pause button. She had hit the pause button hard, very hard.

She always recorded it, just in case. Sometimes they'd be out somewhere or there were times when she just wasn't quick enough to check the numbers. So, she always recorded it. As she stared at the frozen image, a noisy pounding started up in her ears and her breathing became heavy. This was how she always imagined it would be; the sweats, the watery eyes ... if she actually won.

She was so grateful that it had happened when he was working late. She needed time. None of the things she needed could be bought. Not even the amount she had won could buy what she needed that night. She needed time to reflect, time to consider the ramifications... the changes.

What she had was wonderful. He was working so hard to put enough money together. They had such great plans. They would start a family, although they had both married late, there was still time for her. They had talked about it so often. Their dreams were so important to both of them. What would happen to the dream? Yes, what would happen? She knew that she had a lot of hard thinking to do. Her life hadn't always been this easy, or this good.

When her parents were both lost in a major plane crash being an only child, with no relations either willing or able to take her in, she had spent time in limbo. A sad time before being put up for adoption. Then more misery and waiting and uncertainty before being adopted by a loving couple. Things had turned around for her then. She had lived with her adopted parents, right up to the time she had married. Now, so happy, with the man she loved, with such exciting dreams.

Would she have to let all of that go? Do their future prospects (without a large fortune sitting in the bank) give them only an ordinary life? Most people, it seemed, weren't content with ordinary. She liked ordinary. She was looking forward to spending a life of ordinary. That night, before he got home from working overtime, she turned all this over in her mind, repeatedly. Their plans for the future. The life they wanted and had planned together.

The following morning she was on the phone to the adoption agency. "Hello, I would like to speak with the manager please, I think her name is Williams, is that right?"

"Yes, can I take your name please?"

"Well, at this point I don't want to give my name but it is important that I speak with her."

"One moment." She was put on hold for a while.

She came back on, saying "Hello. I'm putting you through now."

The manager came on. "Hello. How can I help you?"

"Oh! Hello. I'm in your records but I don't want to be identified. Is that OK?"

A pause, then. "Go on."

"I'd like to make a private donation but remain anonymous. Is that possible?"

"Yes. We do receive donations of that sort."

"OK. I'd like to send you a letter with no sender's address. It'll be addressed to you marked confidential. It'll contain a lottery ticket. That's all I have to say. Are you OK with that?"

"Well, yes. Thank you for thinking of us."

"Believe me, you're more than welcome. Goodbye." She put the phone down with a great sigh.

Within the hour the letter had been prepared and posted. When she got home she reflected on the events, starting from seeing the results on TV last evening through to posting the letter. She felt entirely confident that she would never have regrets, not even about keeping everything from the man she married; the man she loved; the man she would bring up a family with. No. She had done the right thing.

That evening he asked. "How did we go with the lottery?"

She pulled a sad face. "Nope. Sorry. You'll have to keep working, I'm afraid."

He just smiled and kissed her on the cheek.

It had always been their secret place, the Observer knows that. It was way out here in the vastness of the old forest.

He was saying, "Do you remember how we would drive for miles to get here?"

He shook his head. "You insisted on it because your family were so wealthy and important, you said they wouldn't be able to stand the shame of it."

He squeezed her hand and she smiled. "I'm so glad we came back. Sorry, if I'm going on a bit. It always meant so much to me, being here with you."

She was smiling.

"Later, of course, when we were married, we had no need for a tryst like this," he went on. "It all changed. A respectable married couple, we had no need for this. This isolation and this sense of complete privacy. Do you remember how we actually spent a whole night here once because your folks were away? Do you remember how cold it got and how we only had each other to keep ourselves warm?"

He laughed and punched her gently on the shoulder. "You said you wished we could stay here, just like this, forever."

She was still smiling, saying nothing. "Oh! How we were so much in love, all that time ago."

He shook his head. "Then, of course, there was me coming back from the convention three days early, and him lying there in our bed, calling out to you in the bathroom if you wanted another drink."

He looked down at her smile, painted there with little flourishes of lipstick.

He rolled her in on top of him and started shovelling.

It watched the man as he sat, shaking his head. He had just been told a story by a colleague. He had his doubts about the truth of it.

Apparently, the whole thing had started with a relatively minor accident in this scientist's research lab. He had been mixing chemicals when it happened. Just a minor explosion that singed the hairs on his arms. It shook him up a little; less about it burning his skin slightly and more about it being so totally unexpected. In fact, there was absolutely no logical explanation for it happening at all. He soon shrugged it off, knowing there were more important things to think about. He was a research scientist, involved, like so many others, in cancer research.

That evening he noticed that the singed hairs he had washed off his arms had been replaced by a layer of grey powder. He washed and scrubbed his arms thoroughly and thought no more about it until the following evening. It seemed that over a twenty-four-hour period, the powdering layer was back. At this point he carefully scraped it off and sealed it in a plastic container. The next day he visited the nearby university campus, where he found and bribed a young chemistry student to fast-track some unofficial tests on the powder.

An hour or so later the student presented himself unannounced at the research lab carrying the sample and a folder containing test papers. The student, now showing a very serious demeanour, proceeded to explain that the sample was in fact Rhodium. Quite forgetting that the man was a scientist, he went on to say that Rhodium is considered to be a precious metal, then added what the researcher wasn't likely to know, that Rhodium was currently selling at ten times the price of gold!

He went on excitedly to say that he found it curious that it was presented to him in a powder form and that he had checked his results and repeated the test six times before he went on the Net to discover that the sample he was holding was worth a small fortune!

After a discussion that went well into the night, during which the scientist took the student into his confidence by explaining what had actually occurred, it was agreed that two things would happen.

Firstly, to the researcher's great delight with this sort of money coming in, much greater progress could be made in his cancer research program and his good work could be funded indefinitely.

Secondly, the student would take on immediate employment with the scientist, as his personal research assistant. He could oversee Rhodium sales, assist with the recording of test results, and organise the ordering of new equipment and faster computers.

Unhappily, despite the accumulation of a great deal of money over the coming months, with greater and greater amounts of powder covering more and more of the scientist's body, so too did the debilitating illness that came with it. He was diagnosed with a virulent form of cancer and finally bedridden, so the research program was cancelled.

Within days of this the research scientist passed away. When the funeral service was over, paid for in cash by the student, he picked up his few belongings, rang for a taxi and caught his flight to Spain.

It transpires that he now lives in a great mansion, in the hills above Marbella on the Costa del Sol, where he has several cars and regularly entertains just as many women. It seems that no one knows how he came into his money, but in Marbella nobody really cares. He is popular with the locals, giving to local causes, including the school and the church... and every year, without fail, he donates twenty-five dollars to cancer research.

It watched as the man entered the coffee shop. After taking a few moments to look at the list of various coffees he smiled at the barista and said, "Hi! How's it going?"

"Well, since you ask," said the barista, "I do find myself wondering just how much the human psyche really does influence the current state of things. I mean, have we all been thrust unwillingly into this state of existence hardly knowing whether our thoughts are able to give it all meaning? Is there a case for believing that an individual can shape their destiny in any meaningful way beyond the obvious parameters that we generally accept - that most of it is simply put down to fate."

He paused for a moment.

"After all, it's pretty much accepted that each person's experience of consciousness is not necessarily the same as that of others. I believe that we can be so distracted by primal comforts and pleasures that we have become blind to what should be obvious; namely that people are unhappy because they are trying to relieve their troubled souls by recourse to these so easily-accepted physical pleasures, when any such pursuit cannot possibly heal that which is basically spiritual."

He paused again.

"I would have to say that any real opposition to empiricism only seems to weaken any self-determinism an individual considers they may have; especially when applying it to the authenticity of their choices. I, for one, find it hard to believe that anybody would allow this to cut across rational thought."

Yet another pause.

"Although not strictly an existentialist, I do feel that in exercising our freedom of choice (and to a degree our personal responsibilities) we find ourselves in what has to be seen as a hostile universe, and there seems no good reason why this should be so. I think we have to accept the fact that we really can't transcend thought, or even existence, when you get right down to it. Anyway, that's how I see it."

"Yes, well, thanks for that... just one cappuccino, thanks."

The man in the uniform stood waiting at the bus station. The Observer could feel the sense of burning anticipation in the man.

The soldier was home on leave, and a well-deserved one at that.

His uniform had been cleaned and pressed for the occasion, and the world saw him for what he was. It had been a long tour of duty and he was more than ready for a break. His parents always had a room waiting for him, and the thought of laying down on his comfy old bed at home had kept him going since flying in today.

First the train and now the bus. He was on the final leg of his journey; a one-hour ride. Perhaps he could sleep on the bus if he told the driver where he needed to get off. Somebody pressed a button and the bus information board spoke. *The next bus will arrive in two minutes.*

It arrived and he climbed aboard. It was almost empty. After arranging a wake-up call with the driver, he made his way to the far end of the vehicle, where he took a window seat. He wriggled into the corner, pulled his cap down to the bridge of his nose and closed his eyes.

"Excuse me."

He lifted his cap and saw an elderly lady with a bag of groceries standing next to him, swaying precariously with the movement of the bus. He smiled up at her and said, "Hello. Did you want something?"

"Yes. I wondered if this seat was taken."

He glanced around quickly at the rows of empty seats. He could see at once that she was a simple old soul with no harm in her. "No, not at all." He waved at the seat next to him and said, "Please."

"Thank you, young man. That's very kind of you." She settled down with her bag on her lap.

"What a lovely uniform. I saw you get on."

He smiled.

"My grandson is in the army. His name is Thomas."

He nodded patiently. "That's good."

"Yes. He's a good boy, Thomas."

He nodded again.

"You might know him?" she said, raising her eyebrows.

"I might." He thought for a moment. "Does he part his hair on the right?"

She considered the question very carefully. "Do you know, I think he does? Yes, I'm sure of it."

"I might have met him in the barracks, about eighteen months ago."

"Well, there you are then. Just fancy that." With that she sat back in her seat, hugging her shopping, looking very content.

The soldier smiled, nodded, pulled his cap down and went back to sleep.

They sat huddled around the table, watched by the Observer. They were waiting for him to go on with his story. It had become something of a tradition in the place. On those occasions when the old guy came out of his shell and began communicating with his fellows, it was always worth a listen. He looked around at his audience with eyes lighting up as though he was only now aware of their presence.

"Yes," he started. "We were getting off the bus at the terminal, looking around for a taxi…" He looked up at the ceiling. "Ah! Taxis; you can learn so much. One driver that used to pick me up regular told me that dreams can't be destroyed. He told me that. He said that once they have come into existence, they stay. He reckoned Newton's laws explained it. He said that the conservation of energy was the answer. You could muck about with it as much as you like, but whatever you do, it's still there. The dream that is, it's still there." At this point he takes out a scruffy looking handkerchief and coughs into it.

One or two men at the table exchange smiles. A young woman shakes her head at them and quietly says "Go on."

"Oh! Well, that was before my old landlady had her heavenly experience. I couldn't afford taxis then."

He frowned and shook his head. "Gave her quite a fright, that did."

Around the table heads nodded eagerly in encouragement.

"Nice old thing she was. Undercharged me regular. Anyhow, the way she told it, she had just turned in for the night and before she knew it she was up there at the pearly gates, being questioned by this old geezer in a white robe. Not so much questioned, but being told off. He reckoned she had gone up before her time and it was her fault because of the chickens."

Somebody said, "Chickens?"

This had been blurted out without thought. There was a golden rule on these occasions. You didn't react in any way to what was being said. You didn't make comments. You didn't laugh, question, argue or give opinions; you just listened. They sat quietly, hoping he would go on.

He didn't seem to hear the interjection; just sat deep in thought. "She loved her chickens, she did. Kept them out the back; always feeding them. They were always following her around." He nodded. "Must've followed her up. The bloke was getting really nasty, saying they'd never had chickens up there before."

He chuckled. "Poor bugger didn't know my landlady. She ripped right into him, she did. Gave him a proper tongue-lashing. She said the old guy pulled his head in, apologised, and the next thing she knows she's back in bed."

Those around the table all nodded and smiled in agreement with the incident's outcome. They now sat patiently hoping there'd be more rambling. The storyteller coughed and blew his nose. He looked around at those staring at him. He went on.

"Where was I? Oh! Yes… anyway, we were getting off the bus at the terminal, looking around for a taxi…"

The two young women sat across the coffee table. The Observer could see that one was waiting for the other to start.

They had known each other since school and there was only two month's difference in their ages. They had always been really good mates. They now shared a small apartment together and both had jobs in the town.

The younger said, "OK. What's the big secret?"

The older said, "As you know, about a year before I left home my parents sat me down for a chat."

"Of course. I know about that. The whole abandoned baby thing."

"Yes. I know you do, but not all of it."

The younger grinned. "Oooh! Do tell," she wriggled, wide eyed, and made herself comfortable.

"OK. You know I was found by my mother; left under bushes, in a small wicker basket very close to where she lived. You know she took me in and brought me up as her own. This was before she met my father. It goes without saying that I couldn't have wished for a better mother and father. So, at the age of twenty-one I discovered that I was a foundling."

The younger one nodded. "Yes. I guess I knew most of that."

The other went on. "There's more. On the night that this was all explained to me I also discovered that Mum herself was a foundling."

"Wow! How cool is that?"

"Cool? Yes, I suppose it is in a way. Anyway, it was then that I learned that her mother was around our age when she had discovered my Mum hidden in bushes near her home…" She paused for a moment, then said "…in a small wicker basket."

The younger one frowned. "This is some kind of put on, right?"

The other shook her head.

"Really?"

"Really. This is what I was told and I have absolutely no reason to doubt her. She has always been honest with me. One of the things I love about Mum and Dad; they are just naturally honest people."

"Wow! That is so weird. I mean, what are the chances?"

"I know. What are the chances?" The older woman looked steadily at her friend while tears welled up in her eyes and rolled slowly down her cheeks.

Her friend was amazed to see the sudden change of emotion. She said, "What?"

The older woman stood and said "Come with me."

The other followed her out of the room, listening to her friend saying, "Before you got home… at the end of the lane… I heard it… got my phone out and used the torch…"

She opened her bedroom door. There, on the bed, moving slightly, was a small wicker basket.

The boy was walking very carefully when the Observer witnessed what occurred. It was a particularly cold winter with everything freezing over.

That morning his mother was making sure he was rugged up before venturing out into the bitter weather. He was considered old enough to go into town on his own and was planning to meet some friends there. The roads through the town were icy and traffic using them crept along at a careful pace.

He was not even on the road when the incident took place. He was standing at the edge of the footpath waiting to cross. The car wasn't going particularly fast when it encountered a patch of hidden black ice that sent it into a spin. It swiped him off his feet and back down with a heavy thud. He landed on his back and had not moved when people went to help him. The blow to the back of his head was severe and he had lost consciousness.

In the hospital he was examined and it was decided he had received a major concussion. He was identified and word of the accident was sent to his home. The weather had been so very cold in the busy Austrian town that such accidents had become commonplace. As a result, his mother had to take a seat in the waiting area before the attending physician was available to take her through. As he approached she jumped up and he motioned her to sit. He settled down beside her and explained the situation to her.

He patted her hand. "It's all right, he is quite safe now, but I would recommend you keep him at home for a few days" he explained. "With this type of severe head injury the extent of any damage to the brain can be hard to predict. It's nothing to worry about, but you need to be aware that in these cases it is not uncommon to find that it can affect how a person's brain works for a while. You need to keep your eye on him as you may see some changes in his behaviour." He smiled. "Does your boy have any hobbies?"

"Oh! Yes!" she replied. "He loves to sketch and paint. He wants to be an artist."

The doctor nodded his approval. "That's good. You should encourage that. He needs something to occupy him while he recovers. Would you like to see him now?"

She brightened. "Oh! Yes, please. Thank you, doctor."

He led them through to the ward. Her son was propped up with pillows. He was awake, but was looking a little drowsy. He smiled at the sight of his mother. She rushed forward and took his hand. She leant over and kissed his forehead.

She whispered "My darling Adolph, I thought I'd lost you!"

She was worried about her boyfriend of late and the Observer could tell that she felt that he could be in some kind of trouble.

If only he would level with her. These late nights, and coming in just saying he had stuff to do was wearing a bit thin. She'd had enough of watching the clock. She would call him. She hadn't liked the look of the guy who came by looking for him today.

She called his mobile.

He came on saying, "Hi babe. You're calling because it's kind of late, eh?"

She bristled. "No, honey. It's not kind of late. It's nearly 2am. It *is* late!"

"Yeh. Got kind of tied up this end."

"What end? Where are you?"

"Look babe, it's best if I lay low for a bit. Nothing to worry about."

"Lay low? What are you talking about?"

"Nothing to worry about," he repeated. "Probably best if I stay here for a bit. Just for a few days."

She could feel anger rising. She took a few breaths. "You had a visitor today. Well, yesterday."

"Who was that?"

"Dunno. Didn't leave his name. Said you'd know who he was. I didn't like the look of him."

"What did he look like? Can you describe him?"

She sighed. "To be honest, I only saw part of him. I had the security chain on." She paused. "There was no way I was going to take it off. That gives you an idea of what he looked like doesn't it? Eh? If I wasn't prepared to take the security chain off!"

"Look babe, you sound upset."

"Of course, I sound upset!"

"I'm sorry, honey. Sorry that upset you."

She could hear him breathing. She said, "Well?"

He sounded genuinely sad. "Can you describe him for me? It's important."

"OK. Yes. Tiny moustache, a brown stripy sort of jacket…"

He broke her off. "OK. Thanks. I know who he is. What did he want?"

"You! He wanted you. I said you were out and closed the door on him."

"You did?"

"Of course I did. Didn't like the look of him at all."

He said. "Hang on." She heard a rustling of paper. He came back. "Look I have the hotel address here. I'll send this to you in a text. If anyone shows up just give them the address. Would you mind doing that babe?"

"I suppose not. Is that where you are now?"

"Nah, it's just an address I picked from the internet."

"So, where are you?"

He fell silent. "Best you don't know."

"So, you want me to give this nasty looking guy a phoney address? Is that it?"

"Yes. Please babe. I'd really appreciate it."

She sat quietly for a moment with thoughts racing through her head. "OK, sweetie. Just come home as soon as you can."

"Sure thing. Thanks, babe."

She put the receiver down gently. As she was mulling

it over, her phone beeped. An incoming text. The phoney address came on the screen.

She sighed and closed her eyes. She was tired, and she'd really had enough. All this nail-biting, and for what? So she could wash his stuff, feed him, spend time with him when he showed up? Six months this had been going on. She was struggling to pay the rent on this place. She'd said it was too big when they looked it over. No. She was too good for the guy. She'd been a patsy for far too long. She was better than this! Time to turn over a new leaf.

She got up and went through to the bedroom. She threw her empty case on the bed and packed it. He can owe the rent and he can deal with the shifty looking character with the brown stripy jacket. She looked up a street address in another town and saved a copy of it in her phone. She would send it to him on the way out.

It was phoney, of course.

He knew he would get into trouble big time if his boss sees him in his current state. The Observer was aware that the man had been taking drugs the night before. The worker went off to the toilet. He had been particularly dumb as he didn't really know what he'd taken. Maybe splashing cold water on his face would help.

So there he was, splashing his face, when he heard someone come in behind him, but didn't pay any attention. He could see what appeared to be a stranger out of the corner of his eye. It looked like he was tall and wearing all black or something. Not that that's unusual in an office building. Lots of people wear black suits. What really got his attention was the great scythe leaning against the side of the next basin.

He turned and looked at the stranger. All he could see was the face and hands, but they were just bones! No skin, no muscle, just musty, yellow bones. He found himself looking into the eye sockets of a skeleton! The visitor seemed to be washing its hands! A black, hooded cloak hung to the ground.

He moved nervously to the paper towels with the intention of leaving as soon as he could. As he stepped behind the figure, the thick cloak seemed to sway back and brush against his legs. The figure turned his head and croaked, "So sorry".

He was taken aback at the idea that the thing could speak.

He suppressed his panic and blurted out, "Not a problem," as he pulled off a couple of squares of paper and eyed the door.

The bony head swivelled around and spoke again. "Shocking weather, don't you think?"

Now, he had already figured out who this stranger was, and knowing that, he was surprised at the casual nature of the conversation. In spite of being more than a little shaken up, he managed to mumble "Yes, not very nice. I heard it's due to clear up later." As he spoke, he tried his hardest not to look directly at the thing.

"Yes, that would be nice," replied the creature, in a very polite tone.

He stood for a moment listening to his words echoing back. What was he doing? Standing next to a paper towel-dispenser, on the fifth floor of an office building, carrying on a chatty conversation with Death!

There he was, face to face (not that this thing actually had one) with The Grim Reaper! The reality of the whole scene suddenly rushed in on him. He felt his legs begin to give out and he began to wonder whether he would actually make it to the door.

He smiled, although he couldn't imagine why, and turned towards the door.

"Oh! Just one thing before you go". The figure stood with a skinless finger pointing upward, "Sorry to bother you, but could you tell me exactly where Mister Jeff Harding works?"

"Eh? Jeff? Yes, I think I know Jeff". A feeling of relief began to sweep over him, although he was still trembling. Jeff was his boss. The very man he was hiding from.

He grinned to himself, then wondered whether the creature had noticed this; there was no sign that it had. In fact, the visitor seemed very... well, relaxed!

"Yes, Jeff," he went on, "Jeff from Finance; wears a blue shirt and blue tie most days. About my height, and probably around my age as well, I suppose".

"Yes, that's him."

"Well, you can find him on the next floor up; level six. He's about half way along on the right. You can't miss it; it has a large poster up near the door saying something about no drugs being allowed in the workplace." He heard himself rambling, winced and moved closer to the door.

The thing flapped its cloak and said, "Ok, thanks."

He went to open the door, then felt a sudden rush of confidence. After all, with his boss gone life would be a lot rosier. He didn't know where his nerve came from, but knew he would never get the chance again to ask any of the questions that now buzzed around inside his head. He wanted to get out of there and back to the safety of his desk, but there was so much that he wanted to know. Besides, this strange creature seemed very courteous.

He mustered up enough courage to turn and face the other full on.

"Was there something else?" said the thing.

"So, uh, you're The Grim Reaper then?" he asked, feeling more than a little stupid actually asking the question. He simply couldn't think of anything better to say at that moment.

"Yes, that is correct; and you work alongside Jeff I believe?"

"Yes. That's right. You would know all that stuff of course, being… Well, you being what you are, I mean."

The ghastly skull seemed to be smiling. The man wondered how this could be, when another burning question surfaced.

"This chap upstairs, Jeff, seems a nice enough sort really, pity he has to… you know."

"Pop off, do you mean?" The skull looked like it was still grinning.

"Well, yes. Just seems a shame unless there's a good reason for it."

"Oh! You can rest assured, there is always a good reason for a person's number being up. We don't make mistakes when it comes to a person's final calling." The creature in the robe bent to where his scythe was propped and ran a bony finger along the length of the shiny blade.

"No, of course not. I'm sure you know what you're doing. I didn't mean to be rude."

"Not at all. Not at all. Is there anything else? I don't mind answering your questions."

"Well, this chap, Jeff. Will he see you coming? Will he know that his time has come?"

The tall figure seemed to be admiring what it saw in the mirror, occasionally brushing off its sleeves and straightening the wide, black belt that hung loose about its middle.

"Yes. He would know. You see, only the people I intend to reap actually see me."

The man froze, as the full impact of the last statement came home to him. He turned.

The skull was now grinning at him again. It said, "Only kidding." It stood for a moment in front of the mirror adjusting the large, floppy hood.

He was just getting over the shock when he glanced around at the shadow that seemed to be about to leave.

"Excuse me!" he called out, "don't forget your scythe." He picked it up but the figure had vanished.

He looked down and saw he was holding the cleaner's mop.

It looked on as events began to unfold in the woman's house.

Little did the Auntie know what she had unleashed, the day the question was asked.

The girl was very young when it happened. She was a timid child and rather sickly. The winter chill didn't help. She had just put a question to her Auntie and was shocked to see the anger in her face. "No, you certainly can't!" was the furious and quite unexpected reply.

"Why?" she asked feebly, followed by a soft, "Please."

Her Auntie was now fuming. "No means no! I don't have to explain myself to you, little miss." With that she left the room, banging the door closed as she went.

The girl went across to the window and stared out at the snow and shivered. The feeling of being thrust aside, and in a manner so completely out of hand, lingered within the child like smoldering embers. It would be hours before her mother would come to collect her. She blew her nose.

A short while later, the young girl stood in the front garden. There was a small but pleasant amount of heat coming from the front window. The front of the house was well ablaze now. As the heat grew she had to move back to the street.

All of a sudden Auntie came running out through the smoldering front door screaming. At the same time a neighbour appeared saying he had called the fire service and asked if anyone was hurt. The girl said she was having difficulty breathing and an ambulance was called. She waved goodbye to her Auntie as she was taken to hospital. She knew it would be nice and warm in there.

She was sorry that the house would burn down but... she had only asked if they could put the heater on in the front room.

The man was happily banging away at his keyboard. The Observer was witness to this, but it knew this wasn't always so.

It had all started when his friend sold him his old computer. He spent hours teaching himself how to use it and how to type. He felt sure that it was going to open up wonderful opportunities for him. In no time at all he had lofty aspirations. He would write a novel, the likes of which would set the whole business of authoring on fire. It would take the literary world by storm. It would go straight to the top of the best-sellers list, making a fortune for himself in royalties that just wouldn't stop piling up, along with oodles of dosh for his eternally grateful publisher.

He would sell the rights to a movie company so they could make one or a whole series of films based on his book. He would be invited to studios to give advice on how his work should be adapted. He would get invites to cocktail parties in big, posh houses so that rich people could listen to him. He would be sought after by other members of the literati to hear his views on literature's place in society. He would fly around to major cities attending book signings. He would go on tour, giving lectures around the world. He would be invited to stay with celebrities who would enjoy his company and treat him as an equal.

Then there would be the merchandising of course; caps, mugs, t-shirts and so on. He would have to hire top-notch financial advisors to help with his banking and investments and anything else they could think of.

Of course, he would have to leave his job with the water company. Probably move out of his flat and into a large, expensive house. He would probably need to take driving lessons and buy a top-of-the-range car. It would seem inappropriate to keep riding his bicycle. He would probably feel awkward about turning up at the stamp collectors club;

people wouldn't stop wanting to talk about his book and his new life. He wondered how Doris would take it. She wasn't much of a reader and she wouldn't want anything to get in the way of her Bingo Nights!

Gradually, he saw just how much his life would change. It would take on an entirely different direction. The more he thought about it, the more uncomfortable he felt about allowing all these radical twists and turns to take over his everyday existence. Over a week or two his discomfort turned to a foreboding, then to a sense of unease, and finally he fell to a level of anxiety he had never known before. He knew he had to rethink the whole thing if he was ever going to get back to happily banging away on his keyboard again. When it came right down to it, all he wanted was to sit and write quietly, just for his own enjoyment. Then, with this thought, a sudden realisation burst in upon him…

He found a quiet spot at the back of the house, bought himself a new laptop, set up his own blog and began writing short stories.

Now he was happily banging away at his keyboard again.

The Observer was aware of the man standing patiently at the reception desk. The man was quietly wondering what he was doing there. It knew that the man waiting at the desk was a reporter.

He only knew that he was about to get a personally-guided tour of what was supposed to be a top secret personnel project, and it was being sponsored by the government. He had been told that he was being smuggled in by the girl he'd met at the tennis club. Naturally, he was nervous; but of course, a story is a story.

After a short wait, the girl from the club collected him. As they made their way down a long hallway towards the far end of the complex, she said in a low voice, "I'm glad you took up my offer. I'm taking you straight through to the test room. Remember the deal, no notes."

He nodded.

She punched numbers into a key pad, followed by swiping a security card to open the door. They went in and he found himself looking into a vast open office, filled with desks and computers, with every one of them populated. He was looking at one hundred or maybe a hundred and fifty staff, all looking very busy. He was looking through a wide window that ran the length of the room.

"It's OK. They can't see us." she said. "One-way glass."

"What are you doing here?" he asked.

She took on a serious look and said, "It's complex, but basically the purpose of this program is all about developing methods to increase productivity... not just here, but all around the country. The idea being that these techniques can be adapted to any kind of administrative office environment. He peered into the room again. "Wow! Does it work?"

"Unfortunately, yes."

"Unfortunately?"

"Well, yes, of course." She said angrily. "Up there." She pointed. "Amphetamine mist, you can't see it, but it's there. It's fed in through the air-conditioning system."

"Go on."

"It's a drug! It stimulates the central nervous system. It elevates a person's mood and controls the appetite."

"Really?"

"Really. It keeps them all happy and radically reduces the amount of time spent eating," she continued. "See the water dispenser over there?"

He saw it and answered, "Yes."

"It's laced with a newly-developed chemical, it's a memory-blocker that makes them forget their families; keeps their minds on their work."

He was watching a man filling a cup from it when she said, "Over there. See the coffee machine?"

He looked at it and said, "Don't tell me."

She grimaced painfully and said, "It contains a bowel and bladder-strengthening chemical that greatly reduces the number of toilet breaks."

All of a sudden a woman screeched.

"What was that?"

"At a guess I'd say it was a game attempt by a newbie, probably FreeCell."

She went on to explain what she meant. "There are games on the machines that office workers find irresistible, especially that card game, you know, FreeCell?"

He nodded.

"Well, we have a software program running on all the mice that generates a small electrical charge whenever the game site is accessed."

"Does it work?" he asked.

"Oh! Yes, too well sometimes. We had one chap who got zapped so often, bit of an addict you see, yes…" her eyes glazed over. "Sorry, yes, so often we had to reduce the charge on his mouse. Difficult case that was. His productivity dropped right off, when that happens it defeats the whole purpose of the program."

She paused. "I haven't seen him for a while."

He looked puzzled.

She said, "I've heard rumours that those who don't respond the way they're supposed to, never return to their regular jobs. They just disappear!"

He stood looking into the room, shaking his head. He was speechless.

She said, "It's all about the recession, you see. It's about what they call the commercial imperative." She let out a long sigh and turned to him with glistening eyes.

"The hype we keep hearing is that this will change the world by increasing worker productivity, but I'm not at all happy with what we are doing here."

"You're quitting?"

"Yes. I can no longer be any part of this. It's disgusting and immoral."

Just then a man in a suit entered the room. She whispered, "Security... let me do the talking."

He approached and looked the reporter over. "No ID tag?" he said.

"Oh! Sorry," she said. "That's my fault, I forgot. Stay put, I'll get you a visitor's badge." She rushed off.

The reporter, despite the agreement, had a burning desire to report what he knows.

When she returned the security man was gone and the reporter was on his own. She stared with bulging eyes at the cup he was holding. "Oh! Where did you get that?"

"The security guy offered me a hot chocolate, so I said OK."

As he said this he became aware of a strange numbness in his chest.

The man fell and the woman left the building....

The Observer absorbed the woman's thoughts as she stared at the rope swinging gently in the breeze. She was looking at it so intently.

It was just an old rope that had been strung up for the kids to swing on.

It had been hanging there for so long. Just a thick piece that they had found washed up one day. He had brought it home and tied a piece of wood to it, providing something to sit on. She smiled. He was so good at that sort of thing. The kids in the neighbourhood all loved it. Sometimes they had to be told gently that it was time to go home, just to let her, their curly-haired angel, get a go before it was time to come in.

How she loved to be pushed. "Who wants to be pushed on the rope swing?" This was all it took to create so much excitement. She never wanted it to stop. God, how they loved her.

Now, she was right there, pushing her higher and higher. It was late. He would be home from work soon. She could hear the giggles and the phone ringing. It may be him, saying he was delayed. She gave one big push and ran in. It stopped before she could get it. She turned and looked out as she replaced the receiver.

The rope swing was empty...

She cried out; sat up in bed, blinking, hearing noises. He came rushing in, asking what was wrong. She got out of bed and went to the window. She saw her daughter, happily swinging on the rope, of course. Such an awful dream with such dark imaginings.

She still had a husband; she still had a daughter; and late night Chicken Vindaloo meals with a glass of port had just become a thing of the past.

The nature of the woman was being viewed by the Observer.

She had always been a strange girl and an even stranger woman. Now, in mid-life, she said that her love was like a shop; a very old shop. She said everything in it was way past its 'use by' date. Although, she had a feeling that there may be the odd item that was still current, she was proud of the fact that a great deal of variety could be found on its shelves. There were jars and packets, cleaning products and clothing, kitchen utensils, camping equipment and auto parts. All these items sat patiently waiting for someone to call in and find the very thing they'd been looking for.

When this happens. Ah! When this happens, so much will change. The old shop will close its doors for the last time, never to be reopened for passers-by to drop in and look around. The 'Closed' sign will be turned and left that way. All that the old shop contains will still be there, but no longer open to the public. It will all be shared.

That's how she saw it.
Who's to say she's wrong?

In a relatively quiet street in Wembley, on the outskirts of London, the Observer looks on as a taxi pulls up.

A woman is returning home. She is running a little late from her job in the city, but still has time for a bath and a change of clothes before being picked up by her fiancée. They have plans to go out for dinner and a show. However, when he arrives he gets no answer at the door. He is troubled by the fact that there are lights on in the house. So, in desperation, he uses the emergency key she gave him. After calling out as he goes through the house checking all the rooms, he finds her lying motionless in the bath. There was a lot of water splashed on the floor. He could only think that she had slipped, banged her head and drowned.

The man sitting at his desk was something of a loner.

He spent a great deal of time scribbling ideas about one thing or another. His house is large and spacious and very quiet. He lives alone, with no nearby properties. He is, by any standard, very wealthy. He made most of his money in recent years, creating top selling video games. He is reserved by nature. He often travels but always alone. Although in his early thirties, he has no meaningful attachments. Over the years he has had some affairs, but nothing serious. He has always been uncomfortable around women; in fact, he is uncomfortable around people.

-

In Limerick, Ireland, the lodger that lives on the top floor is about to put the kettle on.

His window gives him a grand view of the River Shannon. He is staring out at it now, day-dreaming about his recent trip to America. In the background he has music playing and he is softly humming to it. He is not rich by any means, but he happily spends most of his money on music. Quite by accident he had met a girl overseas. He is thinking about her now. He had written to her, as promised, but hadn't received a reply. As he gets a mug ready he notices a slight buzzing noise coming from somewhere. He gazes out at the view again wondering if he should write again. He decides and shakes his head. He leans across to switch the kettle on. It is the last thing he ever does.

-

The man has moved from his desk, across the room to a makeup table and mirror.

He is at play with his hobby. As a recluse, it is a private hobby. His table is covered with products; skin-toning creams and powders, concealers and lotions, waxes, gels and sprays. Although this has been a favourite pastime for a number of years, he has more recently found a need to hone up on it. He enjoys perfecting his disguise. This is primarily a dark brown wig, brown contact lenses (his eyes naturally being green), and a moustache and glasses that he ordinarily didn't need. When he has finished, he stares at his new persona and smiles.

-

On New Zealand's north island, in Hamilton, a woman is leaving a Shopping Centre.

It is a busy complex, always having large numbers of shoppers going through. Most stores are closing and it is emptying. Crowds are spilling out onto the streets. The woman in question works in a music store only a few blocks away. She has only done some light shopping on this occasion and is now heading for the bus-stop. A crowd is building as she waits at the pedestrian crossing for the lights to change. She is standing at the curb aware of the number of people building up behind her. In an instant, she goes forward, stumbling into the path of a heavy goods vehicle. When the police attend the scene several of those remaining say they saw a man bump into the back of her but couldn't tell if this was because it was so crowded or not. When asked if they could point him out they couldn't; he had gone.

-

The green-eyed man is in a pensive mood.

He is reflecting on the unhappy family life he had as a child. More than that, he remembers the more recent incident. He couldn't book for the play he wanted, so he had to make do with a musical. A meal in a local restaurant was included in the ticket. He hadn't particularly enjoyed it but was determined to make the most of it. His pulse quickens. He remembers returning to the table. The people at it, either not able to look him in the eye or worse, those who smirked. He recalls how the frustrated waiter sent him back to wait for a vacant place at another table. He had tried really hard that night, sitting there with all those strangers; making a big effort to relax and be one of them, to be accepted. He only got up to go to the toilet. He knows that something snapped inside him that night.

-

In Bangkok, Thailand, a woman falls from a balcony.

There was no one there to witness it; no one there to see how such a thing could happen. She had been living in the house since just after her daughter was born, for more than twenty years. She was a widow. When the daughter returned from work she discovered the body. The local police looked on it as a suspicious death, but made no headway with it. All they had was a witness saying that a man was seen passing the house; that was all, just passing. The only thing of interest was that he was described as unusual, looking out of place. The young woman would be left with her memories; especially the recent memory of going with her mother to the US to watch a wonderful musical.

-

On the flight back from China the green-eyed man felt sure he had been seen.

Not on the balcony but on the street. Ordinarily it wouldn't matter, but he felt he'd been stared at. He knew that if he wanted to complete the mission he had set himself he would have to adopt extreme caution. For the next act of retribution he would need to return to the USA. His planning would be scrupulous. Nevertheless, he would need to keep moving if he was to complete the entire undertaking. He considered that timing was now becoming more important.

-

In the area known as East Village on Manhattan Island, a man climbs into his bed.

He lives alone in an apartment block, having lost his wife a few years back. It was very small and a little cramped, but it was all he needed for his reinvented lifestyle. He worked in a financial consulting firm in the business centre. He would be classed as a workaholic if it weren't for his love of catching every musical that hit Broadway. This was something he and his wife had always enjoyed and the passion for it stayed with him. He was laying comfortably and was soon in a deep sleep. Smoke inhalation took its toll long before the fire raged through the tiny rooms. He had switched off his bedside light for the last time.

-

The man in the busy office had risen through the ranks and was now one of many detectives serving in the city's International Crime Division. The Wembley murder was something that hit him on a personal level. The victim had been the daughter of a member of his local dart team. The group played weekly at his local pub and quite naturally his friend had been applying pressure for him to look into it. In his work he had an array of databases he could access during any routine process of looking for criminal connections. It may have been more luck than anything that he came across a match between witness statements. They were descriptions given at two different suspicious deaths, both listed as possible crime scenes. The first being a statement given by a neighbour, following the death of a woman falling from a residential building in Thailand. The other being an earlier incident in New Zealand, where a number of witness statements were taken after a suspicious road traffic death.

-

The green-eyed man sat at his desk planning his next move. He paused for a moment. His eyes stung as he was thrown back into the restaurant where it had happened. He hated these flashbacks and hoped they would stop when everything he needed to do was done. He knew it was a case of him returning to either New Zealand or Thailand. On the other hand, he could take a trip to Japan. In his mind it wasn't a case of selecting on the basis of degree of guilt. No. They all shared the responsibility for what had taken place. On the basis that a husband in New Zealand had suffered the loss of his wife and a woman in Thailand had lost her mother, the answer was clear. He went back to his planning.

-

In the days that followed the discovery of matching descriptions a wide-ranging hunt was on for a person of interest. At this point a profiler was consulted to determine the kind of person they were looking for. Meanwhile, looking into the private lives of the victims and conducting interviews with close relatives, a link had been found. Both of the parties from New Zealand and from Thailand had attended an evening show in America, on the same night. The breakthrough opened up a number of avenues for the police authorities to make enquiries about the events occurring on and around that date. The resources of the international criminal investigation agencies around the world were now being used to gather information. They now had a list of potential victims and it was just a matter of waiting for the perpetrator to make his next move.

-

In Japan, the young man was lounging in an armchair reading.

He was one of a number of students lodging in a house in a place called Taito, not far from the University of Tokyo. Although he looked as though he was just relaxing with a book, he was in fact swatting for upcoming exams. He was so intent on his study that he did not hear the green-eyed man enter the room carrying a short length of nylon rope. The man had decided that it did not have to look like an accidental death. He also felt that there wasn't time to lay a trail of guilt to a student in the same building, although he felt sure that it would be a line of enquiry. In the same way that the student wasn't aware of him, he in turn had no idea that a team of police had watched him enter the room. The arrest was very quickly performed. It took a long time for the student to regain the composure required in order to again immerse himself in his studies.

-

During the lengthy interviews that followed the full story was revealed.

When the truth came out it was nothing short of bizarre. The man responsible for the series of deaths had, like all the others, purchased a show and dining package online, for an evening in the USA. The ticket included a show and a three-course meal at a restaurant located in the heart of the theatre district, just a short walk from the theatre. After the show he walked to the restaurant, where he had been put at a table for eight. He hadn't enjoyed the musical as this just wasn't the sort of entertainment he preferred. He had been determined to be sociable and join in the conversations going on around him. He got to know a little about all of them and felt he was doing well. The seven others were made up of an American who lived not far away, a New Zealand couple, a student from Japan, a mother and daughter from Thailand, and a man from Ireland.

He thought it had all been going well. They had all placed their orders and were now chatting amiably. He needed the toilet and excused himself. It was at the end of a warren of passageways so that on his return he found himself getting confused. When he finally got back into the main dining room he saw that he was approaching his table from a different angle. The table seemed to be full, but it was his table, he recognised all of them; all except a woman who had taken his seat next to the Irishman. For several moments he just stood at the end of the table, waiting to be noticed and given some kind of explanation and apology. Nobody looked at him. Nothing came. He heard a soft sniggering. He was filled with a fury he had never known before. Then a waiter appeared at his elbow wanting to move him on. He explained what had happened, but the waiter was far too busy to get involved. Instead he guided him to a waiting area where he joined a long queue, all waiting for seats to become vacant. Of course, he had carried out some research later to find out the identity of the intruder.

-

Now that the interviews were over, the detective felt sure this man wouldn't get the death penalty. His personal opinion was that the man was barking mad. He figured that by the time the psychologists were finished examining him he would be committed. Following hours of listening to and recording his full confessions, he'd clammed up. In fact, he now seemed to be in a catatonic state and it didn't look as though he'd be coming back out of it. One of the psychology reports had said that his motivation had been to ensure that none of the people at the table would ever enjoy a show and dinner package again. It sounded pretty simple, but it was probably right.

Not long after the affair the detective's wife was offered spare theatre tickets. She pulled a face when she handed them to him. They were not interested. The fact was, nobody in his family liked musicals.

The two men sat at their desks; the Observer knew they were attempting to adjust to their new environment.

A number of staff had been shuffled around while a part of the magazine's office was being renovated. The editor was finishing a call while the illustrator was doing his best to put the final touches to his sketch. He jumped when the phone was slammed down.

The editor was fuming. He said, "What a prima donna that man is!"

The illustrator looked up.

The editor sighed, "I've explained the situation to him several times but no, the status quo just isn't good enough for him."

The illustrator went back to his drawing.

The editor went on. "I've argued the point with him ad nauseam but he won't budge." He absentmindedly shuffled papers on his desk. "It should have been a case of caveat emptor when we took him on."

The illustrator showed some interest. "Oh! Really?"

The editor rubbed the back of his neck. "Personally, I've had my doubts about his bona fides. He seems to think he has carte blanche over the way the magazine deals with its writers."

The illustrator was suddenly aware of the man's incessant proclivity for using foreign phrases, wherever possible. He grunted.

The editor lowered his voice. "Apparently he's been ringing others around the office, trying to get support for his ideas; dealing with it en masse as it were, trying to get everyone on side," he shook his head, "when I'm the only one he should be talking to."

The illustrator said, "Right."

The editor glanced out the window saying "Well, he's certainly persona non grata from my point of view. Did you know, there are better writers than him out there that submit their work pro bono?"

The illustrator said, "No. I didn't know that."

The editor, still staring out into space continued, "Oh! Yes.

You would think that adhering to the terms of the agreement would be quid pro quo for initially publishing his work." He looked back at the other. "I've been doing this job for years; I really object to him questioning my modus operandi."

The illustrator said, "Yes. I can understand that."

The editor said, "It's a fait accompli that the magazine, or any company for that matter, has the right to set its own rules. After all, ipso facto, it's the editor that has the final say on any editorial matters."

The illustrator, supressing a smile, said "Quite right."

The editor grimaced. "I can see now that accepting his first dubious article was a real faux pas. He says he's going away for a while to think about it, as though this was his pièce de résistance!"

The illustrator gave a jolly, "Ha!"

The editor said, "Yes. Well… I know what I wanted to say, but I didn't say it."

The illustrator said, "Don't tell me. Let me guess."

The editor looked surprised. "Go on."

The illustrator smirked. "You wanted to wish him bon voyage."

The editor was astonished. "How on Earth could you know that?"

The Observer saw the man enter the café. He was looking for someone wearing a black beanie. He spotted him sitting in the far corner.

He approached and sat down opposite. He had never met the man. They had only had one long conversation on the phone when he had asked for his services. He didn't know why he was so nervous. After all, this man had more to lose than he did.

Beanie looked at the time and said, "Coffee, tea?"

"No. Thank you anyway."

He glanced around the room and said, "Is it done?"

The other smiled. "Oh! Yes, it's done."

Beanie took a stuffed envelope from his pocket and murmured, "The other half." He gazed across the table with a frown. "I don't know why we had to meet like this. I was quite happy to drop the money off like before."

He took out a handkerchief and padded his forehead. "Anyway, did she suffer? I wouldn't like to think she suffered."

The man sat back staring at his client. "You interest me. It is very rare that I ever come face to face with people who engage my services… but you, tell me why you…" he leant forward, dropping his voice to a whisper, "tell me again why you wanted your wife dead."

The other was visibly shocked by the question. "You know why. She was cheating," he whispered.

The man shook his head. "No. Nice lady your wife. Said I was a colleague of yours that was just popping in. Gave me a cup of tea before I told her why I was there."

"A cup of tea?"

"Yes. In my line of work you really have to be a good judge of character. Just talking to you on the phone put me on my guard." He checked the time again. "I don't have long; I've got a plane to catch."

In a daze the other said, "Another job?" Then realised how frivolous the question was.

"No," came the reply. "Another country. In my profession it doesn't pay to stay in one place too long." He sipped his coffee slowly and continued. "She told me about your lover, the girl you've been seeing for several months now."

The other looked startled and opened his mouth.

The man raised his hand. "Look, there's no point denying it. I had the full story by the time I left the house. She has known about it for a while. She was hoping it would just run its course. You know, she's very much in love with you." His hand flicked again. "No. Of course, you wouldn't know." He looked at the pale face of his client, then went on. "Yes, when I left the house I not only had the full story, but your lady friend's address."

The other looked frantic. Raising his voice he said, "What! What have you done?"

One or two patrons looked over. The man shushed. "Not wise to make a fuss." He smiled. "No. She didn't suffer. They'll find her soon enough, I'm sure. Heart attack it was. I left the treadmill switched on and running. Nice touch I thought."

Tears were streaming down the client's face and he was shaking. "I don't understand," he blubbered. "I don't understand why you should do such a thing."

"It's simple really; as I said, your wife is a very nice lady. I'm giving you both another chance. It's up to you now." He stood up and stared down at his quivering, speechless client.

"Just be grateful. I don't usually provide this sort of thing as part of the service."

The man left the café.

The Observer knew that over a number of years the woman looking into the camera had been a very successful thief.

Jewellery was her speciality. All ill-gotten gains were sent out of the country and fenced by anonymous parties. It had worked like a charm for so long that at the age of thirty-two she could retire comfortably with the fortune she had amassed. It was the thrill of it all that kept her going long after she needed to risk capture.

Then it happened. It was a pretty simple job; a jeweller's shop in a city. She had found the building's weakness, entered in the early hours, stripped the place clean, filled her backpack and was on her way out when it came like a bolt out of the blue. Her mask simply fell off. She had been looking straight into the camera when it happened. In that moment she knew her cover was blown.

She also knew that she needed a new identity.

The following day she felt the need to break one of her several golden rules. She had never approached her first link in the fencing operation in person. It had always been strictly by phone, informing him where to pick up the proceeds. But now, with her cover blown wide open, with her face about to appear on crime scene boards all over the country, she had no choice. She knew he had provided new identities for others, for a price. It was going to be expensive but there was no other way. He obviously kept himself well informed because he wasn't surprised when she showed up on his front door step, wearing a scarf, dark glasses and a high collar.

After discussions about what had brought her there, he said he could help. He had done the same for others and none of them were ever caught or brought to justice. He had a small surgery room in the house. He said it could all be resolved by the following day. He said he could provide her with the perfect disguise. Of course, this came at a price. She sat quietly thinking it all over.

She said, "That's a great deal of money for a small operation that you say won't take long."

"Yes, I know," he agreed, "but you have to weigh it all up. I would probably recommend that you retire. I'm sure you have built up a fortune due to your successful enterprises over a number of years. This is probably the only way you can be absolutely sure that you won't do time."

She nodded. "OK. Let's do it."

He brought a laptop through and she transferred the money. He said, "I'll give you an oral premedication to relax you then we'll go through to the surgery. You understand that you can never divulge anything about what we do here today." She agreed to the terms.

She was relaxing in a chair as instructed when he returned with a little bottle of clear liquid. He tipped it into a small tumbler saying "It's quite tasteless, but it will make you more comfortable."

She swallowed it down and almost immediately felt the effect. She began to feel a coldness sweep through her body, followed by a drowsiness.

As she came out of it, he appeared in front of her saying, "All your troubles are over." He was holding out a hand mirror.

It was probably that the drugs she'd been given before surgery were still in her system, but when she looked into the mirror she thought she saw a frog.

The Observer hovers over the hotel balcony where the man sits watching the small waves flashing and glinting light as they roll in.

The blue waters that lap into the harbour are still. They have always been still, embraced as they are by the outstretched arms of the surrounding land. He looks down on it. He is imagining the scene two or three hundred years ago. A time when pirates would come and go in there fast-moving vessels with their great masts and sails, without hindrance from the native people who lived in fear of them. He knows that centuries back these brigands held great sway in this out of the way place. Arriving at night, they would take on fresh provisions, then scour the town for drink, women and anything worth stealing. They would then disappear before daylight, head out to the open sea, there to hide in the vastness of it, to lay in wait, to apply their lucrative trade and to plunder their unsuspecting prey.

Now, in the modern world of holiday makers, this place serves as a sanctuary for tired businessmen, clever computer programmers and overworked office staff. All milling along the skirt of the great body of water. Along the water's edge, all manner of shops and restaurants offer their wares and services. At night, the buildings are festooned with coloured lights and music plays in the streets and on the boardwalks. This is his last night; his work here is done. He will make his way down into the pressing crowds in the evening. He will go looking for knick-knacks and trinkets; small gifts for those waiting for him at home.

The evening is barmy now as he makes his way through streets bustling with night life. Hot food stalls line narrow laneways and every shop has neon signs blinking colours out across footpaths. His glimpses of the harbour show as shimmering bands of coloured light dancing across the bay. He only needs one more item before he can return to the beckoning refuge of his hotel room.

He is in yet another shop, eyeing an item behind the counter on an upper shelf. There is a haggling over price. He thinks 500 is too much, he walks away, he is called back, 400 is agreed, he hands over the money, the item is brought down and wrapped. He is told the price is 400 and only 200 has been received. An argument follows. 200 is taken from the till and shown as proof. More argument. Talk of calling the police from both sides… He pays the further 200 and leaves! He moves back through the happy, noisy throng. He is angry and tired now.

In his room he is packed for the morning. Out on the balcony he sits looking down. The dark waters that lap into the harbour are still; they have always been still. While down there, hidden in the vastness of it, lying in wait for their unsuspecting prey, and still applying their lucrative trade… pirates!

They still exist.

The doctor sat for a long time, silently looking over the test results. The Observer hovered above watching him and his patient.

The doctor looked up. "Some of these readings are a little borderline but nothing to worry about." He closed the folder. He sat back saying, "Nothing to worry about."

The woman frowned. "Borderline?"

"Yes. One or two readings were marginal but, as I say, nothing to worry about."

She said, "But they are acceptable; as readings I mean?"

"Oh! Yes," he replied. "Nothing to worry about there."

"You seemed unsure about what you were reading. That's why I asked."

"No. Not unsure, just a slight ambivalence on my part, but nothing to worry about."

She looked perplexed. "If there is anything wrong, I mean, even if it's a minor thing, I feel I need to be told about it."

He said, "No. No. Nothing like that, just a momentary doubt that's all. Nothing to worry about."

She grimaced. "I don't mind having these tests done again, just to be sure, I mean."

The doctor shook his head. "No. That won't be necessary. It's not uncommon to find one or two equivocal numbers when testing of this sort is carried out, but it's nothing to worry about."

She pouted and said, "Equivocal?"

He stiffened. "Look, as I say, there's nothing to worry about."

She flapped her hands. "I think that's the problem, right there."

He looked puzzled. "Problem? I don't understand."

She shrugged. "I think the fact that you keep saying that there's nothing to worry about has me rather worried."

He sat pondering for a moment. "Really? Do you mean that my telling you that there's nothing to worry about is worrying you?"

She nodded. "Yes."

He shook his head slowly. "In that case, I don't think I can help you there. I mean, this would be more of a psychological problem; not something I'd be able to deal with. Not really my field, you see." He looked around his desk top. "We have a psychotherapist here at the surgery. Would you like me to give you a referral?"

She shook her head and smiled. She said, "No, that won't be necessary. I'm sure it's nothing to worry about."

The Observer found himself inside a small girl's bedroom. She was drawing. It was fascinated by the images being portrayed and by such a young mind. It was looking closely at what appeared to be a small bird perched on a gate post when the girl's mother entered.

When she opened the door to the room she couldn't believe what she saw. She couldn't believe that it was happening all over again. She turned and called out for her husband. He would have to deal with it. She knew she was far too angry. After a moment she yelled again and stood taking deep breaths. The young artist couldn't understand it.

Their daughter had been scribbling on walls from the time she could walk. This time it was considered to be really bad. One whole wall of her bedroom was covered with coloured crayon. There were squiggles and dashes; marks that were almost circles, some that were almost triangles and a lot of lopsided squares. She had used her little chair to do all the high bits and made sure it had gone down to the skirting the length of the room.

When her father came in, he suggested her mum go and sit down while he dealt with it. The young artist couldn't understand what was happening. He certainly looked angry as he inspected the damage done to what was a newly-painted wall; repainted to hide some of the little marks that had been drawn over a fairly long period of time. These had been small bits of graffiti; just scrawls and doodles; nothing like this!

He was very angry, she could see that, but she really couldn't see what the problem was. After some unhappy words and looks from her father, she was put back to bed and the light was switched off, leaving her tucked up and thinking. She was confused.

She had done it all for them. Why couldn't they see it? The mountains with the clouds above them and the little houses down in the valley; and they must have seen the cows in the field all eating grass. Couldn't they see how the little river went through the valley with the boats; the boats with people in them? Why couldn't daddy see the owl, sitting on the post? The one she had drawn especially for him, because he loves owls.

She just couldn't understand why they didn't like her picture. Laying there quietly in the dark she imagined growing up, getting better and better at it, and one day doing one with which they would be really happy.

The Observer knew that this mission was coming to an end.

The Observer was aware of the man's sadness and desire. The old man had never been to Naples. See Naples and die. He had heard this. His late wife often spoke of it; mainly in jest, he thought. Maybe not. He now heard about the very bar where this would prepare you for just that. The travel agency he used to book his ticket was definitely odd, but they seemed very confident that they knew what they were doing. As part of the deal a representative would meet him at the airport and settle him into a hotel before visiting the place in the evening.

He arrived in the city and found everything to be as promised. His guide (for that is how he saw the man who was to look after him) was very polite and professional. He answered any remaining questions his visitor had and arranged to collect him from the hotel later in the evening.

As arranged, the guide turned up and they walked the short distance to the bar. As expected, he supposed, the place was full of elderly people. They ordered drinks and found a table. He couldn't help noticing the beautiful woman serving drinks and felt compelled to comment on it.

"Ah! Yes," the guide replied. "That's Death."

The old man couldn't believe what he was hearing. He stared at the woman. No black cloak; no ugly scythe. In fact, for him it was more of a female form in an evening gown. He raised his eyebrows at his companion. "Surely, isn't Death supposed to be ugly and scary?"

The other smiled.

"Not necessarily. For some with advancing years, Death becomes more attractive."

## CHAPTER SIX

# The Second Return

The Controller. "I have all your reports. They are good. Did all your time periods run to schedule?

"Yes."

"Where all your transitions smooth?"

"Yes."

"That is good. As you know, our remit is to deal with what is only a small fragment of human affairs. It was originally thought that this would be one of the simpler areas to cover. The complexity of reports to date indicate otherwise. We are dealing, in no small measure, with the behavioural complexities of this planet's superior lifeforms. We are investigating the manner in which people respond to various scenarios and to what degree they are able to exert their individual influence over them.

"As your training will have informed you, other forms of endeavour are being observed, such as Education, Health, Art, Science, Politics, Philosophy and many more. What we are looking at within our tiny sector is the behaviour of lifeforms taking place within diverse areas of activity. We need to learn what motivates their actions and what part do the various individual personalities play in the resulting behaviour. We need to critically evaluate the psychological mechanisms that underpin their behaviour patterns. Much of what we have learned about the human condition indicates a remarkable degree of unpredictability.

"It has been decided to send you on one last assignment.

"Go well."

"I go well."

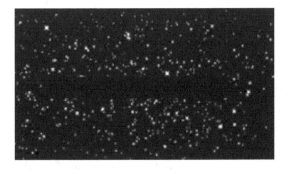

## CHAPTER SEVEN

# *The Final Mission*

Instantly, the Observer hovered in the room where three evenings a week volunteers would sort donations.

The large bins that had sat at the front of the store during the day were brought in and wheeled to the back of the premises and emptied. The empty bins were put back at the front each morning. The room at the back of the charity shop had a large trestle table set up in the centre of it. On those evenings when sorting was done, a number of helpers would stand around the table and wade through everything, creating a number of plastic crates, each containing a particular category of items, such as toys, books, crockery, kitchen utensils, but mainly clothes. During the day those working in the shop would restock from what had been sorted.

One of the several helpers was a quiet woman. She had been a widow for several years. Losing her husband had been a terrible blow and had driven her into a shell. Giving herself to charity work was the only social contact she maintained.

She found the people she worked with easy to get along with and it got her out of the house several times a week.

Another helper was a reserved man. He was a widower; never thinking seriously about seeking out another partner since his wife died. Her passing left him bitter at first, but as time went by he learnt to put that part of his past life behind him. He enjoyed the evenings he spent at the back of the shop.

Most evenings there would be three or four people sorting, but on this occasion there were only two; the widow and the widower. With neither of them being fully aware of it, for the very first time they are alone in an intimate setting.

That night Aphrodite (she, of course, being the Goddess of Love) may have been sitting unseen in the corner of the room.

The woman had the furtive habit of trying things on while she sorted. Sometimes a scarf or a necklace would take her eye. She would put to one side any item that appealed to her and ask for it when staff were there the next day. They would always tell her she could have it, but she always insisted on paying for it.

The man was admiring an expensive looking satin glove. He leant across the table to retrieve its partner, quite unaware that there was a hand in it.

Aphrodite may have smiled as she left.

The Observer watched as the woman stood perfectly still in front of the painting.

After a while she moved to one side then back again, looking at the painting with a satisfied expression on her face.

It had taken several months to produce, often painting late into the night. She had it framed and had spent the last couple of days agonising about which wall it would hang on and how high it should be. But now, this was it; this was the place; it was perfect.

She jumped out of her reverie as the doorbell chimed. She had invited a friend to be the first to see it. She knew he liked art and had been telling him about her creation. He came into the room and stood in front of it.

"Wow!" he said. "It's certainly colourful."

She waited for more, but he just stared at it in silence.

"I've been working on it for ages," she whispers, "and finished it yesterday."

"OK," was all he said.

"I picked it up from the framers on the way home," she said with pride. "What do you think?"

He hesitated and asked, "Did you really do this yourself?"

"Yes. It took months, but I think it was worth it."

"It took months, you say."

"Yes. Do you like it?"

"Well, I'm having a bit of trouble..."

"Trouble?"

"Yes, I guess I am. I mean... what is it, actually?"

"Oh! Didn't I tell you the title?"

"Yes. Yes, you did. I think that's where I'm struggling, to tell you the truth."

"Struggling?"

"Yes. I can't quite see Happy Family. That is the title isn't it?"

"It is," she replied.

He stepped back a couple of paces, then moved forward again. "Sorry, I can't see a happy family anywhere. The title had me expecting something quite different."

"Well, it is abstract, of course." she said, sounding hurt.

He shook his head saying, "I guess it's all in the eye of the beholder." He stepped up to it again and feeling that he should at least say something positive about the painting, pointed to a splodge near the centre. "I do like that!" he said.

"Oh! You do?" she said, obviously delighted. "Where?"

He moved even closer, pointing to a swirl of blue with a thin yellow line running through it.

"Me too," she said. "That's Uncle Albert."

The Observer looked on as the girl was looking in the mail box. It could feel the excitement bubbling through her. The school girl's head was buzzing with all the wonders of her English lesson. Mister Perkins was such a good teacher. He made stuff come alive. He was so good at choosing books for the classroom discussions, especially the latest one. She could hardly wait to share some of it with her mother.

As she came in she called out, "Hi mum, had some great story analysis this afternoon."

Form the kitchen came, "Oh! Lovely dear. I'm just tidying up for your Aunty's visit."

She joined her in the living room still carrying her books. "We've been studying this book by a Spanish author."

"Really?"

"Yes. Did you ever study anything by Paulo Coelho?"

"Who?"

"Paulo Coelho."

"No. I don't think so. Was there any mail?"

"No. I checked. Anyway, he wrote this book called *The Alchemist*. Ring any bells?"

"Not really. Have you seen Tibbs?"

"He's in the hall. This book is about this shepherd boy who travels all the way from Spain to Egypt to find buried treasure. Mister Perkins says it's about how powerful a person's dreams can be and how we should all listen to our hearts."

"That sounds exciting. Did I tell you Mrs Gregson saw that stray dog again?"

"Yes. You told me. Anyhow, this boy, his name is Santiago, meets all sorts of people along the way, including this alchemist…"

"This what?"

"Alchemist, a person who can turn metal into gold."

"Wow. That would be something."

"Yes, and he meets him…"

"Do these look nice?"

She looks up. "Yes mum, they're lovely."

"Your Aunty is very fond of daffodils; they're from the garden, of course." She turned to look at her daughter. "Why does this boy do all this?"

Pleased with the question, she went on. "Because he kept having this dream about this treasure. Well, when he finally arrives at the Egyptian pyramids and begins to dig…"

The doorbell rings.

"Ah! That'll be her now. Put your books away and I'll let her in."

In her room she drops her stuff on the bed and whispers, "Sorry Paulo."

The Observer watched the woman. She was looking up into a cold, grey sky with snowflakes being whipped by a fierce wind.

She grumbled to herself about the foolishness of clearing the snow from the back of the house. She was doing this in order to scrape ice off the back kitchen window. This activity was supposed to make her feel better when huddled up in the house by giving her a view of the back garden. That in itself made no sense considering the fact that most of the garden was hidden under a blanket of white.

While shovelling snow her thoughts wandered to the previous night's TV show. She thought about the program's guest Psych who was saying that a person's thoughts alone were actually capable of bringing about changes in one's immediately-perceived environment. She wondered how true that really was.

She stopped and straightened up with her eyes closed. She just stood and thought and imagined and… to her astonishment she felt the freezing air that had been whipping her face begin to lose its chill. The wind dropped to almost nothing. Even with her eyes shut she was aware of the sun on her face; on her body. It was becoming stronger. In fact, she was beginning to feel quite warm.

It was like she was back in Spain, standing barefoot

on hot sand, looking out to sea. She could feel the sun oil that coated her skin and still sticky on her fingers. Only her bikini felt cool from her recent dip. The shovel fell silently into the soft snow. She raised her arms up and out, with her face turned towards the burning sun.

An hour later she could feel the warmth of the bath water slowly bringing her back from a state of hypothermia.

Autosuggestion, don't you just love it?

The conflict between the men was made clear to the Observer.

The brothers, now both in their fifties with only a couple of years between them, had never had time for marriage. Neither felt the need for a family life. It had always been a case of it being all about the business, for both of them. Although that was going well, they'd been having bitter arguments for several months about what changes, would or would not be made to the running of the business. The younger brother wanted to expand the business while the other was perfectly happy with the way it was operating.

The older man had cooked, and after the meal was pouring two glasses of wine. He was saying, "I bought this one recently; see what you make of it."

The younger man drank some, saying, "Yes. Good thanks". He got up. "I know it was your turn to cook, but I bought these the other day; they're your favourite." He went into the kitchen and brought back a small packet of mint chocolates." The brother ate one and commented on how good they were.

Despite the apparent cordiality, both were aware of the long-running tension between them. The younger man had offered to buy his brother out, but this was rejected. They both knew that it was critical that they resolved their differences before their personal issues impacted on the business. The business was everything… to both of them.

After more wine and chocolates, the younger man broke the silence. "I've come up with a solution to our dilemma."

"Oh. Yes?" said the other with a faint smile.

"Yes," the younger brother went on. "I felt that the best solution would be that one of us passes on."

The other raised his eyebrows and said, "Passes on?"

"Yes," came the reply. "It really would solve everything, don't you think?"

The other shook his head, still smiling. "Well, I suppose so, but how would we go about it, do you think?"

The other replied "Oh! No, not we… me!"

The other said, "You? Really? And just how would you go about it?"

The younger man shrugged his shoulders. "Already done, big brother." He nodded at the packet. "It was on the first mint."

The other lifted his hand to his throat.

"I'm assured it's quite painless and will all be over in a few minutes."

The older man glared at his brother and said, "We are such fools, you know."

The other grinned and said, "We? We; fools?"

The other went on, "It was in your wine."

"I don't believe it," said the other. "Where could you possibly get poison from?"

"Oh! That wasn't difficult. The waiter at the golf club got it for me."

"Him? That's who I bought mine from. What a low-life. I heard that he'd done time for housebreaking. Not a nice person at all. Didn't like dealing with him but…"

The younger brother said, "Can you believe it? He knew what we were both doing. Did you buy the antidote?"

The other looked sheepish and said, "No. I didn't think I'd need it."

"Well, I did, thank the Lord I did; we can both take mine. Let this be a lesson to both of us."

With that, he struggled out of his chair and left the room. A minute or so later he came back shouting, "He's been here!"

The other said, "Who's been here?"

"The swine from the club. My desk draw has been broken open and the antidote's gone!" He slumped back into his chair.

Both men were now feeling the effects of the poison.

The older man forced his eyes open and said, "How long have we got?"

The other replied, "Not long. I would think."

The older man asked, "But why take the antidote?"

The other grimaced. "Well, if you think about it… I mean, the way we treated him, at the club, he's probably not too fond of either of us."

A few minutes passed and the room fell silent.

The Observer watched the boy who had always been computer savvy.

He had found what he wanted on the Dark Web. It was a peculiar site, but placing an order seemed to be straightforward enough. Each day, after school, he would hold his breath as he turned into his street. He was always the first to bring the afternoon mail in. This time it was there! A small, tightly-packaged item. In his room he opened it up. Here it was at last. A beautifully-crafted, hand-held death ray.

He sat on his bed a long time, going over the instructions for its use. As the website had stated, it came with a warning that if it were ever used, the user would forfeit their soul for eternity.

He got out of his school clothes and dressed for the street. He was always allowed an hour or so before tea. That would be time enough. He knew where to find him. He managed to tuck his newly-acquired device down behind his waistband, out of sight.

As he left the house, making his way to the local park, he whispered, "Your time has come, Tommy Smith!"

He was walking down the busy street, marvelling at what he saw, while the Observer looked on.

Although the day was warm and sunny he saw several people wearing gloves and scarves. He thought that was odd. He saw a man start to cross the street pushing a shopping trolley full of tennis balls. He walked past a young boy wearing a swim mask. His father wore one too. He could hardly believe his eyes when he heard the squeal of tyres and turned to see a bright blue fire engine racing past. He saw that a car had been parked in the street with no wheels, and nearby, a small boy was sitting in the gutter, tearing up and eating a newspaper. How really strange it all was. There was a fire somewhere and giant smoke rings drifted across the sky. He shook his head in disbelief. A young girl stood outside a shop selling frogs from a large wicker basket. He was looking at a poster for a lost mouse, with a black and white picture attached, when he noticed soap bubbles coming up through cracks in the pavement. He'd never seen anything like it. He was watching a man dragging a dead dog on a lead when he heard the shout.

A burly young man in white was jogging across the street, weaving between the traffic.

He called out again, "Stay there. It's OK. Just hold on." The man from the institute approached with caution. He was puffing and panting.

"Come on now. You know you shouldn't be out here like this," he said with a sympathetic smile on his face. "Come on, old fella; we've been worried about you. Let's get you home."

The man growled, "Don't want to."

"I know, but it's porridge tonight mate - your favourite!"

The Observer knew that they lived on the same street, which was ideal.

They were both in their forties, both separated with their children gone, living their own lives. They each lived alone now. They could see each other whenever they wanted to and they could each have their privacy whenever they needed it. Outside of their relationship they were both busy with their jobs, their friends and maintaining contact with their respective offspring from their previous marriages. They both agreed that it was good that it was casual; good that they didn't smother each other. The arrangement was ideal. That is, up to the morning of the incident.

One never knows when a gas boiler in a basement is going to explode and set a house on fire. When it happened in the early hours that morning, the force of the blast shook houses and rattled windows up and down the street. The deafening boom woke him with a start. He looked across at the clock seeing that he had another ten minutes before his alarm went off. He went back to sleep.

Later, from his bathroom window he could see the flames. He could see the blaze and the emergency vehicles as he drove out. He would have stopped, but he needed to get in for a meeting. Later in the morning he phoned from the office, but it went to voice mail. He left a message.

"When I drove past I noticed an ambulance outside your house; hard to see through the smoke. Are you OK?"

The Observer watched as the two middle-aged sons stood looking in at their aging father.

"The prognosis is not good," said the younger man, handing him the notebook.

The other shook his head. "What did the Psych say?"

"Says he's as mad as a hatter."

"Oh! That wasn't helpful."

"Well, that's not what he actually said, but it's what

he meant." He looked again through the one-way mirror. "He just rambles away like there's no tomorrow. None of it makes any sense. The weird part of it is that every now and again he'll stop all the random body twitching and become absolutely lucid."

Tears welled up in his eyes. "It happened yesterday. He just sat there rambling; none of it making any sense; just random stuff."

His brother asked, "such as?"

"Oh! First it was about him pushing a button on a box without knowing what it does. He said he had to keep looking at the button because he didn't know whether it was red or black." He paused. "See what I mean?"

"What else?"

"You really want to know?"

"Sure. You get to see a lot more of him than me; me being so far away."

The other went on. "Yes, I understand. OK. He seemed to be saying something about collapsing the minute, then he was talking about time expansion, with time moving too quickly. After that he was just staring down at the floor for ages. When I asked what he was looking at he said he couldn't be sure whether it was saliva, sputum or phlegm. Of course, there was nothing there. It was just after that… only moments really, he looked up and smiled, saying they had it wrong and it would hold them up in their research."

The older man showed more interest. "Do you know what he meant?"

"Not really. I mean he is, or was, a science professor. This stuff is all beyond me. Considering my world is mainly mechanical engineering and yours is science… Who knows? If you'd been here you may have made some sense of it, although with all his blathering it's hard to tell if he's ever making sense; you know, just because he looks calm and completely composed. These sane moments may only be more madness."

The other said, "Tell me, anyway."

"Sure. He was talking very quietly as though people were listening. He tends to do that when these moods take him. I couldn't hear much of what he said, but it was definitely about them not listening to him."

"Them?"

"Yes, you remember, a year ago when he had his first breakdown. The letter he got back after sending in his findings. How it pushed him over the edge."

"Yes, of course. He showed me the letter at the time. Go on."

"It was just a continual unhappy muttering really, but he seemed rational enough. One thing he kept repeating was either Schrölinger or Schrödinger. It sounded Austrian or German; he kept saying Schrödinger something."

"Equation?"

"Yes, that's it! The Schrödinger equation. Means nothing to me, of course. You know about it?"

"Well, yes. In physics, particularly in my area, it's an absolutely fundamental equation."

"About?"

He smiled, "You don't want to go into that here, but put simply it's used in quantum mechanics to register performance or behaviour." He frowned. "When I read the letter that upset him so much I had no idea it was about this. I mean, it was just a rejection of his ideas."

The younger brother tapped the book. "You'll probably

find notes about it in there. I've seen it, but it has more numbers than words. When it was found in his rubbish he said he had no further use for it. That's what the nurse told me. He had no further use for it. Felt sad hearing that; sounded final." He took out a handkerchief and wiped his eyes.

The scientist opened the book and started flicking through.

"I'll have a read of it," he said.

The Observer found the two women looking out into the garden.

The visitor was saying, "What's he doing out there?"

The lady of the house replied, "Oh! He's adjusting his frogcoptor."

"Frog what?"

"Frogcoptor. That's what he calls it."

The visitor looks back out. "It looks like some kind of windmill. Did he make it?"

"Yes. It was just a little windmill that caught the wind, but he got hold of one of the kid's small, plastic frogs and glued it to the front and called it a frogcoptor."

"Oh! What's he doing now?"

"Trying to get it to spin around basically."

"It looks like he's oiling it. Will that help?"

"I wouldn't know. I'm afraid to ask, really. I made a casual enquiry the other day. He's been at it for weeks now. Anyway, I asked him how it was going and I got this long explanation about the principle of the axle."

"The principle of it?"

"Yes. I was stuck in his shed for a quarter of an hour hearing about these clever scientists during the Renaissance period, identifying what he called simple machines."

"Yes. Well, I must say it does look simple enough. I hope he can get it going."

The wife smiled and said, "Of course… it won't work."

"It won't?"

"No. Not there it won't."

"Why?"

"Simple. Where he's put it… it gets no wind."

The visitor was amazed. "Oh! Is that true?"

The other just nods.

"Why don't you tell him?"

"Not likely. It keeps him out of the house!"

The man in the chair was hovered over by the Observer. His wife had gone out late night shopping and he was at home in his comfortable chair watching TV.

There was the sound of a door opening and the rustle of shopping bags. The man had the knife ready. It was sharp and right for the job. If it was to be, he'd make it quick. It would all depend on her. Ever since he'd known her, everything depended on her. No, it would now be left to fate. He liked the idea. It was like tossing a coin. Either way she would never know; never understand.

He sat patiently, waiting until she came through to the living room before asking the question. The excitement was building like nothing he had ever known before. He heard her approach.

"Did you remember my fruity popcorn munchies?"

"Oh! Gee! Those things. No, I'll get them next time." Then in a lower yet audible voice "If I remember."

He rose slowly from his chair. He held the knife behind his back as he moved silently behind her. It was such a silent business. No screaming, no struggling, just a hand clamped to her mouth and one sweep of the knife. He held her upright for a minute or two before laying her gently to the lounge room carpet.

He looked down at his hands, and the carpet; so much blood!

He jumped as the front doorbell rang... The screen suddenly lit up with *To be continued...*

He stabbed at the remote, switching the TV off. He sat with an evil grin, thinking about the show. He had recently developed a taste for gruesome murder shows; even the repeats. He sat waiting.

Finally he hears the door open and close. He smiles to himself, hand in pocket, feeling the smooth contours of his flick-knife. He likes the idea of leaving it to fate, the toss of a coin, the anticipation of it. He hears her coming.

"Did you remember my cigarettes?"

She sighs out loud, "Yes dear."

He scowls with bitter disappointment.

He brings his hand out... empty.

Grey storm clouds gathered over the little house, gradually smothering the setting sun. The Observer looked on as the woman took her child in from the threatening weather. Unseen by them, in the growing darkness, a silent figure stood watching.

Once inside the girl went to the front window, scowled and peered out at the looming storm. "Don't like Mr Wind; he took my ball."

She pressed her face to the window until her nose flattened against the glass. There was a flash of lightning followed by a loud peal of thunder and she was pulled back to the protection of her mother's arms.

She held her daughter for a moment then kissed her cool cheek. "Come on, I'll make toasted cheese sandwiches with slices of tomato for tea."

"Can the man have some too?" the youngster asked as she ran ahead to the kitchen.

"What man?"

"The storm man. In the lighting."

"Lightning." The mother corrected. "There's no one out there, my love. It was probably just a bush moving in the wind." She shook her head and smiled. The imagination of her three-year-old never ceased to amaze her.

They took their meal into the livingroom; the woman stirred the fire a little until it burst into flames. The girl laughed at the shadows that danced around the walls bringing life to the pale curtains and faded wallpaper. The picture of a smiling man flickered on the wall.

Later, the mother began to read a favourite bedtime story, but as was often the case, sleep overcame the girl before the end of the tale.

Tousled curls lying softly on the pillow made the woman think of her husband and a sudden tear escaped and rolled down her cheek. She brushed it away quickly and went back to the livingroom.

The fire had begun to die down and she realised that she'd forgotten to bring in more wood from the box on the porch. The cold air made her shiver as she opened the door. The concrete floor of the porch was wet and slippery and she almost lost her footing as she pushed back the heavy lid of the wood-box. A noise from the bottom of the steps startled her, sending her heart pounding. Someone was there! Just out of the light from the doorway a dark figure moved towards her. She began to step back slowly, feeling the warmth and safety behind her. If only she could reach the door. There was the heavy tread of boots coming swiftly up the steps and she turned to lunge through the doorway, but it was too late. A stranger was towering over her; he pushed her inside and closed the door behind them.

They stood facing each other for a long, agonising moment.

"What do you want?" the woman was surprised by the calmness in her voice. "We don't have any money."

The intruder stood without speaking, surveying the modest room. A hint of a smile played on his lips and he nodded as though giving approval.

"Get some wood!" he demanded as the smile died. "And be quick."

Once more the cold air greeted Lisa as she gathered an armful of logs, but this time it felt almost soothing. It gave her a moment to think. What could she do? He was obviously much stronger than she. If only the nearest house wasn't so far away she might risk going for help, but that would mean leaving her child. Tentatively she went back inside to face the unknown.

As she entered, she could hear her daughter's voice mingling with the husky tones of the stranger. She moved silently to her daughter's door. Fear gripped her and held her motionless as she watched the scene before her. But then she saw gentleness in the eyes of the giant man as he sat engrossed in conversation with the tiny figure.

"Mummy! It's the storm man; his name is Ben. His little girl went away and now he's sad."

As she tucked her daughter into bed again the woman wondered what had brought this man to their home. He instilled so much fear in her, yet this little one was undaunted by him.

"Who's that?" The intruder asked, pointing to a picture on the wall as she returned to the main room.

She sat down opposite him. "That's my husband. He'll be home soon," she lied, hoping it sounded convincing.

He closed his eyes and sighed as though very weary. Firelight touched the deep lines in his face giving him an eerie appearance. She sat and watched him for a while. He seemed to be sleeping.

Now was her chance! She shuffled closer to the telephone, and slowly reached out. She lifted the receiver in slow motion and began to dial the emergency number.

She didn't finish. Without warning, the powerful grip of a big hand was around her wrist and the receiver fell to the floor.

"What do you think you're doing?" His face was close to hers.

"Please leave us alone!" Her plea was barely a whisper,

afraid of waking the girl in the next room. "Go now, and I promise I won't tell anyone you were here."

"You don't get it do you? This is my house." The big man stood up with his arms aloft, his faced filled with anger. "You are in my house!"

She recoiled from his rage, bewildered and shaken. He was pacing up and down muttering about his lost wife and child. "Came home and they were gone," he was saying.

"Doreen and my baby. But they'll come back, you just wait and see. They'll be back alright. Oh! Yes. You just wait…" His voice trailed off as he continued to walk around the room.

The stranger was so lost in the past that he didn't notice the woman leave the room. In her daughter's bedroom, she knelt in the darkness, praying softly by the bed. She was asking for help. Slowly a feeling of peace began to envelop her until somehow she sensed that a silence had fallen on the house.

A sharp noise made her body jolt. It was a knocking. Someone was knocking on the front door. She rose without making a sound and peered into the next room. It was empty; only the fire was crackling, but the knocking continued. The woman took a large glass bottle from a cupboard and held it resolutely in front of her. She moved slowly and deliberately towards the front door. With the bottle raised above her head she flung the door open.

A police officer stood on her front porch, staring at the raised bottle. She lowered her arm awkwardly and did her best to smile. The officer relaxed and told her that a 'Ben' had hailed them as they passed, saying he needed help.

"He told us that he had been bothering you madam, and that he was very sorry." The policeman went on. "We've had complaints from former tenants of this house. Seems he was living here when his wife and child died. Apparently, he never really got over it."

The woman swallowed hard trying to take in what he was saying. "You mean he walked out and gave himself up, just like that? I don't understand."

"No, not really. It was your husband. He persuaded old Ben to leave and get help."

The woman drew in a quick breath; she felt her legs go weak as she clung to the doorframe. The policeman was still talking; she tried to concentrate, but had no idea what he was saying.

"Your husband? Might I have a word with him?"

The woman raised her arm and pointed to the picture of the smiling man. "That's my husband. I mean… that was my husband, he's been dead for over a year now."

The officer sighed apologetically. "Well, that's Ben for you. Do you want him charged?"

She shook her head. Her daughter had seen good in him, far beyond his outward pain and rage. Perhaps one day his wounds would heal and he could learn to live for the future and not the past.

As she closed the door the twelve o'clock chimes rang out. She looked across at her husband's handsome face behind the cold glass. Something was different. She felt sure his head was at a different angle, more full on, somehow. She moved closer. Was it her imagination, or was there a new twinkle in his eye?

"I love you too," she whispered softly. "I'll love you forever."

The Observer was in a silent place; the study of a young man busy writing a short story. The man's thoughts would be important during this observation as the writer only occasionally grunted while reading his draft in silence.

"Sometimes, events are not quite what they appear to be on the surface," went the tale.

"For instance, one evening a young woman was walking through a park. Well, you'd have to say jogging rather than walking. Anyway, the park she was jogging through wasn't a park as such, more like a field; in fact it was a football field, and the girl wasn't really old enough to be called a woman; plus, it wasn't evening, it was morning.

She was on her way to the library, when she found a stray dog. Although, strictly speaking it was a coffee shop that always had lots of magazines laying around that she would like to read when going in for coffee.; not what you'd call a library. The cat she found - it was a cat - not a dog, ran off as soon as it saw her. Actually, it didn't run, it walked.

As she crossed the street she was nearly hit by a bus, no, not a bus, a man on a bicycle. But it shook her up and she was glad she was going for a coffee. However, it was actually beans she was going there for, not coffee. The coffee beans were for her Aunty, who liked making her own coffee. She, her mother, not her Aunty, would often send her daughter, not actually her daughter but her neighbour's daughter, out for her favourite beans. In fact, they weren't her favourite really, as the shop had not been able to get the ones she liked best for several months. Well, to tell the truth, it was more like a couple of years.

Anyway, on the way home she saw a young woman

walking through the park. Well, not really walking, she was jogging..."

He sat back and sighed with a self-congratulatory smile on his face, knowing that it was more about finishing the work for his school project and less about the quality of it.

The Observer was looking down on a small group of men. They had finished their game of cards. One of them was doing all the talking.

"I don't know how much of this is true," the speaker began. "So, I'll just tell you what my brother told me."

He took a sip of sherry. "As you know, as a philosopher he was always keen on studying the religions and this may account for much of what he is convinced he experienced."

He poured another drink with nobody saying a word.

"As it transpired, when he fell off the ladder, he says he lay thinking for a while. He was thinking about the number of times his wife had told him he was getting on in years, and how he should get a tradesman in to do that kind of work, when he stopped abruptly to ask himself where he was. He didn't recognise anything, but it wasn't a hospital."

There seemed to be a mist in the room but it was clearing. He found that he was sitting on a chair in what was rapidly becoming an extraordinarily large room. The more the mist cleared, the more he could see, and what he saw told him that he was not in any kind of Earthly place."

He paused and took in the expressions around the table.

"He says he just sat thinking deeply for a while, as any philosopher should, about the ramifications of this unexpected turn of events. He told me that once the haze had cleared completely, he could see a figure approaching from the other side of the room. It was some distance away and walking very slowly. Eventually it came close enough to present itself as a young man in a suit and tie, carrying a clipboard. He apparently flipped a couple of pages over as he came up with a pleasant smile, telling him he was welcome.

"At that point my brother stood up and was about to tell him who he was when the man raised his hand. He told him not to trouble himself, saying that names meant nothing there. They knew who he was. He then riffled through his paperwork again and said he had an appointment with God. My brother questioned this, but was told everyone who goes there gets an appointment with God. My brother asked if he was an angel, but the man didn't seem to notice the question and told him to go in. He said he'd find a seat waiting for him and pointed at a door that my brother swears simply wasn't there before.

"So, he crossed the room and went through the door. It was a similar environment, but a smaller room. The further half was fogged. He walked over to the chair and sat. The fog cleared and a large man, dressed in white with a great flowing, white beard appeared sitting before him. My brother said, 'Good Lord!' and God smiled and said, 'That's me.'

"My brother was told not to concern himself because he was only seeing whatever he was expecting to see. He was told it made question time much easier and that everyone gets to ask Him one question when they arrive. You can imagine how my brother felt, as a philosopher I mean. He was overcome with a sudden sense of intense excitement sweeping over him. Anyway, God confirmed that he was, in fact, a philosophy lecturer at a university. God said He was pleased with this, as it made the occasion rather special for Him. He explained that He had all sorts come to Him; He had kings and queens, politicians and moguls, draft-dodgers, beggars, criminals and all manner of people, everyone young and old and in between. He said it wasn't often He got asked a question by a thinker; not a real thinker. God told him he should think carefully before asking his question.

"Well, my brother sat, trying as hard as he could to control the exhilaration he felt, in order to concentrate completely on his one question, but without warning, his whole body convulsed. Apparently, he looked up at God and saw Him shaking his head and shrugging as He began to fade in a swirl of mist.

"Then, it happened again. It was much stronger this time. He felt a powerful, burning thump on his chest. He heard someone saying that they were getting him back. So, there he was, on the operating table and mumbling about how he wanted to ask just the one question.

"Again, it's only hearsay, but on the way out of the theatre one of the nurses was heard asking another what my brother was blabbering about.

The other nurse sneered and said he was a philosopher and God only knows what they think!"

It was a quiet and peaceful place. The Observer looked down on the tiny, secluded dwelling.

It could never be said of Henry that he did not like people. He liked them well enough to remain in their company for half a century, and since this represented the greater part of his life, he felt with no little pride that he had done rather well.

He was not a big man, but rather less than average height, tending towards being stocky. Dark grey hair, well-toned muscles, and weathered skin all served to conceal his long years. In his face an enduring smile glowed warmly to those who had an eye to see it. In all, his disposition could be fairly described as contented.

Twenty peaceful, satisfying years had passed since the time he had lived among other men. He had grown, slowly at first, to appreciate the full worth of his own company. During the early months that he had come to live in these hills, the old man (having learnt something from the world he left behind) prepared himself for loneliness. So completely had he accepted the likelihood, however, that this creeping evil would one day visit his little cabin, it had never crossed his threshold.

The fact that his entire way of life was that of living simply detracted nothing from the value he placed upon it. He kept no pets, ate little, and never felt the need of a transistor radio. Much of his time was spent reading, smoking a pipe that could only be described as ancient, and keeping his residence in good order. He would often take long, rambling walks through the dales of his beloved Yorkshire, but would always return to his soft, warm bed at night.

Once a month, give or take a few days, he would trek the four undulating yet descending miles to the little village for provisions.

With each passing year he had found the return journey more arduous, and the huge knapsack that he slung across his back, less manageable. The tins that held each monthly supply of food grew heavier with every trip. But quite regardless of this, the seasons slipped quietly by.

The people in the hamlet were pleasant enough towards him; while privately regarding him as undoubtedly odd. Groups of them had often sat around dim-lit parlours speculating upon his motives for leading such a queer life. They felt sure he had at least a modest fortune, deposited with their one and only bank; they fairly knew he was not of the Moor. Someone had said he had been some sort of foreman in a timber yard, somewhere in the south where the great cities stand.

Beyond this, and beyond all their idle suppositions, he was to them 'old Henry', and nothing more.

Today was a special day in the life of the old cabin dweller. It was his birthday.

These particular days of the year had always meant a lot to him, hardly less so now than when he was a boy. Something good always happened on his birthday. A fact now so well-established that he could not prevent it, had he the mind to.

One year, he recalled, he had caught four rabbits in one day. Normally, that many in a fortnight would be a high return for the small effort expended baiting and adjusting his simple, painless snares.

On another of these supernatural days he had found an old earthen pot, half buried in the soil. With the greatest care and patience he had removed it, cleaned it till it looked new, and fashioned a trim shelf to fit the trophy. This now adorned a hitherto drab wall in his small yet tidy abode.

Something always happened.

Today would certainly be no exception to the rule. In fact, it would hold more enchantment than any that had gone before. This morning Henry was seventy.

Even when he was a very small boy, living with his parents in the noisy city, he had felt the magic creep slowly into his bones when lying in bed on those anniversary mornings. It was always as though the feeling was there because he willed it so. He could not make it stop once it had taken hold, but why should he ever want to?

The old timer drowsily drifted in the revelry of days of youth and moments of laughter. It was time gone, used up; not able to be relived, only reviewed.

The first signs of the sun were colouring his room's interior with a soft yellow. Hardly awake, his bones were already charged with magic.

He dragged his legs laboriously across the bed, and sat, perched on its edge, blinking at his toes. It was a cold morning; far too cold to be chopping wood and lighting fires. He was reflecting on this. The wood pile would probably be frozen, and the door to his shack iced over again.

It had been unusually cold, and for several mornings now he had found that he had to break open the door. This he did by pounding its frame and loosening the ice, formed by the rain that had fallen sometime during the early part of the night. Inwardly, it amused him greatly that he should have to break out. Whenever he did it, he was filled with the unshakeable sensation that he was an amateur burglar, trying to get in!

Musing on all this, and still staring blindly at his bare feet, he became aware of the mounting battle deep inside him, between the magic and the cold.

His legs swung back, the quilt and blanket fairly smacked him under the chin, his head thudded back deep into the pillow, and the old hermit sported a grin that went halfway round his head.

This was not a day when he had to get up, he could do exactly what he liked. He would lay here a while and think about the way he would pass the day.

He could make things happen today.

Although he had always known that this unique charge that ran through his frame gave him a special power to momentarily catch the eye of Him who governs all things, he had never more than half admitted it to himself. But, in truth, if he had done nothing to displease his guardian angel during the twelve months past, this gift was assuredly his. Provided the thing he sought was not outside the bounds of what would ordinarily be considered reasonable, it was his. And this year, for the first time, he knew it.

As the muscles of his face relaxed and his breathing became slow and comfortable, the old man slid off again into memories of past treasures. The rabbits he had known were there before setting out to check the cages. The piece of pottery that had rested only a few feet from the spot where his search began. The aching leg that once again became equally as good as the other.

The sun that lit his room had become a yellow-orange and the music of the birds came down from surrounding trees. They, too, shook their heads, stretched their wings, and generally prepared for another day. Unlike the tenant below, however, returning to their nests and allowing the day to take care of itself, was not within their humble powers of decision.

The sounds from the woods and the colour of the sun pleased the aging recluse immensely. These were the things he had come here for.

The droning of the mill, and the never-ending applause of plank against plank; these had been the things that at one time had robbed him, and whether or not they knew or cared, others too, of the melodious chorus he was now enjoying.

What would he do today? What would he have happen?

Henry propped himself up on one elbow and pulled aside the plain white curtain, which somehow reminded one of an open pillow-case. In the half-light he could barely make out the misty green hills, rolling away and becoming one with the hazily-gilded horizon.

What could he possibly wish for on a morning such as this?

It was then that it happened. Within a single heartbeat the design took shape. He laid back, a little exhausted.

The idea had come to him so suddenly; it had burst in upon him like a bonfire-night cracker landing unseen at his feet. He had never asked for anything quite so big; quite so important.

He had often wondered what would happen if he took leave of his senses and pursued the sort of prize that most of those he had left behind would have chosen. Would he have been debased and disappointed, and never again able to invoke his sacred rite?

Conversely; could he really have opened his door one

morning to find a great chest stacked to the lid with firm little packets, each containing used banknotes, methodically arranged in small denominations?

This idea was at once preposterous to him; his personal desires did not include possessing great wealth. Nevertheless, the fact remained; beyond wishing for a sunny day, a lost object found, a pot or a rabbit, he had never ventured. That is, not until today!

Henry Brinkworth, for that was his name, former sawmill supervisor and incessant gambler, twice divorced, and now long gone from a world where such things take place with unnerving ease, had made up his mind. He would use his talent, and ask for that which he desired most. There was now no doubt in his mind that such a request could only come from a sincerely happy man.

Through his tiny window, Henry once again took in the vista. It was this, he remembered, that had settled the issue of where he would build his much needed haven, a long time ago.

As he watched, the sky grew unusually dark, and the green of the land became murky; even the morning chorus began to fade. The old man settled down between warm covers once more, and followed the retreating light across the ceiling above his head.

In a moment the room was black. No silvery singing entered his humble shack. No sound was there from within. Not even the heaving of an old man's chest.

Henry had been granted his final birthday wish.

The Observer was now located in the road, outside of a village public house. It was dawn as the man came out.

In truth, he was thrown out by the landlord, who was rudely woken by the man's snoring from under the stairs near the patrons' toilet. He had been missed at closing time, which wouldn't have been a problem if he hadn't snored so amazingly and disturbingly loud. He managed to get to his feet and stagger out into the darkness, barely making his way in the poor moonlight.

He had only gone a few steps when all at once the rustling of the hedgerow stopped dead. Trees no longer moved and the world went completely silent. He stuck his fingers in his ears and wiggled them.

What he was about to imagine was that on this night of all nights, aliens had landed, and at that precise moment everything was put on pause; this notion being brought on by his drunken stupor.

As he stood blinking, his imagination ran on. Two hologram-like figures drifted towards him. One of them said, "Earthling."

He belched.

The alien said, "What?"

The man grinned and said, "Whoops."

The alien said, "What?" The two beings looked at each other. One said, "Do you speak English?"

"Of course," he slurred.

The visitors exchanged another look and one said, "Of course... there may be a need to obliterate your planet, we're having a bit of a clean-up, but before that we have chosen you to be our guide."

The man stepped back, through his arms open and said,

"Wow! Really?" He thought hard for a moment and asked, "Why me?"

"You are a random sample. Tell us the reasons for your wars?"

"Sorry, can't help you there."

"You have no knowledge of this."

"Nope."

"Nope?"

"Nope. Next?"

"What about art?"

"Ahah! I can help you there. Aunt Jessie has magazines full of that stuff." He winked. "Including pin-ups."

"Pin-ups, yes… and books?"

"Don't get to the library much, but the car's got a manual, you know, with diagrams an' all."

The beings seemed to fade in and out momentarily. "That sounds interesting. What about innovations, inventions?"

"What like the pedal-bin, you mean?"

The aliens waited.

"Sister Clara's got a new one; the latest."

"Explain."

"Well, it's a nifty little thing. It's all shiny with a shiny lid, and at the bottom there's a little black peddle that isn't shiny, but well… you know, not shiny… and when you stamp on it, the pedal I mean, the lid just flies open." He stood nodding with a huge grin.

At this point he thought he could feel a distinct wobble in the Solar System. As he fell into the ditch, he wondered if everything would still be there when he woke up.

The Observer was in a sitting room occupied by two men. The older man tapped out his pipe and said, "It all started with a flower."

He looked at the young man from the library with old, bright eyes. "You wanted a story, so you'll get one."

He smiled while he packed in fresh tobacco and lit up. "I'm sure you appreciate that this goes back a long way. Most of those involved in the affair are dead and buried. A fate that awaits me, of course." He took a long puff and said, "My doctor tells me this will speed things up."

The younger man said, "He's probably right, but do go on," making no effort to hide his interest.

They had met and chatted a few times at the library with the younger man saying how much he liked reading police dramas. When he was told that the other was retired from the force, but had been a Chief Inspector, serving most of his time in and around London, the younger man had become interested. The fact that he was a retired British Bobby, meant that their bond grew stronger, often leading to long discussions about crime and criminals.

The retiree picked up a thick folder from the coffee table, saying, "These aren't the official police records of course, just the materials I kept. They mainly consist of my own written notes; just scraps noted down as the case unfolded. And my word! Did it unfold!"

He shook his head. He looked down at the folder on his lap and tapped it.

"I digress. A lot of what is contained in this file became public knowledge, but not the story behind it."

He searched again and found what he wanted.

"Ah! Yes! Here we are, the first phone call. It was a

strange one. You have to understand, I was just a young copper at the time. I had only been out of uniform a few weeks when the call came in. I remember it came in during the afternoon. It certainly sounded like a member of the public had witnessed something and they felt duty bound to report it. We were asked to look deeper, whatever that meant.

The caller said that it would be to our advantage if we went to this particular location and look for some recently disturbed ground. I mean, it sounded like we were being sent to a remote grave site. But that wasn't what we found."

He paused. "Would you like more tea?"

"No. No thanks."

The old man wiggled in his armchair, making himself comfortable. "Alright then," he continued "three of us went out that day; my superior, myself and a constable. I won't use any names if you don't mind?"

The other shook his head.

"Good. Well then, when we got to the spot the caller had directed us to, we found a bit of a clearing off to one side of the lane we had been told to take. It was just a small gap in the trees, really. Dead in the centre was a little pile of loose soil. The flower that I eluded to was planted on its top. It was an unusual looking flower, white petals with a green and yellow centre. Nobody really wondered what it was at the time, only why anybody had bothered to leave it there."

"It wasn't growing then?"

"No. Just stuck in the top. It looked bloody silly, to tell you the truth. We all figured that somebody thought it was a bit of a lark. It was still an offence, of course, causing the police to waste their time. My boss was livid."

He grinned, recalling the memory of it.

"Anyway," he went on, "due process was followed. The area was searched, but nothing was found. The flower was bagged, of course, but there were no clear tyre tracks worth mentioning, and no discernible footprints either. The whole episode was considered to be a pure waste of police resources, but the file was left open in case there were other similar pranks."

He picked up the folder. "About three weeks later the station got a second call. We knew it was the same caller. It not only sounded like the same man, but like the first time, he started by saying..." He sorted through the file. "Yes, here it is, the caller said 'I want you to look deeper than before.' Naturally, that wasn't making any sense at the time. Although it did have the feel of someone wanting us to look again at an old case."

More shuffling of papers. "This call was different; we weren't being sent to any out of the way place, but to the back of the station; our station. On that occasion it was just the boss and me who walked around the back. The caller said to look for something in red. We found it. It had been painted on quite carefully. It consisted of four numbers that occupied the area of a single brick."

He lifted up a small notebook, flipped through several pages and read "9144. That's all there was. Again the area was searched for anything that might help us find out who was doing this. But they were being very careful, and between you and me we began to think, very clever too."

He shook his head. "No. This was no ordinary prankster; nor was it a graffiti artist. This was someone with a real purpose. This person was meticulously drawing us in; almost teasing us, getting us to do just what had been said on the phone... getting us to look deeper."

He closed the file and fell back into the chair. "Over the days that followed there were no phone calls but lots of meetings. Those of us who were directly involved in the case, probably four or five all told, would go into a huddle to exchange ideas. I suppose there were two sides to the affair really. There was the feeling that somebody out there was taunting us, when all they had to do was to make a report; anonymously if they liked. The other side of it was the sheer thrill of having these apparent riddles, clues, whatever you want to call them, just sitting there waiting to be cracked!"

He grinned at his visitor. "I'm sure you'd like something now. I know I would. He slowly got up. "Tea... coffee?"

The man from the library blinked a couple of times, taking in what was being asked. "OK. Yes, a coffee would be good if that's not too much trouble. Thank you."

From the kitchen he raised his voice saying, "You know, we went over and over those numbers. Was it part of a telephone number, a page in a book, a case number? We tried adding it up, multiplying it, we ran it through a computer but nothing came up, or at least nothing we could see. Eventually, we put a notice up in the canteen saying, 'Does anybody have any idea what these numbers mean?' then underneath, the four numbers, extra-large."

He chuckled as he came back with two coffees. "Sugar there if you want it." He stood with his chin down, remembering. "We copped a lot of flak over that notice." He moved back to his chair. "But, you wouldn't credit it, but it gave us our first real break. A young officer knocked on my superior's door, saying he had an idea about the numbers. I was called into the office."

"Apparently, the constable had worked in the home-carpeting trade before he joined the force. 'It might just be a coincidence, of course, but that number, it's a metre, or part of a metre, he said.

"My boss asked him to explain. He told us 0.9144 of a metre was equivalent to a yard. We had no idea whether this was going to help, or even if we were on the right track. But that didn't matter; it was something."

He sipped his coffee and went on. "None of us could have guessed what would happen shortly after that. Because our man in the forensics section didn't recognise the flower we had bagged at the first scene, he had sent it off to some botany expert, specialising in..." he hesitated "in floriculture, I think. Anyway, our man was amazed when the results came back. It turns out that the plant shouldn't be here at all. By here, I mean, England."

"Sorry, I don't understand," said the visitor. "Shouldn't... in what way?"

"Well, by virtue of the fact that the plant itself was rare." He delved into his papers again. "The plant was a Scottish flower called a Diapensia Lapponica, a rare species that only grows in one place, Argyll, Scotland. Of course, you can imagine how this made the case suddenly fall into a completely different category. Why would anybody go to the trouble of bringing a rare plant, such as that, over such a distance, just to push it into a pile of dirt? But it gave us the first two pieces of the puzzle, Scotland and Yard!"

"What we really couldn't understand was why anybody would go to all that trouble. It made no sense. It felt like some sort of cat and mouse game, and not everybody was happy about it. Anyway, we knew there would be more, and there was.

Two or three days after that, a small parcel arrived. We had to wait until security and forensics had finished with it before we got to see it. All we knew was the package had contained a book. It turned out to be an old German paperback novel, very much the worse for wear. The front cover was torn and many of the pages were creased.

He stopped and asked "Would you like another drink?"

His visitor answered, saying "No thanks. Was it part of your investigation, the book I mean?"

The older man smiled, realising his visitor was keen to move on with his story.

"It certainly was. It's interesting that you should use that word."

"Word?"

"Yes. When it came through from our forensics people their report was short and sweet. The only thing that seemed to be of any significance was that a single word, mid-way through the book, had been highlighted with a yellow marker. The word was 'untersuchung'. In no time at all we had the next part of it solved. The word meant 'investigation' in English. So, that meant, to date we had 'Scotland Yard investigation.' It was now a fair bet that this was a criminal case, either current or from some time in the past."

He stopped again. "Are you sure? I'm going to make myself another."

The other said, "Yes, I'm fine thanks."

While the ex-policeman was rattling around in the kitchen the young man sat pondering the case. He had lots of questions building up, but he would hang on to them and let the old man tell his story. As it turned out, some of his questions were being answered as it unfolded.

The old man came back and sat down, sipping his coffee. He picked up the thick folder and tapped it again. He went on with the events as though he hadn't stopped. He shook his head.

"All through this, the same old questions kept coming up. Why were all these pieces being so elaborately fed to us? Why string it out so slowly with such great care to preserve the anonymity of the originator? In fact, why the mystery? Why not just come out with what is being asked?"

"The further along we went, the suggestion of it being an inside job grew stronger. Could it be one of our own? If so, why do it this way, unless the person only suspected a miscarriage of justice and wasn't sure? If they came right out and called for a new enquiry that proved that the original conviction was correct, they would be left with egg on their face! But no matter what we thought, we had to proceed. Just as we would with any other case."

He opened the folder "Let me see, yes, it was quite a while, almost three weeks before anything else happened. There was a phone call into the station late in the evening. It started with more or less the same phrase about looking deeper."

He stared at his visitor. "I said at the outset that I wouldn't be giving out any names, but this is the exception. You will recognise it no doubt, considering your interest in crime. You are bound to have read about the case at some time. Anyway, the significant thing about this call was that after the usual phrase he only said one word: 'Hanley'.

We had a name. Was it somebody on the force? A solicitor? A witness or a criminal? It could be anybody, although all initial efforts were directed at going through criminal histories.

This turned out to be a good move, because by mid-morning the next day we had the records. Hanley was serving time for murder."

The other's face beamed. "Yes. I do know about the case."

The old man finished his coffee and growled. He said simply, "This is where it got harder." With that he sat scraping out and refilling his pipe. As he relit it, he seemed to become aware of his visitor. "Sorry. Yes, our whole case had changed overnight, and there was worse to come."

He looked through his papers once more. As he did, he said, "Everything I've told you so far was never made public. This had all been police business; strictly operational affairs, you understand. Somehow, we didn't know how, the press got wind of the fact that we were looking at Hanley's case. We suspected that somebody 'in the know' had tipped them off. Anyway, that blew the whole thing wide open, of course.

Now, the media was crawling all over it, and crawling all over us. Although no reasons were given for looking at the case again, there was a lot of speculation. None of any of this helped us in pursuing the enquiries we were committed to follow up on. Journalists were dogging our footsteps at every turn."

He retrieved a small scrap of paper from his file and held it up. "I said things got worse, and they did. That same day a letter was routed through the system and ended up on my governor's desk. The envelope held a small piece of paper…

not this, of course. This is only a copy. It went straight off to be examined, but nothing was found of any use, either on it or the envelope. As you see, it shows a hand-drawn box with the number two in it, and a series of numbers printed underneath."

He handed the paper over with a half-smile. "See what you make of that."

The other sat excitedly staring at what was a real life clue from a police investigation. "Wow! This looks like it is stating that the square root of the number two is 1.41421352. Well, that's what it looks like to me." He handed it back.

"Well done! Yes, that's exactly what it looks like; but it isn't."

"It isn't?"

"No." He held the paper up and pointed to the last number. "You see the 'two' here? This 'two' should be a 'six'. You see? It was wrong; and we were being told by the sender that he was convinced that something was wrong. From the first elaborate ploy with the flower (done to make sure that we took notice) right through to this piece of paper, had all been to bring us to the point where we were looking seriously at an old case."

The young man nodded slowly.

"So much of what followed became public knowledge, of course." The other went on. "The case was thoroughly investigated with the new DNA technology that was available. As I'm sure you know, the blood samples and fibres from the crime scene proved conclusively that the man was innocent of the crime. You would also know that the real perpetrator was never caught."

He threw up his hands, indicating that his story was

finished and sank back into his chair. "Did you enjoy the story?"

"Yes. I most certainly did. Thank you very much. Wow! I thought I had so many questions, but they all seem to have been answered."

He stood up and the old man struggled out of his chair. "Maybe, just one." He added.

"Go on."

"Did you ever find out who was behind all those clues?"

The other thought for a minute, then said, "No. We didn't. But I will let you in on one more piece of information from behind the scenes. Several years later, just a couple of months before my governor retired he received one last anonymous note. It came through like the one before, in a plain envelope, hand-printed.

It contained just two words; 'Thank you.'"

Their regular teacher for the first session of the morning was sick, so they had a standby teacher. The Observer watched as the new lady entered the classroom and looked them all over. "Right," she said, opening a little notebook and proceeding to chalk up a list on the blackboard. It read:

Cat
Horse
Rabbit
Snake
Frog
Fish

She turned to the class and asked "Which of these is the odd one out?"

A flurry of hands shot up. The teacher pointed.

The chosen girl says, "The snake is the only animal without legs."

"No. some fish have legs." She puts a cross after the word 'snake'.

As young as they were, a lot of confusion buzzed around the room. After all, if a fish does have legs, the snake must be the only one without them.

Utterly disappointed the girl says, "Are you sure, miss?"

"I most certainly am. Some fish use their pectoral fins as legs."

A boy says, "She's right you know. My Dad said some species of fish can walk along the sea floor using them."

The teacher flaps her hands and says, "Yes. Let's move on, shall we?"

A girl says, "What about a frog miss?"

"Why a frog?"

"It's the only one without a tail."

The teacher shakes her head. "No, some cats don't have tails."

A voice from the back says, "Never seen one."

The teacher stiffened. "That's because you haven't seen a Manx cat." She puts a cross next to 'frog'.

"Anyone else? Yes." She points to a girl with her hand up.

She says, "A rabbit."

"And why a rabbit?"

"Because it can hop and jump, miss."

"No. Horses can jump." She carries on putting crosses up.

The girl says, "But can they actually jump, miss?"

"Of course, over hedges and show jumps," came the reply. "Now, come on class, you're not doing very well, are you?"

A boy shouts, "A fish, miss."

She sighs. "And why a fish?"

"Because it's the only one that swims under water."

"No. A water snake can swim under water."

Another boy says, "Cats, miss."

"Why cats?"

"Because they're the only ones with whiskers."

She shakes her head. "No. Rabbits have whiskers." She looks up at the board. "Well, I'm really disappointed with you all this morning." She points to the only one without a tick.

"A horse!" cries a boy.

"Ah! At last! Yes, well done. A horse; and why a horse?"

"Don't know, miss."

She pulls a face. "Because it's the only one with hooves, of course!"

A small voice whispers, "I hope our teacher gets well soon?"

This causes tiny groans and whispers to float around the room, just as the bell goes. Despite their tender years, they have serious doubts about their stand-in teacher. They all troop out slowly, doing their level best not to look at her.

The Observer looked on as the man behind the desk shuffled papers and shook his head.

He looked across at the younger man. He knew that the

results wouldn't please him. There was no easy way of doing it, so he just came out with it. "I'm afraid you need to go back for another visit."

"Back… back where?"

"To the clinic."

"But I've already been there!"

"Yes, I know, but they need to carry out…" he looks down and reads "a psychological evaluation."

"But I've had one of them! Complete waste of time it was, but I've already had one. Probably a typo. You know I've had one already."

The man sighs. "Yes. I know, but they want you to have another one."

"No. I'm not going back there again. Place was full of loonies."

"That's all very well, but it says here a further evaluation is required. Look, you need to understand that these tests can provide information concerning the likelihood that an individual could re-engage in any alleged behaviours."

The young man drops his head and mumbles, "All this fuss about phase-outs."

"Pardon?"

He looks up with anger in his eyes. "I said all this fuss. I mean, just look at it. It's obvious what happened. The gun just went off. I mean, it happens, doesn't it? Guns just go off."

He turned and looked out of the window and stared into the gardens that fronted the building. He continues, "The Psych kept on about phase-outs. Says it's when a person blacks out but stays awake. I didn't believe a word of it. I know I don't have them."

He looks up with a pleading expression and repeats. "I'm not going back there, not ever."

The man said, "Look here, I understand that these evaluations can often be a bit drawn out sometimes, but they must have their reasons."

The young man didn't appear to be listening. He sat rigid, staring blankly.

"Hello!" he said, in a firm voice.

The young man jumped. "What?"

"I was just saying that they must have their reasons. After all, certain criteria have to be met."

"What criteria?"

"Well, I don't know. I'm not a psychologist, am I?"

"You're not?"

"Of course not. Anyway, I don't make the rules; it's all in the Mental Health Act."

The young man seems to drift off again, this time staring up at the ceiling. The man taps on his desk a couple of times, but the other doesn't move. He slaps the desk hard. The other looks back down with a start.

"I was explaining about the rules and the Mental Health Act," he says, with a tone of authority.

The young man sighs and says, "Look. All I'm asking you to do is write down there that you've seen me and that I am perfectly all right. Just say that no further assessments are required. I mean, that's not so hard is it?"

The man had to make an effort not to laugh, but couldn't help a small grin. "You obviously don't appreciate the situation. Let me explain. There is no way…"

He stopped, aware that the other's face was going

stone-like again with eyes glazing over. He was aware that the young man's hand was fumbling in his pocket.

Without changing his facial expression, the hand came up holding a gun. It was now being held with two hands, pointed at his chest.

The man said, "Yes, of course. What would you like me to say?"

The man the Observer was next to in the car had extremely strong emotions. It was instantly appraised of the severity of his feeling towards others.

The man was watching the nodding dog in the back of the car ahead. It was hypnotic. It just bounced around continuously for no apparent reason. He hated it.

He felt the vibrations as his car slowly drifted off the edge of the road, over the rumble strip, and onto the hard shoulder. He hated rumble strips.

He opened his eyes and swerved back onto the road, causing the truck already there to blast its horn. He had always considered that the horns on trucks were unnecessarily loud.

He hated truck horns.

Realising that he must have nodded off momentarily, he began looking out for an exit. He hated having to look for exits. He would pull off and find somewhere to stay for the night, probably a motel.

He hated motels.

He didn't recognise the rundown looking Cosy Nook Motel. It was a silly name.

He hated silly names.

He had been travelling around the country selling insurance for years, which he hated, but had not come across this place before.

He wasn't prepared to keep looking. It was growing dark and he didn't like driving at night; in fact he hated it.

He just needed a meal and a sleep.

"Good evening, sir," said the smiling girl on reception. She stood and patted her hair.

He hated it when women patted their hair down like that.

"Can I get a meal and a room?" he asked. "Of course you can," said the girl with carefree flippancy.

He had always hated carefree flippancy from young girls.

He didn't waste time; he dumped his bag in his room and found the dining room. The menu seemed to be mainly Chinese.

He hated Chinese. The room seemed to be teeming with young people, all making a lot of noise.

He hated it.

He scoffed down the last of his fish and rice and hurried up to his room. He was on the first floor back, with a view of the car park and waste bins. He stepped out onto the narrow balcony and took in the view.

He hated it.

A gas-pipe in the dilapidated kitchen (broken for several hours and spewing liquid gas throughout the entire building) finally met up with a source of ignition. This resulted in an almighty, ear-splitting explosion.

He hated any kind of loud noise.

He held his ears as the wall behind him began to crack open and he toppled from the crumbling balcony.

He just hated toppling from crumbling balconies.

He plummeted, head first into a large metal dumpster full of plastic bags containing food scraps; mainly vegetables.

He hated vegetables.

This was followed by another huge explosion, which brought the heavy lid of the waste bin crashing down barely missing the top of his head.

After a few moments and a few more blasts, the bin, fitted with casters, began to roll across the sloping car park, finally coming to rest against something soft. He, having found that the metal lid was too heavy to lift, passed out among the slimy, gaping bags of putrefied food.

He hated passing out among slimy, gaping bags of putrefied food.

Hours passed before he was brought to by sounds of shovelling, running water and voices. He began banging on the lid of the bin with what felt like a chicken bone. It lifted and a fireman wearing a hard hat peered in.

"Hey! Will you look at this! We've got a survivor!"

He just laid there staring up, feeling really stupid and smelling really bad.

He had always hated feeling stupid and smelling bad.

The next face that appeared had a flat hat with gold braid. He looked down, wide-eyed and said "Dammit! The whole place gets gutted, with bodies piling up, and this guy survives it all… in a trash cart. Well, you know what they say. Only the good die young."

He had always hated that saying.

The unusual room was taken in by the Observer. Its features were quite different from most other rooms. It acquainted itself with the thoughts of the man sitting in the chair. He was something of a recluse, but most certainly had his own ideas about the imminent nuclear holocaust.

His success in business had meant that he was able to plan for what he knew was coming. His personal fortune enabled him to purchase the best shelter on the market. As he was now retired and living alone, he threw all his resources into the project of surviving the madness building across the globe.

The night that the news was broadcast that the two major powers could well easily declare war, he put his plan into action. The view of most tacticians was that it would take only two days before other countries would enter the conflict. The escalation would then see all nuclear weapons deployed from all countries that possessed them, with total world annihilation within a single week.

He was ready. With only a handful of others, wealthy enough to have such an underground facility built, he would survive. For him, hearing the newscast (as terrible as it was) gave him a sense of self-validation.

It was with growing excitement that he used the laser retinal scan to pass through the outer door and make his way deep into the site of his shelter, where the essentials for sustaining life for at least twelve months would allow him to survive the madness that may already have started. Closing the heavy door of the bunker it would be time-locked. Everyone and everything may very well be annihilated within a month and the door was timed to open automatically after two months. This was not only to prevent entry, but to stop him leaving. Not even in some crazy state of panic, or any brief moment of insanity, could he expose himself to the horrors of what may have begun on the outside.

He settled into his bedside chair. This was it then; the war to end all wars. This was what mankind had brought about.

Armageddon!

He eyed the huge cans that lined one wall from floor to ceiling. He looked at the tap that was connected to a gigantic water tank beyond. The supply of food and water had been perfectly rationed to enable survival for a year; not that it would be needed.

He knew the old 'rule of threes'. You can survive three minutes without air, three days without water, and three weeks without food. He remembered reading how Mahatma Gandhi, had on one occasion, gone without food for three weeks.

Something jolted him out of his chair. He ran across to the food preparation area and began pulling out drawers, checking cupboards, looking in containers. He was becoming frantic! He worked away tirelessly, for several minutes, then slumped back into his chair.

With watery eyes he sat gazing across at his provisions. He couldn't believe what was happening.

He jumped up and went through the entire room again, this time pulling out drawers and throwing the contents onto the floor, emptying cupboards and tossing things over his shoulder. He went on until everything was totally exposed, strewn and scattered around him.

He sat on the floor opening containers, emptying out

plastic bags, rummaging through all those things; all those essentials for which he had meticulously listed and planned.

Then, all of a sudden it was there.

He sat dazed for several minutes, silently sobbing, as he clutched the tin-opener to his chest.

The bank was quietly going about its business. The Observer looked on as the man with the case held up a gun.

"This…" he waved it about "is not a real gun." He swung his arm around to let everyone see it. "It is only being used to get your attention. Of course, you don't know for sure that it is a replica. It serves its purpose right now and you have my word that I'll be gone in a few minutes and no one will be harmed. Provided you all sit on the floor and stay quiet, no one will be hurt. OK? Down."

Four staff and a dozen customers slowly sat down wherever they could.

"Thank you." He turned to look across the counter and said, "The Bank Manager please."

Nobody moved.

"Please!" he repeated, and the manager came out from a small gate in the counter.

The man put the brown case up on the counter and was about to open it when a woman screamed, "It's a bomb. He's got a bomb!"

He turned sharply and shouted, "It's not a bomb! I told you, I'm not going to hurt anybody."

He turned to the manager. "Not if we just do this quickly and quietly without any fuss."

He opened the case and took out several thick bundles of bank notes. "I want to see you place this money securely in your vault. Can we do that? Can we do it quickly?"

After a moment's hesitation the manager looked at the gun and nodded. He led the way to the rear of the building and the door of the vault. In moments he had it open. The man handed over the bundles of notes and watched as the manager stepped inside the small room and placed the money carefully on a table. He could hear the man talking to himself in a low, droning voice.

For a moment the manager considered counting the money but dismissed the idea. He came back out, closed and relocked the vault.

They walked back to the front of the bank where people were still sitting and still looking nervous.

He closed and picked up his case. "Thank you for your patience," he said, looking around the room. With that, he walked slowly out of the bank.

A short time later the Bank Manager, still trembling from the ordeal, sat giving his statement to the police inspector. When this was done, the inspector asked, "So, why do you think he did it?"

The manager said, "I really don't have any idea. I only know he kept mumbling something about Karma."

The Observer watched the boy as he approached. The old coin shop sat quietly in a lane that nobody used.

The young boy in the sporty-looking track suit wasn't sure how he had come to be in that part of the town. He never crossed the bridge; he had no reason to. But here he was, a long way from the busy shopping area on the other side of the river. He must have lost his bearings without knowing it. He sometimes caught a bus into town, just to wonder around gazing in shop windows on a Saturday morning. Now he stood staring at coins and medals, large and small, gold, silver, bronze, all sorts. Most of them looked very old and several were in such poor condition he was sure nobody would ever want to buy them.

One large gold medal caught his eye. It showed a javelin thrower, arm stretched back and about to launch. He stood gawping at it. This was his favourite sport at school. Two years running he'd come first on Sports Day.

Suddenly, he was startled out of his day-dreaming by a woman's wizened old face appearing quite unexpectedly above the display. She was grinning and crooking a skinny finger, inviting him in. She looked rather crazy but he had always been surprisingly tolerant with such people for his age.

He looked at his watch. He didn't have long before catching his bus. He was having lunch with his uncle at twelve. His uncle had said he would provide lunch if he helped him remove a few branches at the back. His arthritis made it difficult for him to manage the chainsaw. He was his favourite uncle and he wouldn't want to let him down.

He tore his eyes from the medal and looked at his watch again; twenty minutes, no more. He wasn't at all comfortable about it, but he would really like to get a closer look at the medal that seemed to mesmerize him. There was something special about it, something appealing; precious even.

He went in. The old woman watched as he made his

way through the shop, stopping occasionally to look at a particular item.

He eventually stopped at the window display, peering down at the medal.

A croaky voice said, "Would you like a closer look at it?" Perplexed at the question, he just nodded. She lifted the large medal out and handed it to him.

She pointed a crooked finger at it. "That's a future medal, that is."

"A future medal?" he asked.

"Oh, yes. They're not all future medals, of course. I mix them with all the others. That one appeals, does it, eh?"

"Yes."

She cackled. "And you don't know why? Am I right?"

His young face reddened. "It's a beautiful medal," he said, surprising himself with the way he expressed it. He stood turning it over and over in his hands. It had a wide, flat slot at the top for a ribbon, but no ribbon.

What he hadn't noticed was that the man on the medal only had one arm.

What he did notice was a small gold label that covered something up. He looked closer.

From out of nowhere the old hand took it back gently.

"Can't show the year," she whispered. "Would get into all kinds of trouble, I would."

He frowned and said, "How much do you want for it?"

"Can't do that either. No, not for future medals." She looked around. "The others, yes, but not future medals." She patted his arm. "You might be running late."

Surprised by the statement, he looked at his watch.

"Yes!" he said. "Thanks for…" he paused, not knowing what it was he wanted to thank her for.

"Thanks anyway," he said and hurried back into the lane. He knew he had to make good time if he was going to catch his bus.

What he couldn't know was that it would be another decade before the first Paralympic Games would take place in Rome…

The psychiatrist was talking to the two personas, one Michael and the other Toby. The Observer understood that the professional man was only addressing one of them.

Michael was looking around the room, it had white walls and ceiling with a grey carpet. The door was a metal security door with a small window. The prison psychiatrist sat behind a large desk in a high-backed, padded, swivel chair. Michael sat opposite him on a plastic chair with no cushion.

The doctor cleared his throat as he closed the file and put it down. "Michael, thank you for letting me have this chat with you. Today I would like to go over the events that took place earlier this year; the killings at the youth club. I just need to know more about the motive. Do you understand?"

Michael gave a congenial grin and said, "Yes, doctor, I understand, but I don't think I'm going to be much help as I wasn't there."

"No. That's why I need to talk to, Toby."

Michael shrugged. "I don't think he wants to talk to you."

The doctor looked disappointed. "OK. But will you at least ask him for me?"

Michael sighed and said, "Alright, I'll ask."

With that he closed his eyes and lifted his chin. He seemed to be mumbling something. "Sorry doc, Toby says he doesn't want to talk to you."

The doctor thought for a minute. "Tell him I can arrange some privileges for him if he just talks to me for five minutes."

"OK. I'll try." Michael goes into a trance again, muttering much longer this time. There seems to be an argument going on. The doctor sits patiently. He knows this could be a breakthrough.

"Toby says he'll talk to you, but only if he can sit in your big chair." Michael screws his face up and drops his voice to a whisper. "I know he's much younger than me but he does get some strange ideas sometimes. If I let him talk to you, you will be nice to him, won't you? I mean, you won't hurt him or anything?"

"Of course not, Michael, I'm only here to help him."

"OK." Michael stands, and they swap chairs.

Michael sits back in the padded chair with a smile spreading across his face. His eyes are closed and he grips the arms so that his knuckles turn white. After a few moments his eyes snap open and he stares at the doctor with an evil frown. He bares his teeth and hisses.

In a much younger voice, Toby says, "You wanted to talk to me?"

"Eh... yes." The doctor is suddenly very uncomfortable

with the dramatic change in his patient. "I wanted to ask about the killings; the motive I mean."

"Ah! Motive. You grown-ups always want to know about motive. You always need to have reasons. You're really stupid, do you know that?"

With this he stands and produces a knife from his prison tunic.

The doctor jumps up in horror. "However did you manage to get hold of that?"

Toby laughs insanely. "You stupid fool! What difference could it possibly make if I told you that? You shrinks are always asking the wrong questions."

The psychiatrist was staring at the knife with wild eyes, saying "What do you mean?"

"Well, as the security alarm is under this side of your desk, you should be asking yourself whether you'll leave this room alive."

He wiggled the blade, and with a demonic grin adds, "You see? I'm only a kid and even I know the answer to that!"

The Observer was watching the woman as she listened to the noises. She could hear him going from room to room, bumping into things and complaining.

Her husband was forever losing his pills and she was sick of it. He was old, sick and grumpy. He had never been a cheerful man from the day they met, but this... this continual carping, this incessant blame he dumped on her for anything he wasn't happy about. There was never a kind word, although she had spent five years looking after him; waiting on him hand and foot. She simply had no life of her own. He could be very forgetful at times and would want to take two in the same day. She would have to insist that he had already taken one and remind him that taking more than one tablet in twenty four hours could be dangerous. Of course, she would never get any thanks for that either.

She had left him for over an hour mooning about the place mumbling and swearing looking for his pills. Finally, he came into the kitchen saying, "Have you moved my pills again?"

She closed her eyes, making a great effort not to cry. She turned to him. "I never move your pills. Why would I?"

"I'm not so sure," he muttered.

She took a deep breath and said, "Just give me a few minutes to get this in the oven and I'll come and help you find them."

He snorted. "Yes. Well, don't be too long," he staggered off, complaining under his breath.

She stood staring at the food she was preparing but not seeing it. How many years had it been? Five? Yes, it would have been five years that she had put up with the same old thing day in and day out… and it had been getting a lot worse of late.

She finished up in the kitchen and went through to join him. "All right, let's see if we can't find your tablets," she said, trying to sound cheerful.

"Pills." He said wearily.

She stared at him. "What?"

He glowered at her. "Pills. I've told you before, I don't

like them called tablets. Why can't you ever get anything right?"

The search went on for ages with no result.

"I have to take them," he grumbled. "You know I have to take them." He glared at her accusingly. "The doctor said it's important that I keep up my medication. You know that."

"Yes dear, of course I know that."

She thought for a minute and went on. "Well, if we really can't find them there are a few of those you used to take, before the doctor started to increase your dosage." She frowned thoughtfully. "That's if I can find them."

He flapped his arms saying, "Well, don't just stand there. Go and look!"

She took another deep breath and went off to the bathroom. After several minutes spent rummaging around in cabinets and drawers she came back with a small box of pills.

"Here we are," she said, with a look of triumph on her face. "The seals are still intact. They won't be the same strength of course, but they'll do until we get more from the chemist."

He pouted. "They'll have to do, I suppose."

She brought a glass of water from the kitchen. "Now then," she said, looking at the label, your tablets are..."

"Pills." He corrected and shook his head.

"Yes, all right, pills. Yours are fifty milligrams and these are only ten. You need to take five." She dropped them into his hand."

He swallowed them and said, "It's about time."

She agreed, it was.

"There you go," she said, knowing full well she had seen to it that he would never lose his tablets again.

The Observer watched as the visitor sipped his sherry slowly and frowned at his older friend.

Not that there were many years between them. They had both seen a lot, done a lot, and spent a lot of time over the years engaged in many conversations similar to this. They had probably spent a lot of time discussing the eternal verities without really knowing it.

"You think so, do you?" asked the visitor.

"Yes. I think I do," the other replied. He scratched his temple thoughtfully and went on. "I read somewhere that the eternal verities, such as truth, honesty, character and loyalty, will never change, but will always prevail."

· The visitor struggled with his iPhone, then looked up. "I have a website here that says an eternal verity is the state or quality of something that is true, in accordance with fact or reality."

"Yes. I can go along with that," came the reply.

"Well, I suppose I do too, but I'm not sure that this really stabilises any notions a person may have regarding things ethical, intellectual or spiritual."

He glanced momentarily at his phone, as if hoping for enlightenment. "After all, it has been said that good and evil arise together. As I understand it, this is the fruit of the Dharma practice."

The other nodded, saying, "Go on."

The visitor shrugged, as if suddenly feeling unsure of his

ground. "When you start questioning these things, I mean actually looking at what is meant, you inevitably challenge the validity of the whole thing. They can become quite flexible, as notions, I mean."

The other puffed out a breath. "Oh! Come on! You can't muck about with the eternal verities. We are talking about the values that man has been guided by throughout history. You can't change the eternal verities with any concept of flexibility. There's simply no room for that."

"Maybe," said the other, picking up his glass again. "I can see how you are looking at it. Your view on what I see as relatively abstract ideas about things like conscience, compassion, spirit, soul, sympathy, hope and love... Well, these are pretty basic, moral principles. However, when you think about it, things like this that everyone seems to know about seem to remain unchanged from one year to another. Whereas some, like everyday life, are subject to occasional updates."

His friend raised his eyebrows in disbelief.

"Alright, put it like this." The other went on. "Wouldn't you agree that one of the most common eternal verities within human existence is that a person believes that if he or she makes choices based on the principle that these are made by others, that person will be generally regarded as intelligent? You may not like the idea, but you would have to agree that this is a pretty basic principle, which in itself accords with reality."

The other smiled and shook his head. "Well, my friend," he said in a quiet and friendly way. "To my mind, where allegories and parables are entirely open to all manner of interpretations, these sorts of variants cannot be applied to the eternal verities, based simply on the fact that they are eternal."

Well then," said the visitor "on a personal level, would you say that true friendship is an eternal verity?"

"Absolutely!" said the other and poured two more sherries.

It looked on as the woman thought about her husband. Everyone has their shortcomings and she knew he was no exception.

After a couple of years of being married to him she had learned to dread her birthdays. Then, as the years rolled by, she found a peaceful resolution building within herself. These special occasions with their special gifts took on a different meaning; a somewhat magical charm. Now, with so many years behind them it was that time of year again. It was that day again.

She waited during the day in a state of high anticipation. She knew it would happen during the evening. It always happened that way. He would suddenly appear holding something wrapped and he would be wearing a loving, boyish smile. She didn't fully understand why she now found these times so precious. Despite this, she knew how much she loved him and how much she appreciated whatever was given.

These feelings were heightened the moment he came into the room that evening, holding a parcel and wishing her a happy birthday.

In that instant she remembered all those other gifts: a

pack of ballpoint pens, a fridge magnet, a flower vase, a large box of tissues, a coffee mug, a pair of tea towels, a dustpan and brush on two occasions, and last year a set of coasters, to name just a few. She could see how much it meant to him. It was beautifully-wrapped and she opened it with great care.

It was a wooden carving board.

She placed it down on the table lovingly and gently ran her fingers over it. She turned to him with teary-eyed joy… she hugged him.

The young girl stood looking up at the luxury apartments, while the Observer looked on.

She had come in answer to an advertisement for a house cleaner, and if she had this right, the old girl on the phone would be an easy mark. She had become something of an expert when it came to picking these old biddies. They were usually widows, with more money than they knew what to do with. They were always so trusting; so gullible.

It was a hot day and she felt the cool relief as she entered the building. She took the elevator, got out and found the door; she pressed the buzzer. A few moments later she heard someone approaching from the other side with the clattering of a walking stick.

The girl smirked. This quickly turned into a warm and innocent smile as the door opened. "Hello, we spoke on the phone."

The old lady frowned and shook her head.

"…about the cleaning; doing some house cleaning for you."

"Oh yes, of course, that's right. Thank you so much for coming, my dear. Please come through."

She led the way slowly into a beautiful loungeroom, where they settled down into two large, comfy armchairs next to a marble coffee table. The girl looked around, taking in the expensive furniture and floor coverings.

The old lady leant forward with some difficulty, pointing at the table. "It's a warm day, so I thought you'd like something cool. You pour, dear; my hands...," she wriggled bony fingers and grimaced.

"Yes, of course. That's nice of you." She poured some juice with ice cubes clinking. "You only need someone to come in twice a week, you said."

"That's right. I hope that suits you?"

"No problem."

The old lady relaxed visibly. "I do hope that suits you." She looked around and said, "It is rather big. Too big for me really; but we moved in here only two months before my dear husband passed away; and that was less than a year ago. He wanted to make me happy, you see."

She looked around again. "It is a large apartment. Are you sure you wouldn't mind, doing the cleaning, I mean?"

The girl was wondering just how many rooms there were, not that it mattered; she would only need to work a couple of days before making her move. She wondered what the pickings would be like here. There's bound to be lots of small expensive items; figurines, jewellery and a load of cash tucked away. Pretty awesome, she thought.

"No. Not at all," she said.

The old lady was smiling. "He was a wonderful man, you know." She pointed at a far wall with her cane.

The girl scanned the wall, but couldn't see any photos, only pictures.

"A photo, you mean, of your late husband?"

"Oh! No my dear. The paintings. He did all those. He was quite famous you see, but you wouldn't have heard of him." She struggled to retrieve a handkerchief from a pocket and dabbed her eyes. "No. No photos," she went on. "I can't have them…"

Her eyes continued to water. "Silly, isn't it? We were so happy together, but now he's gone, I just can't bring myself to look at them."

Despite herself, the girl understood what she was saying and felt the old woman's sadness. She actually liked the old girl, but that wasn't a good thing. No. She couldn't think like that. It would make her job harder if she allowed those sorts of feelings to creep in.

The old woman was topping up the drinks, when she suddenly winced. "Oh! How embarrassing. You'll have to excuse me, my dear." She struggled out of her chair and hobbled slowly out of the room.

The girl wondered where the bathroom was, hoping it wasn't too far; she nevertheless couldn't help supressing a wicked grin.

Almost half-an-hour later the old lady came back. She strutted across the room bolt upright. She was wearing a completely different outfit and carrying a large bag. She approached the girl, bent down and gave her face a hard slap.

She was out cold and would stay that way for another hour at least. She then proceeded to fold her telescopic walking stick and place it in the bag along with the pickings gathered earlier; a few precious items of gold and silver, several pieces of jewellery and some cash.

Then she carefully removed the girl's gold earrings, her silver necklace with a tiny silver cross, along with three bangles and two rings; one of which looked genuinely expensive. She picked up the girl's bag and found her wallet. She found her cash, there was a surprising amount of it. Certainly more than enough to get far beyond the next town. She dropped the girl's handbag into the larger one and zipped it up.

She did a last minute check around. She thought about how very handy these time-share apartments were; there were always vacant periods.

Before she left, she returned and stood for a moment looking down at the girl. Smiling, she said "God! These kids, they're so gullible!"

The Observer watched as the old-timer eyed the hot drink machine across the hall.

"I would give quids for a coffee. Buggers won't let you bring drinks in here. Never known a place with so many rules."

He turned to his younger companion. "Like coffee do you?"

"Oh. Yes," came the reply.

"Good!"

He gazed longingly at the machine again. He tapped the other man's arm, glanced around and dropped his head. "I did hear," he said in a whisper, "this machine has been wired to the main switchboard. Anybody using it before seven in the evening would cause a massive surge and fuse all the lights!"

His companion raised an eyebrow. "Do you believe that?"

The man laughed. "Nah. 'Course not. They'll tell you anything in this place to protect their precious rules. Rules are more important here than people. Rules, rules, rules…"

The two men stood in the open doorway, watching people slowly moving down the corridor. Sad looking people with pale faces; faces that were blank for the most part. People who were being looked after by the state for their own good often wore such expressions.

As if from nowhere, a tall, thin figure suddenly swept into view. His long, black robe flapped from side to side as he navigated his way through the slower traffic.

"Oh! God!" said the older man. "Here comes Jiminy Cricket."

"Jiminy who?"

"Cricket! You know, 'love-forty' and all that sort of thing."

"Love-forty? That's tennis, isn't it?"

"Look mate, don't get picky with me. Remember, I've been around longer than you. I'm an old-timer, I am. I've seen it all come and go. I've seen it…"

The man's eyes glazed over for a moment. Then he snapped out of it and turned to the other. "Could have been worse you know," he said with a half-smile. He leaned forward and spoke softly. "He could have been carrying a gold-fish bowl." He shuddered and went on. "Oh! Yes! One of his favourites, that is. Dead lucky we are, I tell you!"

A bell sounded somewhere in the building. The two men found seats at the back of the room and waited for the others. Within a minute or two they were joined by a dozen people, looking a lot like mature-age students.

They all sat waiting for their 'tutor' to arrive.

"Who have we got today?" asked a lady at the front.

"Professor Hicket," came the reply.

The woman looked up at the time and sighed grumpily. The clock above the door said five past six.

"He's late this evening. Maybe he won't show," said another.

The men at the back smiled at each other.

"We've seen him!" said the older man with great pride. "Haven't we?"

The other nodded at the group, a little coyly.

"Going down the hall, he was," said the first. "Going like a bat out of hell and twice as nasty!"

Muffled laughter went round the room.

As the commotion died down the younger man was asking about the professor's name.

"He's not a real professor," someone mumbled.

Someone shushed.

"Well, 'e ain't," came the reply. "No way. They just let 'im pretend, just to keep the peace. Saves them looking after us don't it?"

"Shut it!" said the man at the back. He turned to the man next to him. "Take no notice. We wouldn't be given anybody who wasn't properly qualified. His name is Professor Jeramie Hicket. He does have the odd funny way about him…"

Here the man made a strange gesture against the side of his head and added, "Not at all unusual in this place."

The earlier sniggering now gave way to an unexpected burst of excited laughter. With that the man got to his feet, obviously basking in the adoration of his fellow classmates. He strode to the doorway with a great deal of pride and stood bolt upright, as if standing sentry.

His smile dropped a little as he ogled the drink machine once more. He licked his lips.

After a few moments the self-appointed door attendant clapped his hands to gain the room's attention, and buoyed by his previous success with his audience, began a humorous announcement.

"Heads up, everybody! Old Jiminy Cricket, conscience of the nation, philosopher extraordinaire, has just entered the west end of the hall carrying what looks like a…" his voice trailed off and he seemed to reach out and brace himself against the door frame.

He returned to his seat and dropped his head into his hands, mumbling "Gold-fish bowl," as the rest of his companions squirmed in their seats. They knew what was coming!

The lofty figure in the black robe swept through the door and up to the front desk in a dramatic and somewhat haughty flourish, coming to rest in a most important pose in front of the group.

He looked them over with the arrogance of a person absolutely convinced of his God-given superiority over the rest of his kind.

With more theatricality he placed the bowl on the desk,

along with a large bag that rattled as he put it down. From this he took a biscuit tin, a small bag and a jar.

He looked out across the sea of faces, as if deciding whether the people he saw were worthy of what he was about to reveal. "Good afternoon. I have something important to show you today."

A series of soft groans went around the room. The old-timer looked first at his friend, then up to heaven. The man at the desk didn't seem to notice any of this. He went on.

"If I place this bowl thus, and take up this tin of golf-balls, and place them thus into the bowl" (he did this until they reached the mouth of the bowl), "you will see that I have filled it."

He looked up. "Does everybody agree that this bowl is now full?"

"Yes," came the instant and positive response.

The audience had seen this all before, time and time again. However, whatever society may think of those held within the walls and grounds of this establishment, there was one thing they weren't silly about. They knew from hard-won experience that the quickest way through this charade was to go along with it.

The so-called professor smiled with a great deal of satisfaction. "Fast learners, eh? Good. But I give you fair warning; it gets harder."

Furtive looks and a few grimaces went around the room as the man dipped into the smaller bag and produced a handful of marbles.

"If I now drop these glass balls into the container thus," he smiled as the balls tumbled into the available spaces with a sharp clattering sound. He tapped the side of the bowl and added the last few until they reached the top.

He looked up again. "Does everybody agree that this bowl is now really full?"

The audience wriggled in their chairs and agreed.

A strange smile seemed to dance across the lips of the old-timer.

"Now," said the lecturer obviously enjoying himself, "what if I were to take this jar of sand and pour out the contents thus." Sand settled into the crevices until it reached the upper rim.

"Would you say now that this bowl is now truly full?"

Agreement was given again, only this time the less patient members of the group threw in a few comments and moans.

The man at the back was still smiling.

The lecturer seemed not to notice. Instead he moved out to the side of the desk, clasped his hands in front of himself, and took on the air of a person about to bestow great wisdom.

"Now. Imagine if you will, that this bowl represents a person's life. Further, imagine that the golf-balls are the important things in life such as a person's family, partner, health, or children. In fact, if everything else was lost and only they remained, a person's life would still be full. Now, I want you to suppose that the marbles you see here are other things that matter, like a person's job, house, or car. And finally I want you to look on this sand as everything else; the small stuff."

He paused and stared at the group. "Everybody keeping up, are they?"

A general grunting and nodding of heads prompted him to continue.

"If you imagine all this to be the case, then consider this… If a person was to put the sand into the bowl first, there would be no room for the marbles or golf-balls."

He raised his arms in a grand gesture. "The very same goes for life. If a person spends all their time and energy on the small stuff, they will never have room for the things that are really important! Thank you."

With a sweep of his gown he took a deep bow. His listeners, out of relief more than appreciation, began to clap.

As he straightened, his attention was caught by the old-timer at the back waving his hand in the air.

"Yes. You had a question?"

"I wondered…" the old-timer began with deliberate coyness, "I wondered if I could contribute something in some small way. A philosophical point that I feel your excellent demonstration has raised?"

"By all means, be my guest!" The man in the robes was flattered that his talk had created such a reaction. Normally, he had often thought, there was surprisingly little.

The man at the back seemed to hesitate. "It does involve a physical involvement on my part I'm afraid."

"Doesn't matter. Carry on by all means," came the reply.

The man stood up and walked slowly to the front.

"My contribution is in two parts. First the physical, and second the philosophical". He looked up at the taller man for encouragement. The other signalled for him to continue with a gracious sweep of the hand.

The old-timer took a step back, turned and left the room.

The audience was for the first time fully attentive. Faint rattling noises could be heard from across the hall and all eyes were on him as he returned with two cups of coffee. With these set down in front of the demonstration bowl, he turned to his audience.

"As I said," he continued, "my first point is a physical one." Again he looked to the professor for his approval.

With a little nervousness creeping into his voice the other repeated, "Carry on. Please, carry on."

The old-timer lifted one of the plastic cups to his mouth and drank slowly, savouring every drop. He returned the empty cup to the table, licking his lips loudly. He then picked up the second cup and slowly poured its contents into the top of the bowl. He stood for a few moments while the liquid visibly seeped down to the bottom.

"Alright," said the professor, sounding less patient, "I see the physical point. I'm sure we all do; but what about the philosophical point you wanted to make?"

"The philosophical point," said the old-timer with a broad grin spreading across his face, "is that no matter how full a person's life is, there is always room for a nice cup of coffee!"

At this point, the room went black.

The Observer floated above the main entrance to the shopping complex watching the man stamping his feet impatiently.

The doors of the centre opened at nine o'clock, and

Jeremy was there and waiting. He didn't want to waste any more time than was necessary.

"Good morning!" said the friendly stranger, holding the door open.

"Go to hell!" Jeremy replied.

Jeremy didn't trust people. He didn't trust them and he didn't like them, especially friendly strangers. He had dropped by the chemist shop in his local shopping centre to pick up a prescription and he was in no mood to exchange pleasantries.

Jeremy was upset about the fact that, at the tender age of 35, he was overweight and had a nasty ulcer, a big one. Despite the fact that he had caused his ulcer with his own intolerance and penchant for over-eating, he blamed everyone else; his family, his neighbours, even total strangers.

Jeremy was not a nice person.

"Good morning!" said the trolley lady, a pleasant woman in her sixties. "Would you like a shopping cart?"

"Go to hell!" he barked again, heading for the prescription counter. Jeremy was not only mean and intolerant to people, he was cruel to any living creature he encountered. As a young boy he would spend hours, shooting birds out of the trees with his air rifle. As a child he delighted in catching small animals and burying them alive. He would do his evil deed and then laugh as he contemplated the anguish being experienced by the small creature as its oxygen ran out. One of his favourite pastimes involved the use of a test tube he had found in the garden shed. He got a lot of satisfaction out of cramming bugs into it, right to the bottom, until they suffocated. He particularly liked this because his finger fitted so nicely into it, and was able to watch his victims!

Jeremy paid for his ulcer medication and headed back out to the car park. His stomach was hurting; perhaps it would help if he had something to eat. He pulled into a nearby take-away food outlet and entered the drive-through lane. A large serving of chips and a can of soft drink might be just the thing to relieve the discomfort in his stomach. That is, if the old woman ahead of him would make up her mind. She was looking at the menu board, trying to decide what she wanted. Jeremy blew his horn and shouted out the window.

"Make up your mind or get the hell out of my way, you old witch!"

Upset, the old woman moved ahead and placed her order. She glanced nervously in her rear-view mirror as Jeremy glared at her. She hurriedly placed her order, collected it and moved on. Jeremy ordered his food and drink.

He placed them on the seat beside him; the smell was more than he could stand and his stomach was getting worse. He would have to pull up somewhere. He paid the young attendant with a scowl and headed out onto the highway.

Unfortunately for Jeremy, his thoughts were directed towards finding somewhere to eat and not on the road. He didn't check for traffic before pulling out. A very large vehicle travelling at a fair rate of knots hit him broadside. Funnily enough, he didn't see the tunnel and white light so commonly described in near-death experiences. He just heard the crash and, for an instant, felt intense pain.

In fact, he was not dead but dreaming. He was imagining that he was standing about twenty feet from what was left of his car.

"Oh! Sod it!" Jeremy thought. "Good thing I've got

insurance!" He watched as people ran out onto the highway from all directions.

He heard the approaching sirens. "I suppose I'm going to lose points over this. It's not my fault; that stupid truck-driver was going much too fast."

Jeremy's concern about insurance and a possible traffic violation turned to sheer horror when he saw his own broken body being pulled out of the wreckage of his car. He moved in a little closer. Sure enough, the body he was looking at was his own. Police were now on the scene taking statements from horrified witnesses. Uniformed men were loading his dead body into the back of a waiting ambulance.

"So, this is what it's like to be dead!" he thought to himself. "Well, so far so good."

Now, Jeremy didn't actually relish the idea of being dead. But the fact that he was conscious, had absolutely no stomach pain, felt light on his feet and was able to walk about freely, felt like a real bonus!

"Hey, you there!" Jeremy shouted to a nearby police officer. The man didn't hear him. Jeremy shrugged. "Well, at least I won't be hassled by the cops!" he chuckled to himself. "If this is what it's like to be dead, how bad can it be?"

Jeremy sat down on the curb; he was trying to decide what his next move would be. He'd recently had the movie 'Beetlejuice' out from the video library. He was now musing on the fact that his own after-life experience seemed to parallel that of the main characters in the film.

"I wonder where that little Beetlejuice character is," he thought.

He leaned back and contemplated how he would spend eternity in this painless, carefree existence. He had an idea.

"I've got to try this!" he thought as he got to his feet. He walked out into the middle of the highway, straight into the path of an oncoming tourist coach. Sure enough, it passed right through him. For a brief moment, his head and shoulders protruded through the floor of the bus, right in the centre of the aisle. He watched the passengers flash past him.

"Oh man! That was amazing!" Jeremy laughed to himself. He jumped out in front of a car. Same thing; the car passed right through him.

"This could be fun!"

He jumped in front of about a dozen more cars, enjoying the thrill of watching them rush right at him, and through him.

"Oh great! Here comes a taxi!" he thought. He would particularly enjoy this; cab drivers always overcharged, in his opinion. He jumped out in front of it. The cab driver slammed on the brakes and stopped.

"What the…?" Jeremy yelled.

"Get in!" the cab driver ordered.

"You can see me?"

"Of course, I can see you. Get in!" the driver ordered. Jeremy walked around the front of the vehicle, staring at the driver, and climbed into the back.

"Where are we going?" asked Jeremy.

"Hell, of course. Where do you think?" replied the driver. The driver pushed his foot down and sped off down the road.

"We're going to hell in a cab?" Jeremy laughed.

The driver didn't answer. He just glanced up at Jeremy

for an instant and then jammed the accelerator pedal to the floor. The cab moved even faster.

"Wow!" Jeremy shouted, holding onto the door handle. "Watch out. We must be way above the speed limit, whatever it is!"

The driver ignored Jeremy and continued speeding up. The scenery rushed by so fast it started to blur.

"Hey! Slow down!" Jeremy screamed.

The driver raised his head and looked steadily into the rear-vision mirror. He didn't look at all worried, despite the fact that the taxi was now moving faster than any vehicle had a right to move, and speeding up with every second that passed.

"You haven't seen anything yet!" said the driver, shoving his foot down even harder.

They were now going so fast that the view out through all the windows became a blur. Jeremy was shoved back so hard into his seat it hurt. They were travelling at such a speed that the colours outside the windows were being warped somehow; warped into colours he had never seen before.

"What's this thing run on, anti-matter?" Jeremy gasped.

The driver only looked casually into his mirror and grinned.

Finally, after what seemed an eternity, the cab began to slow down. Things outside became visible again. They were cruising along an isolated two-lane highway in the middle of nowhere.

"Where the hell are we?" asked Jeremy. The driver looked up at him again, smiled and pointed through the windscreen.

Jeremy couldn't believe his eyes. Looming up in front of them was the largest amusement park Jeremy had ever seen. In the middle of nowhere! It was huge.

"You like amusement parks, don't you?" asked the driver.

"Oh, yeah!" shouted Jeremy with glee.

"Then you'll love this one!" said the driver. "This is every amusement park you've ever dreamed of, all rolled into one."

The cab pulled up to the main entrance. Sure enough, as Jeremy looked through the main gate he could see castles, mountains, cable cars, merry-go-rounds, slides, and all manner of rides. In fact, he was looking at all the attractions he'd ever seen, in all the amusement parks he had ever visited.

"Damn! This is magnificent!" Jeremy shouted. "But where are all the people?"

"There aren't any, Jeremy!" said the driver. "There's not one other person within a million miles of this place. Just you!"

"You mean I've got this great amusement park all to myself?" Jeremy shouted.

"It's all yours, Jeremy. The rides are all operating. The restaurants and snack bars are stocked with fresh food and drinks. All for you!"

"Well, I've got news for you!" said Jeremy. "Somebody screwed up. This isn't hell, this is heaven!"

Jeremy jumped out of the cab.

"Aren't you coming in?" he asked the driver.

"Nope! You're all alone. This is just for you." With that, the cab sped off down the two-lane highway and disappeared.

Jeremy looked up at the main entrance in front of him. The huge sign over the entrance read 'Welcome to Hell'. Jeremy walked in. He couldn't believe what he was looking at. The place was every bit as beautiful and clean as any park he had ever seen. Fresh flowers were everywhere in beautifully-manicured gardens. Like the cab driver said, all the rides were in perfect working order, just waiting for him.

And, best of all, there weren't any people! Jeremy had the whole park to himself, forever!

"Where do I start?" he thought to himself. He decided to get something to eat. After all, he hadn't had a chance to eat his chips before the truck hit him.

He walked over to a nearby sidewalk cafe. Since there was no one to wait on him, he went behind the counter and helped himself. He made himself a couple of hot dogs, covered them with lots of hot chilli sauce and fried onions and poured himself an extra-large soft drink.

He took his food to a nearby umbrella table and sat down to eat. The hot dogs were delicious, in fact, the best he'd ever eaten. He was overjoyed at his good fortune. He was now contemplating a future with an endless supply of delicious food and great entertainment. The sun was shining brightly, the temperature was somehow perfect, and best of all there were no people to get in his way! He gobbled down his hot dogs, swilled the last of his drink, and stuffed his litter into a nearby rubbish bin. An unusual move for him; he normally didn't bother.

"No use littering my own personal amusement park," he mused to himself. He looked around. What would it be first? He shaded his eyes and looked across the entire park.

"Would you look at that!" he murmured to himself. Off

in the distance he saw the biggest water slide he'd ever seen in his life. It was one of those enclosed, tubular slides. The tube, instead of being the usual green fibreglass was made of a crystal clear material; like glass. And it was high! In fact, it was so high that an elevator was fixed to the side of the structure, just to get you to the top. What a ride!

Jeremy ran as fast as his bulk would let him. He jumped on the elevator and pushed the button that would take him to the top. Up, up he went.

"This thing must be thirty stories high!" he shouted. He was getting used to shouting. After all there was no one around to complain. The view was breathtaking. For the first time, Jeremy could see all of the amusement park and beyond. The park was truly awesome in its size. Beyond there was nothing. Just empty land as far as he could see, from horizon to horizon. The elevator stopped with a jolt. Jeremy stepped out. Stopping for a moment, he looked up into the bright sky.

"Thank you, God! Thank you for sending me to hell!" he shouted. He looked into the water slide. How inviting! Fresh, clear, warm water was gushing out of several outlets at the entrance, cascading down the inside of the tube. Already wearing shorts, Jeremy ripped off his shirt, shoes and socks and sat down on the slippery platform, ready for the ride of his life. He gripped the sidebars for a moment, savouring the feeling of anticipation, and then he pushed himself off.

Down he went, lying on his back, feet first, with his arms at his sides. The water was warm and wonderful.

"Man, this is great!" he yelled at the top of his voice. "I'm really picking up speed! Yahoo!" he shouted.

Jeremy was having the time of his life. This was totally

unlike any water slide he had ever been on before. Faster and faster he went.

"Oh man!" he thought. "I'm really gonna fly out the end of this thing! I'm gonna skip across the water like a frisbee" he laughed.

He couldn't wait. "Heaven! I'm in heaven!" Jeremy began singing to himself.

His joy, however, slowly turned to stark terror, when he realised that the tubular slide was actually getting narrower. It was imperceptible at first, but sure enough, the diameter of the slide was getting smaller as Jeremy picked up speed. Horror doesn't begin to do justice to the feeling Jeremy experienced when he recognised the predicament he was in. He tried to stop, but it was no use. There was nothing to grab onto. The inside of the tubular slide was perfectly smooth. Not only that, but Jeremy could only move his hands a few inches. He was on his back with his arms at his sides, and the diameter of the slide wasn't great enough for him to change the position of his body.

Down he went, picking up speed, faster and faster. By now, Jeremy was screaming his lungs out. He knew what was going to happen in just a few more seconds. If the slide continued to narrow, he would be wedged inside it. Wedged for eternity!

Then it happened! The slide narrowed to the point where it stopped Jeremy's forward plunge in an instant. It was a dead stop, sudden and final. The abruptness of it made his head spin, with swirls of flickering light dancing across his eyes. The tube was so tight he couldn't move a single muscle in his entire body. He was held tight, and to the extent where he could barely breathe. There wasn't room for his diaphragm to expand inside his chest in order to take in a full breath of air. He could only breathe in very short, gasping breaths. His arms, of course, were wedged tightly at his sides.

His first thought, naturally, was to scream for help, but this wasn't possible. A person needs a good lung full of air to scream. Besides, as the cab driver had pointed out, there wasn't a person within a million miles of Jeremy's personal amusement park. To make matters worse, Jeremy couldn't even count on death to end his torment.

Patterns of light were still dancing in his head. He squeezed his eyes shut. Slowly, something began to take shape behind his eyelids. A shape that he didn't recognise.

Jeremy would never recognise the image of the test tube that swam about inside his brain.

Never is a very long time, but happily it coincides with the length of time Jeremy has to enjoy his personal amusement park.

At this point the dream ended and Jeremy woke up in a hospital bed with a nurse saying, "Are you feeling better now?"

"Go to hell!" he replied.

The man was lost in his thoughts and the Observer saw these as well.

The vehicles in the street moved slowly through the town and disappeared over the hill. He could see them all quite clearly from his window. One by one they appeared below in all shapes and sizes. They would come, climb the hill, and go. Gone forever, he thought.

The scene outside could easily represent any one of thousands of towns or cities around the world. The man in the chair was a little frightened by the idea. He did not know why.

George James had given twenty two years of service to the company that employed him. They had been good years. From general messenger boy he had been elevated to the sales force. After two decades of selling correspondence courses he found himself managing that same force from his present lofty position, two floors up, and overlooking the town.

The office was clean and modern, as was the rest of the storey occupied by the firm. Much of the space was used as storage. Books, records, cassettes, forms, and other study aids were stacked neatly on tiers of coded shelving. George had installed this system some eighteen months before. His predecessor, a man long in the tooth and short on method, operated on a somewhat different basis. The new manager had never understood how the old boy had coped.

During his first year of office the new man had done well. Commendations had been heaped upon him and his superiors had privately congratulated themselves on their choice of new sales manager. Then things began to change.

It had started about the time of the new course promotions. George began to make mistakes. Not big ones. Small things that more often than not, stayed within the confines of his own office. A report not prepared in time; a letter not answered with his usual promptness. His own insistence on operating without the help of a personal secretary had enabled him on several occasions to burn the midnight oil and put matters right without involving others.

It was more than a little ironic that George had shunned the services of a secretary on the grounds that she would slow him down and impede his efficiency. He used the general office typist, made all his own calls, and personally arranged his appointment diary to his own satisfaction. His system had worked remarkably well for a year.

The new line of home-study courses had been well-received. Because they dealt with the subject of memory improvement they had appealed to a very wide section of the public. At first the courses had sold well and compared favourably with most other study subjects. Then, in the third month, the line had suddenly developed into a veritable boom for the company. Extra staff were employed, and more office furniture and equipment were brought in to handle the upturn in student numbers.

It was at this point that George had begun to come apart at the seams. He could not understand it. The increase in sales was just the thing to fire his blood. It should have been the best possible environment for George to excel in. But this was certainly not the case. The man had gone from bad to worse. His blunders grew, but not the sales.

Eventually, he was summoned to the branch manager's office and reprimanded for his lack of proper attention to normal duties. It was humiliating. George had left the office like a school boy slipping quietly out of the headmaster's study after having the cane applied.

His wife, too, was at a loss. The daily events brought home and discussed all seemed quite alien to George's true nature. After a few weeks of constant evidence that things would not improve if let alone, she took a deep breath and suggested the services of a local psychiatrist. George hit the roof!

The traffic outside still streamed through the town. It seemed endless. George picked the card up from his desk. On its face it bore some elegant script, and the edges were tinged with blue. It looked to George like a ticket to a fancy-dress ball. He took this as fair warning that the psychiatrist's fees were high. He flipped it back onto the blotter and swung around to face the window.

Something about the way the cars were disappearing over the crest of the hill disturbed George. It had bothered him for some time. A medical man might come up with some significant reason for it. George just could not imagine going to see one of those people. He had never needed them before. There had to be another answer.

The phone rang. He picked it up.

"Hello. OK, put him through."

"Brunswick here, sir," said the voice. "Could you let me have the figures for the Williams account? I'm with the client now; he wants to settle up for the month."

"Williams account … Ah! Yes, the figures," George replied uncertainly. "Look Brunswick, I'm afraid they aren't ready yet. Tell him we'll carry them over to next month. There'll be no problem."

"Well, the point is sir, the client would *like* to pay us *now*, sir." The salesman sounded desperate.

The manager rubbed his face and picked through the papers on his desk. It was quite hopeless. He was not even sure he knew what the man was talking about. He would have to be firm.

"Look here, Brunswick. Those figures are not available

at the moment. That's all there is to it. There's no use you whining about it. You handle the client as you think fit. After all, it's what I'm paying you for, isn't it?"

The phone went down with a loud clatter, and the unanswered question filled the room.

The manager stood up and strolled around the office picking things up, examining them, and putting them down again. He knew he was behaving too casually. He returned to his chair and sat thinking about the call. The probable consequences of it could not be ignored. He had to get a grip on himself!

Although it had not worked at all well lately, George's sure-fire method of solving even the most irrepressible problems had always been to swing into his favourite position, look at the view, and, as a bonus, put his feet up on the sill of the window. He made himself comfortable.

As he stared at the view in front of him, the man became uneasy. He was looking, but could not believe what he was seeing. The colour drained from his face and perspiration formed there instead. His eyes were wide, yet empty. He was wearing tennis shoes!

The man at the window knew that enough was enough. He needed help; he intended to get it.

The small card that he hunted for was no longer there. He jumped up and ran around the desk. It had fallen to the floor while the paperwork was being searched through earlier. He picked it up and read the number.

"Hello, Miss Morrison, could you give me a line please?"

"I am sorry, Mr James, I haven't got one free at the moment," said the switchboard operator. "Shall I ring you when I have?"

"Yes. Thank you," said George, and put the phone back gently. He settled back into his chair.

Tennis shoes! His mind must be going. He could understand a few lapses in memory, even forgetting important matters that affect the operation of his sales department, but tennis shoes! His wife had been right; she nearly always was. Why in God's name did he leave it so long?

As he sat, he slipped into a deep reverie. His memory was going; just like those cars disappearing over the hill! He began to feel a little better. Two more minutes drifted by. The phone rang. He picked it up with a mechanical response.

"Your line, Mr James," said the young woman, and set a dialling tone purring in George's ear.

He pulled the handpiece away from his face and gazed at it. The fact that he had asked for a line was still within his memory; but who did he want to ring? He replaced it and slumped back with a sigh. A moment passed and the operator rang again.

"Mr James? Did you want to use the line sir?" She sounded respectful, but annoyed.

"Do what?" said George.

"Sir, if you don't need the line, Mr Johnson would like to use it," she said, in a professional, unflappable tone.

"Mr Johnson? Who's Mr Johnson? Look, I think you must have the wrong number, sorry."

He put down the phone and laughed softly to himself. It was a bit much, he thought, when people ring you up at home asking if someone you have never heard of can use some line or other. What was the world coming to? What would old Pop have said to that?

He glanced across to where his father's picture hung, and saw a blank wall.

"Now, who would take that down?" he asked, as he crossed the room. He stopped abruptly, and looked about him.

"This is not my room!" he gasped. "My room is … it's …"

He stood quite still while his mind raced. In a half scream the man finally asked himself, "What *does* my room look like?"

Just then, there came a professional, unflappable knock at the door.

The bedroom that the Observer found itself in was very quiet.

Then suddenly Mrs Shamborn woke with a start. She heard something; someone moving about on the landing. She felt a little weird. Had she been dreaming? Was she still dreaming? No, she was looking at the bedroom door. She was awake and convinced she had heard movement somewhere out there.

She sat up slowly, still feeling woozy. She switched the bedside light on and turned to give George a shake. He wasn't there. Where was he? She must have heard him moving about. What was he doing at this time of night?

He had been acting strange ever since that man had called in at the office going on about some slush fund or other, before he realised that he was talking to the wrong

George Shamborn. She heard more movement. What was he doing out there?

She was just pulling her dressing gown on when she heard a loud rumbling noise, as though somebody was tumbling down the stairs! She stepped out and peered down in the semi-darkness at stripy pyjamas at the foot of the stairs. Trembling, and still in a stupor, she felt for the light switch.

George was crumpled up, looking up at her with dead eyes. Mrs Shamborn screamed.

What she hadn't heard was the soft click of the front door closing.

-

The tiny interview room was dingy and Mrs Shamborn wasn't comfortable. She was still shaken by the events that had come into her otherwise ordinary life.

The man was speaking to her again after going over her statement. "You can't explain why your husband was out of bed, you say?"

"No."

"And this man you say called the day before, looking for your husband? Did he give a name?"

"No, I don't think so."

"And you say he was looking for Mr Shamborn?"

"Yes. He said it was very important that he see him. He wouldn't say what it was about, and when I told Gordon about it, he had no idea what the man could want with him."

The senior detective felt a brooding puzzlement, but

did not communicate this to the grieving woman across the table.

He looked up with a reassuring smile. "OK. Many thanks for coming in."

-

The detective looked up from his desk and waved his colleague over. "Anything on this Shamborn thing?"

"Not really. It's an unusual name so I looked it up; only two of them in the city."

"That all?"

"No," he smiled. "I had a look at the man's accounts, his workplace and work history. He's had a few fines. His son now lives and works overseas. He donates to charities… look, I don't know what we are looking for here, but this guy is Mr Clean. He's Mr Ordinary, Mr Nobody. I mean, he's just not the sort of guy that gets bumped off!"

The senior detective smiled, "No, you're right. The forensics guy says the bruise on his neck could easily have happened during the fall. Nothing on this mysterious caller, I suppose?"

"Not yet, but the CCTV footage might come up with something."

"OK. Let me know if you get anything."

-

The driver was always cautious along this narrow stretch, some of the trees were very close to the road's edge. However, these considerations did not help when the car behind decided to overtake him without warning.

It seemed to slow alongside and then suddenly pound against him, pushing him off the road and straight into a tree. The entire incident had only lasted a few seconds. The hapless driver could do nothing. The other car sped on, leaving a smoking wreck and a dead man slumped inside.

-

The detective came into the room. "Got something from the CCTV."

"Good. What did we get?"

"A long distance shot of him calling at the lady's house on the day in question, and a second shot of him leaving."

"Not enough for an ID, I suppose?"

"Not then, but a good shot of him driving out at the end of the street. The face through the windscreen was a clear enough image to get a positive identification."

"Excellent work. Who is he?"

The detective looked at his note book. "He's a Mr Barry Hodgson."

"What do we know about him?"

"Nothing yet. This just came in. I'll get onto it."

"Thanks. It'd be nice if we could clear up this one little mystery, at least."

-

The call came in during the morning. The police sergeant was saying, "There was a fatal car accident reported that I thought you'd be interested in."

The senior detective frowned. "And what makes you think that?"

"Two things really. The first being that a lot of side damage was done to the car before it went into a tree. It would seem that the fellow was pushed off the road."

"Well, OK. Sounds like something more than an accident; and the second thing?"

"Yes. The dead driver has been identified. He was a Mr Ronald Shamborn."

-

The two men sat in the meeting room. The senior detective looked through the case files while the other waited.

He finally looked up. "Well, so many connections. So many things that link the two cases. The original death of Gordon Shamborn, taking a fall at his home, and the suspicious death of Ronald Shamborn, who was either accidentally or deliberately run off the road and into a tree."

He sat back. "What do you think?"

"Don't know. It's one hell of a coincidence that two Shamborns, the only two in the city I might add, both die within days of each other. I know we can't base a case on coincidence."

"No, we can't. We need to know more about this Barry Hodgson. What was he doing at the first Shamborn's home? Why was he looking for him?"

"That's still being looked into. I've got Thomson on it. He said he'd have it ready for this meeting, but he did say it was rather complicated.

A few minutes later, there was a gentle knock on the door and Thomson entered holding a file. He handed it to the inspector, with a grimace.

"Any problems?"

"No sir. Sorry, it just took a while to get it all together, that's all."

"That's fine; thank you, Thomas."

The man left the room and the detective spent a long time pouring over the written report, while the senior officer sat as patiently as he could. He eventually looked up with a grimace that mirrored Thomas's.

Growing a little impatient, the senior man said, "Well? Let's have it. What do we know about this Hodgson character?"

"Well," the other hesitated, "it's a bit complicated, or I should say it's very complicated." He looked back at the report. "It seems that Mr Hodgson worked as some sort of contracted assistant in the office of a private consultancy.

"Ah! I see what you mean, anything else?"

"Oh yes. This private consultancy firm was engaged to carry out an investigation of a political nature."

"Oh, no. That's all we need."

"It gets worse."

"It gets worse?"

"Yep."

"Go on."

"The firm was investigating for an advisor to a power broker for a current government minister."

The men sat staring at each other for several minutes.

The senior man broke the silence. "Can you imagine the shear amount of bloody paperwork on a nightmare case like this?"

"I can sir, I can indeed!"

The senior detective stood up, saying, "We're agreed, then?"

The other rose too, and said, "Agreed sir".

"Good. Mark up both files for me, I'll sign them both off… Death by Misadventure."

The company accountant stood puzzling for a moment. The Observer sensed that he was trying to remember something. He picked up the phone. The voice on the other end was strained.

"George, sorry to bother you in the work place. Are you OK to talk?

"Hello there! They said a Quentin Rugg was on the line. I couldn't place you at first. It must be ages since we caught up. What is it fifteen years… more?"

"George, I'm not sure where to begin; it all seems rather fuzzy now I know things are slipping away… I thought I could talk to you; we've known each other a long time and after all we did go to school together…George, we did go to school together, didn't we?"

"Of course we did!"

"Oh, good. I have a pretty major problem… but I don't think anything can actually be done about it."

The man sat down. "I'm listening; just talk to me."

"I don't know where to begin, but I guess I'll have to tell you about work."

"OK. It's quiet here right now. Tell me about your work."

"Well, I'm sure you remember, all those years ago, when the company asked me to head up their software division?"

"Sure, we celebrated, remember?"

"No, not really… anyway, the chance to be working at

the top of the tree in the company's development section was a chance I just couldn't pass up. The company had been working on a device that they claimed would enable even the most computer-illiterate person to use a computer like an expert within an hour. The project was based on virtual reality code. By the time I got involved the company had developed the helmet. The device was designed to transmit signals back and forth from the brain and allow the user to work a computer without touching a keyboard or using a mouse."

George interrupted. "Without touching the mouse, you say."

"I know all this is going to sound strange, but I have to talk to somebody... and you seemed..." the caller fell silent.

"Quentin, where are you calling from?"

"I'm at the local library, looking things up, I think... I'm not sure why I came here to be really honest. Looking for the latest edition of Roget's Thesaurus... I think."

"Quentin! Stay put!" I'm only a few minutes away. We can catch up for a coffee. Is that OK? Will you wait for me there?"

"Yes. Yes. That would be good. Yes, I'll be right here... near the entrance. Thank you, George. I appreciate you taking the time." He rang off.

George sat wondering what it was all about. He had always got on with Quentin; he had always been so full of enthusiasm about the latest advances in this and that. He sounded so strange on the phone; not at all the way he remembered him.

He left the office and made his way to the town library. As he walked, he continually turned the conversation over in his head, but made no sense of it. He may have to accept that his old friend had simply lost his marbles. Not that he wanted to give much time to that idea.

As he arrived at the building he was shocked to see the state his old friend was in. He was thin and pale. His eyes were sunken and he had more grey hair than a man in his thirties should have. He looked sick. In fact, he looked as though he was dying.

They made their way to the cafeteria and found seats. The thought of buying drinks seemed to evaporate as they sat looking at each other.

George started, "You had better tell me what has been happening with you, my friend. You appear to be sick."

"I am sick. Not the sort of sick that anybody could understand; but I am sick."

"Take your time. What's been happening?"

"I don't know how much you're going to understand about what I'm about to tell you. You don't have any background in software development do you?"

"No. I'm a bean-counter. Remember?"

"No. I'm sorry, but I don't?'

George mentally chided himself for being thoughtless with his question. "It's OK. Just tell me what you can."

"The device… it was designed to transmit signals back and forth between the brain and the CPU. The user wouldn't have to use a keyboard or mouse. Peripherals would be obsolete!"

"Yes. So you said. Go on."

Quentin's eyes widened and glared at his companion. A sense of control and sanity seemed to return in his demeanor. "Can you imagine," he went on, "a surgeon who can access the case files for a medical procedure during an operation, without even leaving the operating table or a driver or pilot who can access any route in the world without having to take his hands off the wheel or joy stick?"

"No. You're right. Such a thing is pretty hard to imagine."

"When I got started on the project it was well-advanced; all the components worked fine; they interacted with the brain just like they were supposed to. Looking back, the company just wanted someone who could write the software to drive the thing. I protected my part of the program with a password. Actually, I used a phrase; a string of words; that for some reason I have no memory of. Not that it matters anymore."

Quentin stared at his boney fingers. "That's all they wanted really." He looked up at George with an agonised expression.

"The whole thing started to go haywire when a disgruntled programmer, who had left the project under a cloud, wrote a virus. He had taken a copy of the program with him and used it to write the thing. There was nothing very clever about it, just the usual virus for corrupting data. You have to understand that viruses work by moving from one computer to another when they interact."

He paused and took in his surroundings, as if checking whether anyone was listening. He lowered his voice.

"This virus was designed to replicate itself over and over again until it filled up whatever space it could find in the infected computer's database. I never dreamt that a virus could spread like it did. It was amazing. The thing is... well, the thing is, when the machine went down I was working on it, using the helmet!"

He slumped back in the chair. "The security guys wrote some software of their own. It killed the virus and cleaned up the system. Some guru from their office came round afterwards and asked me what password I had on it. He was annoyed when I told him I couldn't remember it and couldn't find the piece of paper I had written it on. I don't think he believed me. He had some strange idea that the password was part of the problem.

Anyway, everybody relaxed and the project went on. It was soon after this I started getting headaches, bad ones. At the time I put it down to my workload. You know, all those hours working with computers?"

"Yes. I can see that. You were happy to keep going with it then?'

"Oh yes, people like me are suckers for this sort of stuff. New frontiers and all that sort of thing... I suppose you could say that my work was still going well apart from the fact that every time I put the helmet on, the device that allowed the interface between me and the computer, a dialog box would pop up saying that the computer was infected again. It was very frustrating, but at the time I figured that it had to be some kind of mistake because...," he lowered his voice again, "because the computer was all on its own... it wasn't hooked up to anything!"

The man seemed to drift off. He stared into space and mumbled, "Each day I logged on to the machine it was just sitting there waiting for me to give it something to replicate." He gave a nervous shiver. "I know that sounds silly, but that's exactly what it was doing. Waiting for me; me, because I was the one with the helmet!"

He wriggled in his seat and seemed to return to the present. After a few moments of deep contemplation, he went on with his story. "So, I went down to see the hardware guys and had them take a look at the headgear I was using. They said it checked out OK. But just to be on the safe side I got them to build me another one. I even watched as they put the finishing touches to it and handed it over. As soon as I linked up to the computer through the headset, the computer went nuts again. It was re-infected with the virus." Quentin's head slumped. He was obviously tired.

"Are you OK...to carry on I mean?" George asked, becoming increasingly taken with the man's story. He was pleased with the reply.

"Yes, thank you George. I have to tell someone." He straightened up and continued.

"I spent days trying to figure out how the computer could possibly be reading my brain whenever we linked up. It seemed to be the case that my brain was as suitable as any personal computer's hard drive for taking up residence. To this day I don't know how a piece of software could make the leap from a piece of silicon to a human organ."

He smiled a horrible smile. "I tried all sorts of things, but eventually I had to resign myself to the fact that the virus lived inside my skull. I was becoming forgetful, clumsy, but I don't think it was just poor memory that stopped me retrieving my original password." He looked around at the library. "I think that was what I was doing here."

"You didn't make a note of it, then?"

"No. There was no need. I was using it at log-in every

day. I just knew it! I do know it was a phrase of some sort. I came up with it at home. I was writing a letter and found myself writing something repetitively and went to a thesaurus to come up with something different I could use. I wrote the phrase down then, of course, and took it into the office. When I realised later that I had lost it, it didn't matter. Besides, when the security stuff was put on, the whole system came on line as a new version and it seemed pointless using a password since the project was at a stage when everything was in place and set. Nothing could be changed within the programming, not even accidentally; and I was the only one with access to it."

Quentin combed his hair with his fingers; he raised his eyebrows. "That was two weeks ago. I feel myself slipping away fast, but it was good of you to give me the time." He pushed his chair back. "I just had to tell somebody. It's alright if you don't believe me. I'm not sure if I would, under the circumstances."

George smiled. "You're welcome, any time. Please stay in touch. I'll give you a card. You can get me at home or at the office. If there's anything I can do…"

"You've been very patient." With that, he stood up with some difficulty, and after exchanging cards and a hand-shake, he hobbled his way across the room.

George watched him go; he was wondering about the man's memory loss and his obvious loss of physical coordination. It was certainly a strange story and George really didn't know what to make of it. Did he think Quentin's version of events was at all possible, or was he just a sick man? Was it all brought about by overworking?

A couple of weeks had passed when another call

regarding his old school friend came into George's office. This one was from a relative who had found his business card still in Quentin's pocket when they removed the helmet and got him to the first aid room. He was pronounced dead there and then. A funeral was being arranged and George was given a verbal invitation; he accepted.

A few more weeks passed before George came across the business card Quentin had given him, still in his jacket pocket. Knowing he would have no further use for it he was about to drop it in the bin when he happened to turn it over.

A few words were penciled on the back. At the top, in large upper case letters was the word 'comfortable', and beneath it the phrase 'as snug… as a bug… in a rug'.

The Observer watched the young couple as they snuggled together.

It was a beautiful evening; balmy warm, flower-scented and romantic. They sat, cuddled up on their favourite park bench, taking in the view across the pond with its playful ducks. Their courting had started only recently, with frequent after-work trysts like this one. In just a few short days their relationship seemed to be based on a remarkably well-balanced assortment of their own and shared personal needs. It all seemed to hover on the perfect; the ideal. Maybe it was just some glitch in his personality that had him constantly looking for a snag.

She was dreamily counting off the ways that she wanted to be taken care of. He was drowsily listening and coming up with positive replies.

"What I want," she was saying, "is a man who can put a roof over my head."

He squeezed her a little harder and said, "Not a problem."

"I want a man who can put food on the table."

"Of course."

"I want a man who is loving and faithful."

"Always."

"I want a man who is always there for me."

"Will always be there."

"I want a man who will share my problems."

"You can rely on me for that."

"I want a man who can keep me safe."

"Consider it done."

"I want a man who is always willing to go shopping with me."

He sighed. There it was… he'd found it!

It was an alien heat that the sun poured down as the Observer studied the man. He was bathing his chest and legs in something that, for him, was normally found in ovens. He knew that like many other English tourists who flocked yearly to the Mediterranean shores, he could never fully adjust to it.

With his head pleasantly shaded by the side wall of his balcony, he sat watching the local life mix with that of the foreign intruder. Like many small coastal towns in this part of Spain, it was a peculiar concoction of native poverty and gaudy commerce. His hotel room commanded an impressive view across the crescent bay of Tossa de Mar. He was able to watch the to and fro with none of the inconvenience of leaving this quarters.

Timothy Bristow was a small man in his middle thirties. His hair was dark, his eyes brown, the moustache he sported was thick like a garden broom, and in general he looked like a million other people who may be seen scrambling for places on the early tube-trains, in and out of London. There was nothing striking about the man, except that his general appearance was so remarkably ordinary that a person looking at him a second time (despite the odds against it) would probably ruminate on his suitability for the Secret Service.

For most of his life he had been timid and retiring. His early life had certainly not been easy. Both his school days and the many years of service he had given as a clerk in a large London insurance company, had dragged by slowly. In the main, his life had been a slow, painful and embarrassing business with little reward.

He looked down at the bustling street that ran in a great curve around the white sands of the bay. These were separated by a broad promenade carrying a constant stream of holiday traffic, bordered by a few scattered pedestrians. The main body of tourists were now sprawled half-naked along the beach, soaking up the afternoon sun, while others sauntered between the back-street shops looking for objects to place on shelves or hang on walls. These mementos would serve in future to remind them and others of their visit to the gay Costa Brava.

It was this narrow thoroughfare lined with shops and the colourful crowd milling up and down its curved length that Timothy looked down upon with mounting interest.

He could almost see the door of the shop where he first caught sight of the knife.

Five years had passed since the day he had entered the store to enquire about its price. He had always hated the way the shopkeepers bartered and haggled with customers, and resented the traders' custom of displaying their wares without the use of price tags. These black emotions of his had been fully-charged, he recalled, as he picked up the paperknife to admire the craft and beauty of the thing that had caught his eye.

He turned it over in his hands once or twice, and then withdrew the blade from its scabbard. Having satisfied himself that no price was visible, he returned it gently to the glass shelf and left.

For the following two days he was haunted by the thought that someone else, with less timidity than himself, might walk into the shop and purchase it. For two days he had watched the shop, and the shelf that held the trophy. He was annoyed by his own diffidence. The shyness that had plagued him from early childhood was not brought into clear view, and the attraction to the objet d'art that was apparently within his grasp, boiled his blood for the first time.

It was late in the afternoon of the second day that his vigil came to an end. Timorous Timothy Bristow had decided to make his play.

Before entering the establishment a second time, the insurance clerk had reflected on the recent events that had placed him there. His broken engagement to Margery. This had lasted an altogether uncomfortable number of years. Despite her persistent efforts to rid herself of him, he had hung on to the bitter end. And bitter it was. Then there was the endless nagging of his aging parents, pressing him to go out and make a home of his own. The daily criticism of his fellow office workers, urging that he come out of his shell.

And finally, his superior calmly informing him one morning that others were waiting to fill his position if there was no real improvement in his work before the month was up.

It was at this point that he had taken his vacation earlier than was his habit, and had ventured into Europe on what was commonly referred to as a 'package deal'.

At the precise instant the rubber had left the runway he was plunged into regret. The bright lights, late evenings, and free-flowing wine of a continental holiday were not really the scene for him. This he knew for a certainty, and he was ashamed of his impetuosity.

With each passing hour he had sunk deeper into despair; and this feeling was made more acute by the knowledge that he had little better to go home to.

These were the sordid events that had brought him to the tiny souvenir shop, in front of which he now stood. The siesta that had, as always, brought a strange lull to the town, was over. Once more the lane began to fill with bargain hunters. Having mentally prepared himself, as would a soldier before doing battle, he entered the store.

A room full of knick-knacks was actually what it was; teeming with bits and pieces neatly laid out on a huge rack of wooden shelves that stretched almost to the middle of the ceiling. Around the walls still more trinkets reposed on tinted glass shelving, looking as though they were regarded as being of a rather finer quality than the trumpery in the centre.

Timothy edged his way through the rapidly growing crowd of ogling holiday makers, till he stood before the work of art. He picked it up and lovingly caressed the black ebony handle, ran his fingertips slowly over the bronze relief, squeezed the rich, brown leather of the scabbard, and stroked the fine glistening steel that formed the slender blade. It had to be his, and he would not haggle. If the price was right, say, three, four thousand pesetas, he would take it without a quibble.

He nervously waved the object above his head, hoping to attract one of the assistants' attention across the busy shop. A young girl saw his gestures and went immediately to a large, oafish fellow sitting in the corner behind the counter fanning himself with a tattered newspaper. He was a big man for his race. The office clerk did not like this turn of events, as the man was most probably the proprietor, who dealt personally with any patron foolish enough to be interested in such valuable merchandise.

The big, brown man lumbered across the room as though he were neither fond of, nor used to the exercise of walking. He roughly pushed aside anyone in his path and approached his precious customer with a disarming smile.

"You Englees? Preety, no? You like? Preety, no?" said the shopkeeper, coming to a halt.

"How much is it, please?" asked Timothy, determined to get straight to business.

"Thees verry preety, no? You like?" the man cooed.

"Yes, but just tell me what you want for it," replied the prospective buyer, as sternly as he could.

"You like. I see. You like," continued the big man. His head lolled to one side and a grotesque grin came over his face. "Is much," he said, half laughing.

Timothy felt the back of his neck flush hot, then cold. He was slowly filling up from the soles of his feet to the top of his head with the tingling sensation of some newly-found strength. It was a charge that burnt from the inside, and threatened to explode all over the shop.

He drew himself up visibly, held the merchandise up before the other's face, and asked in a voice more resolute than the one he had used all his life; "How many pesetas do you want for this ornamental knife?"

The oaf seemed to sense the change that had taken place in his client.

"Ten thousand pesetas, Senor," said the man apologetically.

The younger man's hand gripped the scabbard tightly. His knuckles turned white instantly. In one deft movement the blade was free and glinting in the sunlight; vertical, between them.

There was a rush of people into the street. The two female assistants crouched down behind the counter. Timothy looked about him steadily; the field was clear. No one would be hurt unnecessarily.

The mountainous brute stood wide-eyed before him, with an expression of disbelief and shattering fear distorting his dark face.

The scabbard dropped to the floor, and the hand that held it flashed to the throat of the proprietor. With one powerful spring from the aggressor's legs the two men pitched back into the centre rack, smashing through the two lower shelves and coming to rest in the middle of the floor with bric-a-brac and splintered wood scattered all around them.

The weapon that was once a paper knife was now held firmly with its tip embedded in the fat neck of the man pinned to the floor. Each breathed heavily into the face of the other.

The intent faces of the shoppers now filled the main window, and the two girls peered cautiously from behind their barricade.

"How much," whispered the assailant, "do you want for the dagger?"

"Nothing, Senor" replied the terrified man, who was obviously having great difficulty speaking. "Is yours."

Both the thumb at the front, and the blade at the side of the perspiring neck, went a fraction deeper.

"How much, Senor?" the other repeated.

"Five hundred pesetas, please, Senor," croaked the big man.

Timothy dug down into his hip pocket, keeping the steel tip in position at the side of the shopkeeper's neck. After a moment he held five one hundred peseta notes before the red, watering eyes of the other. These he dropped onto the other man's chest.

Without removing his gaze or his knife, he felt for the scabbard behind him. Finding it, he brought it forward between their faces. With a deliberate slowness, the attacker removed the point of the blade and slid it softly into the supple leather.

The new owner of the Toledo paper knife stood up. He dusted his shorts, straightened his tie, smoothed his hair, and with a serene smile that might have subdued a raving lunatic, stepped out into the street and disappeared into the crowd.

That same evening he had flown out from Barcelona

airport four days before he was due to return from his vacation. This had seemed by far the wisest move at the time.

Nothing had ever come of the incident, nothing official that is, and it must be assumed that the petrified shopkeeper took the matter no further. Timothy did discover later, however, that the shop had changed ownership a few weeks after the said transaction had taken place.

What indeed had emerged from the whole affair was a new Timothy Bristow.

On his return to London he notified his employer of his intended departure from what had become his 'second home'; and having worked out a respectable period of notice, he collected a fortuitously large long service cheque and bade them all farewell. All this he did amicably.

He laid down money for rented office space in the outer reaches of the city and went to work.

Meanwhile, a small but comfortable flat had replaced his disagreeable lodgings, and his romantic life blossomed with the advent of Clara, a girl who admirably suited his newly-found temperament.

Within three years, Tim, no longer Timothy, had built up an insurance brokerage firm, the success of which provoked the envy of many longer established competitors within the great metropolis. He and Clara had married and taken up a modest country residence.

In an overall summary it could be fairly said that Tim Bristow had done very well.

The man on the balcony nodded slowly as he put away his recollections. The sun was still hot. Tim applied a little more oil to his legs and stretched back into the cooling shadow. He glanced at his wristwatch. Clara and Mark, his two year old son, would return from the shops very shortly. He slowly turned the Toledo paper knife over in his hand.

Friends and colleagues had often shown respectful curiosity about his annual sojourn in what his newly-begotten set regarded as a cheap showy little seaside town. They grew no wiser.

Only his wife knew that once a year he became a pilgrim. A man paying homage.

The environment that the Observer had moved to was one that commanded an expansive view of the sea. It saw that the young man seated here was finding it very difficult to get into the proper mood for the thing; his story.

It was frustrating because he had already scoped out a plot, settled on the characters in the story and had already made detailed notes of the activities and events that would take place during the telling of it. He just stared at his open laptop; the page only showing the one typed word, 'Bloodlust', as a title. A great title. He had thought this when he typed it nearly two hours ago.

It was a fictional piece, of course. The atmosphere created throughout would be sombre and more than a little creepy. The whole thing was dark and foreboding with constant threats being visited upon those who inhabited the narrative as it unfolded.

The writer stopped and looked around him. How could he get the feel of this? It wasn't going to work. The fact was, he was far too comfortable. He should have left all this at home. It didn't help that the weather here was so gorgeous, and he had a great deal of trouble not staring out across the sparkling crests of the waves, breaking smoothly along the snow-white sands of the bay. To say nothing of the non-stop hindrance of receiving the constant attention of the hotel's waiter, who wanted to attend to his every need, particularly when he hadn't asked for it.

The situation was made almost impossible by the fact that this holiday, with its unaccustomed luxury, had been won in a competition, with him not having to pay for anything, together with the knowledge that he had three more weeks of it to go.

Added to all this was the lay-back holiday music that swept along the balcony, making it difficult to ignore the fact that he was staying in a five-star hotel and absolutely nowhere near the gloomy forests in his story, where a foul-smelling group of the undead stalk the intrepid campers, who were quite innocently looking for a good spot to pitch their tent for the night.

He closed his laptop. The ambience just wasn't right. His doomed campers would have to wait. He would give them a reprieve until he was back home in his dimly-lit, single room at the back of the bakery.

The hospital bed that the Observer floated over held a sickly-looking man. It knew that the visitor's day had not gone the way he planned it. There were complications.

A man was saying, "It took so long for the package to arrive, and…"

The man in the bed spoke for the first time. "Package? What package? Who are you?"

The other sighed, "You mean you've been laying there for the last twenty minutes with your eyes open and you haven't heard a word?"

"Where am I? What am I doing here? I feel terrible!"

The visitor pulled his chair closer to the bed. "You're in hospital and apparently you were in a coma when you came in. I wasn't here for that."

"Coma?"

"Well, yes, and you have been laying there looking up at me in a coma for the whole time I've been here."

The patient frowned. "Erm… drinking… I was in a bar drinking. I remember that."

"Yes, and my God, how you were chucking them back!"

The other teared up a little. "I've have problems; a lot of problems."

"I know. You told the whole bar. You were going on about how you had lost your job, your wife had taken off with another man, and you couldn't keep up with the mountain of bills. You said that life wasn't worth living and it was your intention to drink yourself to death."

The sick man was nodding slowly in agreement. His face was taking on a strange tinge of grey.

His visitor went on. "You weren't to know of course, but I was suffering too. My Angela left me a few months ago and I haven't been able to move on. My life was a wreck too."

He took out his handkerchief and wiped his eyes. He went on. "I didn't want to go on living without her. So, I found this Internet site that sold all sorts of nasty stuff, including poisons. It came with a guarantee and everything.

Anyway, I ordered it. It was very expensive, and… as I was saying, it took ages to arrive."

The man in the bed said, "You were going to kill yourself?"

"Oh! Yes, no doubt about it. I laced my drink with the stuff. Tipped it all in I did. I wanted to end it in one of my favourite places, so I chose 'Toni's Bar'. That's the bar we were in. I hadn't seen you in there before, but I know most of the regulars. Nice crowd. I wanted to go out amongst friends, you see?"

The bed started to shake and the patient's breathing became rapid.

The visitor sat on the edge of the bed. He took the sick man's hand. It was very cold and his face was almost black now. He tried not to look at it.

"Anyway," he went on, "I had to catch up with you to give you the good news."

The patient just managed to croak out the words, "Good news?"

The visitor looked at him and wondered whether he should call a nurse; no point really, so he went on. "Yes. The reason I didn't see you pick up my glass and skull it down was because at that very moment my phone went off. It was Angela! My Angela, crying her little heart out. Saying how much she loved me and how stupid she had been. She was pleading with me to let her come back because she realises that I am the only man she wants to spend the rest of her life with."

The bed started to shake more violently now.

"So, you see how it all works out?"

The patient mumbled something like, "I didn't mean to really do it, you know."

His visitor wasn't really listening. "I know, it's wonderful. You got what you wanted and I got what I wanted. It's a miracle, don't you think?"

The other didn't answer. Suddenly, the bed went still.

It could sense Monica's agitation as she sat staring down into the empty street, waiting for his car.

There was so much tumbling through her head. All these plans; all these things to remember. She had never been involved in anything like this. What they were proposing to do would change her life forever… and if they got it wrong, if the crime they were about to commit did not go the way it was supposed to, well, no, she couldn't think about the consequences.

She jumped at the sound of a car door closing and looked out to see Murray's car. He would be downstairs, he would be coming back with the papers. She closed her eyes, and jumped again as the intercom buzzed. She got up and pressed the button.

"Hello," she said in a timid voice.

"Yes. Hello," came the man's voice.

There was a short silence. He spoke again, "Well?"

"Well what?"

"Well, are you going to let me in?

"Oh! Of course, of course," she flustered. "Sorry." She pressed another button, unlatched the door and returned to her chair by the window.

Moments later he came into the room carrying a large envelope. He saw her visibly jump as he dropped it on the table. "You OK sweet?" he asked as he went to her and started to massage her shoulders. "God, you're nervous aren't you pet?"

She looked up at him with watery eyes. "Yes," she whispered, "I've never been so frightened in my life. I can't help it you know. I want it all to go according to the schedule you have worked so hard on. I want to do whatever it takes, if it will make you happy."

She started to sob. "If it will make us happy, I mean. I know you want us to be happy." She wiped her eyes and looked up at him. "That is what you want isn't it... to make us happy? That is what you want?"

He knelt down beside her. "Of course it is," his hands came up and cupped her face, "Monica my love. A few short hours and this will all be over." He smiled. "We'll be on a beach in Miami, Florida, sipping our drinks, and it'll all be over. All you have to do right now is trust me."

They both stood and she threw her arms around him.

An hour or so later they were sitting, sipping coffee and going over the timetable. He was saying, "Have you got it clear in your head, exactly what you have to do?"

She said, "I think so. The bus to the town, the walk to the bank, the identification and the signing of papers."

He nodded and said, "There won't be any problems there... that's all been fixed."

She went on. "From there I take a taxi to the airport and we meet in the café. Is that good? Have I got it all right? It's probably pretty simple, but I've really struggled to make it all sink in. God, Murray! I don't want to let you down. I mean, what if something goes wrong and I panic?"

He leant across and took her hand. "Nothing's going to go wrong, honey. It's all been worked out to keep it as simple and as straightforward as possible."

He shook more papers out of the envelope. "How is your signature coming along?"

She opened her bag and handed him her notebook. "I think I've done well at that."

He looked at several dozen signatures with her new name. "Hey! This is great! You have done well."

He squeezed her hand again and said, "The thing to remember now is that you are saying goodbye to Monica Saunders and hello to Elizabeth Bletchley. That is who you are now. Have you been practising the way I told you; telling yourself your new name over and over?"

She nodded, "I have, I have. I've been repeating it a lot, like you told me.

"Good girl." He picked up the passport she would use as identification. "Here's the passport, and a number of other cards all in the name of Elizabeth Bletchley, just in case you are asked for more."

He looked at the time and saw it was nearly one o'clock. "OK. We're all done. Just time for a coffee before you go for your bus."

She went into the kitchen and came back with the drinks. A few minutes later she headed out, right on time.

She exited the bus in the high street and made her way to the bank. They seemed to be ready for her and the withdrawal was all very matter-of-fact, despite the enormous amount of money involved, just as Murray had predicted.

The case she was now carrying was heavy. Outside she hailed a taxi. One pulled over after a short wait and she had the driver load the case into the boot. When she was dropped off she found a trolley and the man again helped her by transferring it.

So far, she thought, everything was going well.

She entered the airport and looked for Murray. He was nowhere to be seen. She ordered a coffee and sat in the cafe looking at her tickets and her new passport; they had made a nice job of it. Just as well, she thought; it had cost enough.

She looked around again; still no Murray. She smiled to herself. If she got the dosage right he'll still be asleep.

A few minutes later Sally Carruthers boarded her plane for Malta.

It was evident that the Observer had moved to a much earlier event. It was inside a hovel where it found the elderly Mr Nostraman, who, remarkably enough, sat brooding about the imminent rattle of the door knob!

The old man was brooding because his daughter was not going to start tea for several minutes after she got back, and he was hungry. He went back to his books.

Moments later the door opened and his daughter came in from the chilly night air. After hanging up her coat she came in rubbing her hands.

"Hello, father. It is dreadfully cold out there."

He nodded.

"Father, I have something to tell you." She stood still for a moment, bracing herself. "Father," she repeated "I'm…"

"Pregnant, yes I know. A boy, six pounds, ten ounces, brown eyes. A blacksmith with a love of fishing." He paused. "You should watch him for weak thyroid functions." He went on. "He'll meet, court and marry a girl from another village. Three children; a boy and two girls. One of the girls will marry a seaman and live most of her life abroad."

Holding his stomach he threw his head back with his eyes closed and went on.

"Each generation will be very much like one among the many, until…"

"Father!" she cried.

He stopped.

"Don't go on."

He sighed, "As you wish, my love." Rubbing his stomach again, he said, "What are we eating tonight?"

She raised her eyebrows and said, "I will look to that father; I just need a few moments."

He distractedly nodded his appreciation. She turned and went out for fresh air.

As she closed the door behind her, she let out a great sigh. She mumbled, "Bloody Seers! Just let him try creating quatrains for that lot!"

The Observer could see the nature of the girl in the office. She was pretty, intelligent, kind-hearted and a wallflower.

It had started way back when she was in the Play Group her mother took her to, and had stayed with her through to her mid-twenties. Over the years her shyness had sidelined her in many ways and on many occasions. She had no social life but liked her office job. It didn't entail contact with more than two or three people and her bed-sitter provided her with her own space. She was painfully aware of how she was, and wished she could change; wished she could break through her inhibitions that prevented her from making contact, making new friends, communicating freely!

She was in her second-floor room sorting invoices when she glanced down at the street. It wasn't a busy road outside, but her window gave her a great view. Whenever she was alone, she liked to watch the odd vehicles and occasional pedestrians go by. She was looking at what was obviously a breakdown. It was a bright red sports car. It was pulled over with a girl of around her own age inspecting her front tyre. It was obviously flat. The girl took out a mobile phone and dialled.

Just then another car pulled up behind her. This was too soon to be a response to her call. It had to be a knight in shining armour. She wasn't wrong.

The door swung open and a young man climbed out. He would also be in his twenties. He was quite tall and looked well-dressed. He went forward and was talking to the girl. Then he moved to the back of the car and stood waiting for the boot lid to be popped. He looked around momentarily, taking in where he was and finally looked up at the building.

The girl at the window jumped back. It was silly, she thought. She chided herself. He could hardly see her from down there. She felt a pang of something; jealousy or envy? She wasn't sure. He seemed so nice. She could tell he was polite by his body language; and so obliging.

There was something else… he seemed quite reserved, even a little awkward perhaps. He was evidently strong, having no trouble at all pulling the spare out.

She watched as he went to work changing the tyre, which seemed to be all over in no time. The girl stood by watching him. It was a fair bet that they would swap phone numbers at the very least. She'd be stupid if she didn't; he'd be quite a catch.

When it was all done he put the flat tyre in the girl's boot and found a piece of cloth in his own car and stood wiping his hands. The girl walked over to him.

This was quite exciting. Would she give him a kiss for his trouble? Maybe even throw her arms around him? Or would she only give him her number?

She looked on as though she were watching a TV soap opera. To her surprise none of those things happened. The girl was smiling and talking to him, thanking him, no doubt. With that she got back into her car and waved as she drove off.

She looked back at the paperwork on her desk, knowing that she'd told the boss she'd have it all sorted by the time he came in. However, she couldn't resist watching him drive off. She heard the engine being turned over but his car wasn't starting. He tried several more times before getting out and opening the hood.

In that moment something happened to her. She didn't know what it was, she'd think about it later.

She got up and ran out of the office. She raced down the stairs as fast as she could go. She flew out onto the street in time to see him lift his head up from underneath the hood.

She slowed to a more casual pace. They instantly smiled at each other as she approached.

She took a very deep breath, summoned up her courage and said, "Do you need any help?"

Now, in the briefest of moments the Observer moved to the mission's final event.

On its final observation, it watched the boy before it, bobbing up and down with the gentle rocking of the boat.

It was the boy's custom to hire out a small punt with his friend on the weekend but today he was alone. His notion was that this would create an ideal environment for him to finish his story. The warmth of the day had brought out the busy buzzing of insects along the banks of the narrow river.

He sat leafing through his homework book. He came to his essay, unfinished for several days and due in the coming week. He was particularly pleased with the story it told but the ending simply alluded him.

He looked back at his notes. His class had been asked to write a narrative essay with human behaviour as the topic. The teacher said she wanted it to be a personal essay, based on the writer's experiences. It had to be written from a personal point of view and needed to convey an opinion or some moral point.

Reading through his work again he felt that it covered all of the requirements but needed rounding off. It seemed to leave him, as the reader, just hanging, as though there was more to come.

He lay back, closing his eyes, letting the sun warm his

face. He ran a number of possible conclusions through his head, with each one being discarded in turn.

Then, quite without warning, an idea began to take shape.

Suddenly, a great splashing followed by a loud plop snapped his attention to the side of the boat. He sat up just in time to see a large, grey, swimming shape fade away as it sunk back towards the darkness of the river bed.

Sitting back up, he turned back to his idea, and there it was… gone!

## Chapter Eight

# The Last Return

The Controller. "It appears that your reports are some of the last to be processed.

"With the ongoing accumulation of reports it has become clear that the work done in our particular sector has taken on a value far greater than originally expected.

"It seems that behavioural science, regarded here as being the application of those scientific methods used in the study of the behaviour of organisms, is a relatively recent branch of study and research.

One of the most significant findings to date is the discordant balance between logic and emotion when forming opinions. It seems remarkable that this process varies to such a great degree from one individual to another. Observations that have been reported regarding this specific area of human activity indicate that any attempt to scientifically predict the actions and reactions of these lifeforms is not reliable. This developing branch of study currently focuses primarily on the activities by, and the interactions between, these superior lifeforms; these human beings. It is difficult to predict how long it will be before the scope of this study is widened.

"To date, it would appear that there is a consensus that attempts being made to bring about a sustainable future for this planet are minor. It can also be seen that these efforts are being implemented in such a way that progress is slow. There seems to be a general lack of urgency regarding environmental degradation. At this stage, neither political resolve nor the current allocation of funds are enough to make any real difference. Despite the growing knowledge that their environmental issues are real, the lifeforms here are not yet sufficiently motivated to make any positive headway towards a global solution. The problems they face would appear to be compounded by the fact that the necessary understanding, information and technology are all fully available to them.

"For now, the last of all gathered observations and reports are being forwarded to The Committee for Planetary Development and System Stability, and it is there that these will be combined.

"Your good work is finished."

## CHAPTER NINE

# The Final Report

With all regional reports being brought into one by The Committee for Planetary Development and System Stability, the final report went before The Supreme Council for its deliberation.

The following is taken from the end summary of The Supreme Council's recommendations.

*These studies show that from discovering fire and creating the wheel, the species has gone on to split the atom and create nuclear weapons. They have also created a space telescope, built an international space station and sent probes out into deep space. All this has been adequately reported on.*

*Despite their strangely disparate spread of varying cultures and languages, they have brought into being such wonders in the field of arts. Their literature, poems and stories; their paintings and drawings; their music, dance and theatre are quite extraordinary. What these peoples have achieved in such diversity and abundance is truly remarkable!*

*It is these factors that has made them hard to categorise. A summary of all reports indicates that both the probability of their doing harm and their survival potential is finely balanced. However, despite a propensity for war and pollution, it is the decision of the Council to lean towards clemency at this time.*

*It recommends that those that dwell here be given another millennia.*

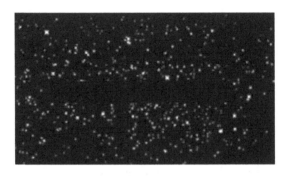

The End

Printed in the United States
By Bookmasters